M000249896

GHOST MARINES

BOOK 2

UNIFICATION

Colonel Jonathan P. Brazee
USMC (Ret)

Semper Fi Press

Acknowledgements:

I want to thank all those who took the time to offer advice as I wrote this book. Thanks first goes to Micky Cocker, James Caplan, and Kelly O'Donnell for their editing. And thanks to my friend, retired Marine Craig Martelle, who besides being a valuable sounding board, helped me with the Imperial Marine Corps collar device as well as the book's blurb. A special thanks goes to fellow writers Lauren Jankowski and Karen Herkes for exposing me to more of the many facets of the human condition. Finally, I want to thank Melton A. McLaurin for his book, *The Marines of Montford Point: America's First Black Marines* and Henry Badgett for his book, *White Man's Tears Conquer My Pains*. Without these books, *Ghost Marines* would not have been possible for me to write.

A few hours after I wrote the above acknowledgments, I found out that Mr. Badgett passed away a week ago on April 24, 2018. RIP, sir!

Cover by Jude Beers

DEDICATION

This book is dedicated to the Private Kenneth J. Tibbs, USMC.

KIA 20 June 1944 on Saipan

The first Montford Point Marine to be killed in combat during the war.

CAMP MARTELLE, NORTHUMBRIA

Chapter 1

"Fuck you, *Corporal*," Lance Corporal Jeremy Stone said, as he lay in his rack, not even looking up from his scanpad. "I don't take orders from no caspers."

Leefen a'Hope Hollow, newly promoted to corporal only three hours before, stood there, his mouth gaping, but shocked into silence. His mind couldn't comprehend what the lance corporal had just said for a moment, and once it sunk in, he had a sudden urge to grab the Marine and drag him out of the rack. It took an effort of will to push back the anger that started to burn within him.

If they had been alone, he might have very well done that. But he was also very aware of Private First Class Harper Sousa and Private Ke Win, the other two Marines in his new fire team, who were deliberately looking away, but whose body language confirmed they were paying *very* close attention to what was happening between Stone and him.

Leif couldn't ignore Stone's disobedience, and he had to react to the situation, but what he did next would brand him for the rest of his time in the battalion. This was a nexus, not only in India Company, but as a Marine NCO.

"You must not have heard me," he said, trying to inject steel into his voice. "Sergeant Zoran told me we've got a work detail at the armory—"

"So, tell her to come get me. I'll follow *her* orders," the lance corporal said, still watching a sports feed on his scanpad.

Leif reached up to touch his collar device, wondering for a moment if Captain Tzama hadn't fastened them on well enough that morning at his promotion ceremony. No, Stone had called him "Corporal." He knew his rank.

"I don't need Sergeant Zoran to tell you anything. In case you haven't heard, I've been Second Fire Team's leader for all of twenty minutes now. In the Marine Corps, that means I own you, *Lance Corporal!*"

"Oh, I know who you are. They told us one of you caspers was coming over. That still doesn't mean I'm going to be taking orders from you. You can go crying to the first sergeant if you want, but that won't change a damned thing."

Stone's audacity gave Leif pause. As soon as he found out he was coming to India two days ago, he asked Manu about his prospective fire team. Manu had said Stone was a gung-ho Marine, one of the best. This Marine lying insolently on his rack was not "one of the best."

He stepped into Stone's room just as a voice called out from down the passage, "Corporal Hollow, where's your team? Top Somersett's waiting. Stone, Sousa, Win, get out here."

Lance Corporal Stone tubed his scanpad and got up, yelling, "We're coming, Sergeant!

"I'll follow her orders," he said quietly as he stepped past Leif, who was struggling with his temper.

"Come on, you two," he said to Sousa and Win who were now standing in their hatch watching them. "You heard the sergeant."

This wasn't over. Leif couldn't let it be over.

But as he stepped up to Stone, Sergeant Zoran called out again, "Hurry your asses, Second. I promised Top you'd be there five minutes ago."

Leif clenched his fists, his nails biting into his palms as he followed the other three Marines down the passage. He was at a loss, and it took an effort to keep from lashing out. He had to keep repeating Ferron a'Silverton's constant refrain of not letting the humans get to them, of taking whatever they dished out and letting it slide off his back.

That had been vital when there were only 50 wyntonans going through boot camp. There were over 800 wyntonan Marines now, but that didn't mean he could afford to draw the ire of the humans. He had to maintain control.

"Even for your first day as an NCO, this wasn't a good effort, Corporal Hollow," his new squad leader said as he passed her. "You're already late getting your team together. You've got to do better next time."

"Yes, Sergeant," Leif said through gritted teeth as he followed his team—*yeah, my team, right*—out of the barracks and across the quad to the armory.

****

Leif sat alone in the chowhall, slowly twirling around the onionmac on his plate as he brooded. He hadn't even put his spice on it, which was almost sacrilege for a wyntonan. This should have been a banner day. He was only the sixth wyntonan to make NCO, and that was something to be proud of.

Instead, he felt like a failure. No, he *was* a failure. He hadn't been able to handle a lance corporal and had let matters slip out of his hands. He should have acted immediately and snuffed out the sparks of insubordination before they could be fanned into a flame. His ability to lead depended on the respect his subordinates had for him, and his reputation was probably finished before it was even started.

Why the hell couldn't I have stayed in Kilo? At least they already know me there.

Kilo had been his home for over four years now, and he was comfortable with his fellow Kilo Marines. But he'd been promoted out of a billet. Every fire team leader billet was filled, and none of the other corporals were up for sergeant in the near future.

India Company, however, had two empty billets thanks to a discharge and a promotion to sergeant, so Leif and Corporal Adair Toms from Lima, also newly promoted, had been transferred over to fill those slots.

"Glad to see you're eating with all your new friends, big guy. Mind if we join you, if you can put up with us Kilo scum?" Lori and Donk didn't wait for an answer but sat down. "So, how goes it in Glorious India?"

"It's OK. You know, it's just India."

"Yeah, India, the colonel's favorite child," Donk said. "Now, you're one of the chosen."

"Yeah, chosen. Don't worry, I may be on my way to glory with India, but my heart's always going to be with Killer Kilo," he said with a wry chuckle as the other two broke out into a laugh.

The late Captain Formington had insisted on calling the company "Killer Kilo" as a lame attempt to connect with his Marines, and it had become a running joke.

"Yeah, you love us so much you've left us twice," Lori said, giving him a soft elbow in the side.

"Not fair. I didn't actually leave the first time."

"We did your hail and farewell, Leif. We even got you a Golden Lion," Lori said.

Leif's gave a real smile at that, and he started to relax from his funk. He had been about to leave the Marines, his enlistment over, and at his hail and farewell, the rest of the platoon had given him a small stuffed lion, a note that said "My Hero" attached to its pink bow. It had been both an honor and a joke, a reference to the real Golden Lion he'd been awarded in the fight to take down the slaver in the Peitriov System. The next day, he'd changed his mind and decided to reenlist, but he'd kept the small lion, and it was one of his prized possessions.

"You didn't give me a farewell this time," he said.

"That's 'cause you're just across the quad. We had PT right after your promotion anyway," Lori said. "They look good, by-the-way," she added, reaching up to give his new collar insignia and imaginary buffing. "You're still the boot NCO, though, so don't forget that."

"How can I forget that when you've been reminding me of it ever since I made the cutting score?" he asked with another laugh.

"So, how's your squad? How's Sergeant Zoran? Is she really that much of a hardass?" Donk asked.

India and Kilo were two companies within Third Battalion, Sixth Marines, so most of the Marines knew of each other, even if not always that much about the specifics, but

Zoran had a battalion-wide reputation as a hard-charging, demanding NCO.

"Already got my ass handed to me," he said, even if that was stretching it a bit.

"Why, what'd you do?"

"Had some issues with getting my fire team ready for a work detail. No biggie."

But it was a biggie.

"Can't let them walk all over you," Donk said. "You're an NCO now."

"Yeah, like you should know. You've just got a month on me."

"A month might as well be a year, my son. And with that, I'm getting drinks. Anyone need anything?"

"Hey, you OK?" Lori asked as soon as Donk left the table.

"Sure. Why?"

"Well, I don't know how long you've been sitting there, but you obviously haven't taken a bite of your food."

"Eh, it's just onionmac."

"Onto which you normally pile on your spice and shovel it in. 'Sides, I know you. Something's up."

Leif shrugged. If any human could understand him, it was Lori. After the incident on Tee-Double-X where they'd been jumped for being a human and wyntonan together, they'd become very close, best friends, even. Leif wouldn't admit it to any of his fellow wyntonan Marines, but he felt closer to her than to any of his own people.

"I just had an issue this afternoon with one of my Marines."

"Who?"

"Stone."

"Him? He's got a good rep. What happened?"

He almost blurted out that Stone was a racist insubordinate, but he bit that back. Even with Lori, he wasn't about to pull out that card. More than that, he knew if he told her, she'd march up to the sergeant major in righteous anger to demand justice.

Even after four years living among the humans, Leif was often confused by their thought process and actions, but he knew if he allowed Lori to defend him, all his credibility would vanish—if he even had any left.

No, this was something he had to take care of himself. He couldn't rely on anyone else.

"Nothing much," he lied, afraid Lori would see right through him—the wyntonans had many strengths, but lying effectively was not one of them.

He looked across the chowhall to where most of India was sitting. It took him a moment, but spotted Stone. The broad-shouldered Marine was listening intently to Jelly Kopf go on about something, and while Leif watched, he roared in laughter, his bug juice snorting out of his nose. The entire table of mostly lance corporals laughed along with whatever Kopf said, and Leif felt a pang of regret.

He had some good friends with Kilo, but except for Manu, he had no friends in India, friends with whom he could sit around and tell stories.

And that made him angry. Angry that he'd been taken from Kilo. Angry that no one had made him feel welcomed into India. Angry that Stone was such a *minta*. Angry that he'd been *promoted*, for the Mother's sake.

He wasn't going to stand for it. There were ways to address Stone's insubordination, ways that could have unintended consequences. No matter what he did, it was probably going to go wrong, so he might as well do what would give him the most satisfaction.

He dropped his fork in his still uneaten onionmac, stood, and said, "I've got to go do something."

Lori put out a hand, grabbed his arm, and said, "Don't let them give you any shit OK?"

"Don't worry. That's not going to happen," he said, staring hard at her.

"OK, then," she said, dropping her hand. "Meet me at the club later?"

"If I'm still around," he answered as he took his tray to the conveyor.

Straightening out his utilities, he strode through the tables, heading to India's unofficial section of the messhall.

"Hey," one of the other India corporals whose name escaped him said as he walked by, "Welcome to India. Come to the club tonight and let me buy you a beer . . . uh, do you people drink beer?"

"Yes, the *People* drink beer," Leif snapped, using the Uzboss word for the People.

He knew his tone wasn't warranted. The corporal was reaching out, after all, but Leif's mind was on a certain lance corporal. He pulled away and continued on, stepping around the end of the table and over to where Stone was sitting. Someone gave the lance corporal a nudge, and a dozen faces turned up to Leif, most of them quietly snickering, eager eyes taking in the confrontation.

This is wrong, Leefen. Not like this, his voice of reason protested.

Leif shoved the voice down right quick.

"Lance Corporal Stone," Leif said, his voice quiet but ice-sharp. "Stand up."

"Well . . . uh . . ." Stone said, looking around the table with a smile on his face before he turned to look up at Leif. "I seem to remember telling you something about you giving me orders."

There were more sniggers from the others.

"I don't care what you said, Lance Corporal. I said stand up. You're coming with me."

"And why should I do that? I haven't finished this good Marine Corps chow yet."

"Because we're going to the gear locker."

There were intakes of breath from around the table. Eyes pivoted back to Stone to see what he was going to say.

"Ah, so that's the way it's gonna be. Fine with me. Better now, I guess, and just get this settled," Stone said, making a show of standing, puffing out his chest.

Lance Corporal Stone was a big Marine, a gym rat, from the looks of it. He didn't have the bulk of a heavyworlder, but for a reg, he had an impressive physique. Shorter than Leif, of course, the human still probably out-massed him by 20 kgs.

"You sure you want to do this, *casper*?" he asked quietly.

There were more intakes of air as those closest to the two heard his words.

"Jer, no cause for that kind of talk," one of the others said.

Stone waved the protest back, then asked, "Well? Last chance to back out."

"Yes, we're doing this."

"OK, then," he said. "Rak, take my tray back, would you?"

He stepped back from the table and made his way through the general hubbub to the entrance, Leif on his heels. Sergeant Wyndam from Kilo looked up and started to give Leif a wave, but something about the two Marines ticked off a warning bell, and he started to rise. Leif waved him back down.

Neither of the two Marines said a word as they made their way to the company barracks. Leif hadn't seen the India gear locker, but all of the buildings were the same, so he was pretty sure it would be in the same relative place in the building. They walked down the empty passage, and sure enough, there it was.

Lance Corporal Stone opened the hatch, looked inside, the stepped back, saying, "After you."

Leif brushed by him, ignoring his vulnerable back as he entered the locker. It was no different from Kilo's. A locked cage spanned the entire back bulkhead. Along the side bulkheads, mops, brooms, and a few other assorted tools hung on hooks. The entry was a large, unencumbered open area, about five meters wide by four deep, which was coincidently just a little smaller than a regulation MCCCP sawdust pit where Marines practiced hand-to-hand combat.

"Last chance, *casper*."

Leif calmly turned around. Stone was slowly taking off his blouse, flexing as he did so. His muscles were much more pronounced than Leif's, and he looked huge compared to Leif's far more slender frame. The wyntonans were pretty strong for their size, however, but if Stone knew that, he didn't seem concerned.

"You disobeyed my order to you today, and you did it in front of the rest of the team."

"Like I told you, I don't obey caspers. Any of the dung-races, for that matter. You caspers, and now even fairies are coming into the Corps for all the PC reasons, but you're never going to be real Marines," he said with real fervor.

"And yeah, I know all about your Golden Lion. I had to stand out there in formation to listen to you get it. But I know the real story, not the shit they passed. You didn't fucking do shit that no one else did. It was all politics, trying to show that you caspers are as good as humans. I know the truth. I heard it from those who were there."

Anger flared again, and Leif wondered if that was true. Not about what happened on the slaver, but that some of those with him then, who saw it with their own eyes, were saying he didn't do anything? That it was all politics?

Truth be told, he'd always felt a little guilty for accepting the award. Yes, he'd helped turn the tide of the fight, but he'd been taken over by *musapha* at the time. Humans had the myth of running amok, where fighters could perform superhuman feats of combat. For the wyntonans, it was true. A small but significant percentage of them could call forth *musapha* when the situation was dire.

Leif didn't "call forth" *musapha,* however. With him, it came raging forth as if under its own will.

Stone's accusation hit too close to home about his own doubts, and the thought that fellow Kilo Marines were downplaying the fight made him angry. He felt the stirrings of *musapha* as if it was awakening.

He had to tamp that down. If it came, he'd not only beat down Stone, he'd probably kill the Marine. No, he had to fight this as himself, and take the chance that he'd be the one to win. No matter what happened, he couldn't fall under *his mistress's* unrelenting grip.

"So, I don't give a good goddamn if you've been made a corporal, or if you are part of the fire team. You stay out of my way, and I'll stay out of your way. Just don't think you can tell me to do anything."

"That's not the way it works, and you know that, Stone."

"And we don't let the dung races into the Corps, either, yet here you are."

"Yes, here I am. And I'm here to stay. I don't care what fucked-up racist beliefs you carry, but you gave an oath to the Corps, and part of that was to obey those appointed over you. So, you're going to do that."

"And are you going to make me, you skinny-ass casper?"

"Yes, I am," Lief said, stepping forward.

His *musapha* started to rise, and he hesitated a moment to push it back. Stone took that moment to strike, hitting Leif right at the edge of his mouth, rocking his head back.

The lance corporal was incredibly strong, almost as strong as a heavyworlder, but Leif had faced down a charging *wasilla* to become an *a'den*, and adult of the People, and he wasn't going to let this . . . this, *monkey*, overcome him.

Stone bull-rushed him, and Leif backpedaled to open up some room between them. He shot out a hard left that snapped against Stone's chin. Anger flared in the human's eyes, and he lowered his chin to his chest, then charged forward.

Like a siren, his mistress called out, a sentient force wanting nothing more than to flood his limbs, giving him the power to rend and destroy. He almost accepted it, giving himself up, but he held firm, keeping Stone at bay with a flurry of light hits that did little damage.

In control of himself, he stepped forward, swinging a wicked elbow at Stone's nose, but the lance corporal had been through MCCCP as well, and he'd anticipated it. With Leif's right arm raised high, his side was exposed, and Stone leveled a nasty one-two right in his ribs. Grunting in pain, Leif almost folded over as he tried to jump back, but he was up against the bulkhead, knocking two mops down onto the deck.

With a grin, Stone charged forward, bent over and ready to grapple. More in desperation than anything else, Leif raised his knee, connecting solidly with the human's face with an audible crunch of cartilage. Stone grunted and raised his hands to his broken nose, and Leif lost it. With a little bit of a distance between them, he started landing huge blows to the side of Stone's head. The human withstood three, legs wobbling, before he went down, arms feebly raised in a futile attempt to ward off the attacking wyntonan.

Leif didn't stop, dropping to his knees so he could keep hitting the defenseless Marine.

"Does this feel like ghost arms? Does it feel like casper fists, you shit-monkey?"

Stone's arms dropped limply to the deck, his head lolled to the side, but Leif got in a few more strikes before he could control himself. He paused, lungs bellowing in and out, each breath bringing sharp lances of pain to his right side.

"Hell, are you with me Stone?" he asked, reaching out to grab the Marine's chin.

Blood was pouring from a smashed nose, and the human's face was already swelling up, but his was breathing steadily. Leif moved behind him and pulled him to a sitting position, back against the bulkhead. His anger was still running strong, but he didn't want Stone to drown in his own blood.

"You OK, Stone? Are you with me?"

He gave the Marine a little shake, which was probably a bad idea given the damage the human had taken. He was rewarded with a groan, though.

"OK, wait here. Let me go get somebody."

He cracked open the hatch and looked out . . . to eight Marines, who looked up in unison, then groaned when they saw it was Leif, not Stone, who was emerging from the field of battle. Leif looked at them warily for a moment, and he almost struck out when Lance Corporal Hystaff stepped forward, but the Marine was only pushing the hatch open and stepping inside.

"Fuck, Corporal, what did you do to him? There's no need to take things that far," he said as the others pushed inside. "Mouse, go get Doc. Doc Mason, not anyone else."

That made sense. Doc Mason was an HN, which was the same rank as a lance corporal. Not that it would make any difference after Leif did what he knew he had to do.

Leif walked out of the gear locker and started down the passage when a Marine, "Mouse," he thought, ran past and out the main hatch. Leif touched his mouth, which was already swelling up. With his alabaster-white skin, he knew it would be turning a bright strawberry red, not something that could be easily hidden even if he wanted to.

The India Company barracks was next to the battalion CP. Moving slowly and holding his right arm against his side, he shuffled down the walk between the two buildings and in through the main hatch.

"Hey, Leif . . . I mean, Corporal, now, what's going on . . . and what the hell happened to you?" Lance Corporal Jen DuPont, from Lima Company, and the duty asked.

"Pitchball game," Lief said. "Is the sergeant major in?"

"I hope you won," Jen said. "And yes, as usual, he's still in."

Sergeant Major Crawford worked longer hours than anyone in the battalion, and Leif had hoped he was still in. India's first sergeant, First Sergeant Gorter-Darrooca, was on leave, and Leif didn't think it would be appropriate to go to Kilo's First Sergeant Popiel since he was no longer in the company. That left the sergeant major.

Leif shuffled to the hatch and rapped on the frame.

"Who is it?" the rough, gravelly voice yelled out.

"Lance . . . uh, Corporal Hollow, Sergeant Major."

"Come on in, Corporal," the sergeant major said, "And congratulations on the . . ." His voice faltered a moment as he took in Leif's visage before continuing, ". . . promotion. It was well deserved."

"Sergeant Major, I—"

"No, really, it's well-deserved," he interrupted Leif. "Making NCO is an honor. I loved my time as one. You know, down in the dirt with the Marines. Best time of my life."

"Sergea—"

"Yes, best time of my life. Difficult, too," he said, stepping out from behind his desk and walking up to him.

"Being in charge for the first time, making decisions. No, not easy at first. It gets easier though. Not easy, but easier. Nothing about being a Marine is easy."

Leif tried to talk again, but the sergeant major wouldn't let him get a word in edgewise.

"You're a good Marine, one with a bright future. The Corps needs Marines like you, but you're green still. You're still learning. Sometimes, things don't work out the way you think they will. Or should. You've got all the Marine Corps regs behind you, to guide you, but sometimes, they don't have all the answers."

The sergeant major's almost frenetic pace had slowed down, and he was speaking normally now, in an almost father-son tone.

"When that happens, you have to do what Marines do best."

"What we do best?" Leif asked, caught up in what he was saying.

"Yes. We make do with what we have. We improvise. We simply get things done. Even if what we do isn't exactly in the regs. Do you understand what I'm saying, son?"

"Uh . . . I think," he said, mumbling through his swollen mouth.

"Good. If you do, then you can make a career out of the Corps. Know when you can step out of the regulations for the good of the mission. But know when you have to adhere to them. Take me, for example. I'm a sergeant major, a glorified paperpusher. If certain things are brought to my attention, then I can't step outside the regs. I'm required by law to take action. Do you get what I'm saying?"

Leif nodded, but he was lost and confused.

"I have to report certain things, especially when, let's say, there is imperial interest?"

He means me. Us. Wyntonans, Leif realized. *We're still in the spotlight.*

"But as far as I'm concerned, if my NCOs take, shall we say, corrective action, as long as no one is killed, then why do I need to get involved?"

Leif stood silent a moment. *Is he telling me not to report what I just did?*

"So, I have to ask myself, was anyone killed? Seriously maimed?"

Only he wasn't asking himself. He was asking Leif. Leif thought back to how he left Lance Corporal Stone. The Marine had a broken nose, to be sure. Maybe a concussion, but then again, humans were remarkably thick-headed. Stone was moving when he left, so he was pretty sure he wasn't badly hurt.

"I can understand that question, Sergeant Major," he said tentatively. "I . . . I would guess that someone would tell you if that ever happened."

The sergeant major visibly relaxed before saying, "So, unless someone was killed, or unless someone was making a civil rights complaint . . ."

Meaning if I was going to complain about discrimination, he'd take action, but the battalion would suffer in the backlash.

" . . . then I would ignore what my NCOs had to do to get their jobs done. Unless they insisted, of course."

"I understand completely, Sergeant Major," he said, feeling a weight lift off his chest.

The sergeant major stared at him for a long moment before saying, "Well, I'm glad you stopped by. So unless there's anything else?"

"No, Sergeant Major. That's all."

"OK, then. Why don't you head on over to sickbay. You need to watch yourself when in the gym. Easy to get hurt, you know. Basketball?"

"Pitchball."

"That'll do it to you."

"Thank you, Sergeant Major, for your advice. Being an NCO is well, it can be challenging."

"And I know you're up for it."

Leif started to leave, and the sergeant major called out, "One more thing, son. As a team leader, you have some say in who is in your team. If you think you need to make a change, then let me know. I'll call up First Sergeant Gorter-Darroca and pass that on.

He knows I've got a problem, and he's giving me an out.

Leif almost jumped at the opportunity. Send Stone packing and let him be someone else's headache.

Is that what I want to do, though? Let others take care of my problems?

He wanted to ask the sergeant major to transfer Stone to another company. He ached to do it. But is that what a real Marine NCO would do?

He knew the answer to that.

"Thanks, Sergeant Major. But everything's fine in India."

"OK, then. Go get yourself to sickbay."

Leif stepped out of the office, then leaned back against the bulkhead beside the hatch, trembling. He'd just been about to turn himself in, expecting not only to lose his new corporal's chevrons, but that his career would be over, but he'd been given a reprieve. He still had a Stone problem, but it would be up to him to fix that.

"Holy shit," he heard the sergeant major, speaking to himself. "That was a close one."

He didn't mean to eavesdrop, so he crept silently down the passage a few meters before he switching to a regular, if limping gait.

"Take it easy, Corporal," Jen said.

"You, too."

His mouth was swollen, and his side was on fire. But he was almost skipping as he made his way to sickbay.

Chapter 2

"You're falling behind," Sergeant Zoran passed on the 1P. "Tighten it up."

"Roger that," Leif acknowledged, then pumped his fist up and down a few times before picking up the pace.

It was up to the other three Marines to watch him and guide on him, but he sought out and caught Stone's eyes, who nodded his understanding.

This was Leif's first field exercise since coming to the company, and he was determined to show he could be a leader. He'd been acting fire team leader many times back with Kilo, but he was no longer simply filling in a billet. Team leader was now his job, and he was going to make sure each of his three Marines did theirs—including his HG-man.

Lance Corporal Stone was not a happy Marine. Leif could see the resentment in his eyes every time the human looked at him, but after a week, the bruises from the fight already faded, and he had yet to challenge Leif. He was sullen, but he did what he was told. That was good enough for Leif. He didn't need Stone to like him, only obey him.

Leif was still somewhat on tenterhooks in the squad. Not with the sergeant—she was hard on him, but she was hard on the other two team leaders as well, and if she knew about his "counseling session" with Stone, she gave no indication of that. Leif was more concerned with the rest of the squad and platoon. First and foremost were Win and Sousa. Win was a short, stocky Marine who was off in his own world half of the time. He seemed to accept whatever came his way, and Leif got the feeling that the human considered him a Marine NCO, not a wyntonan Marine. Leif also got the feeling that Win had not completely bought into the entire Marine rank structure. The fact that the private didn't seem overly impressed with

NCOs didn't matter to him, however, because he had the same attitude toward all NCOs.

Sousa, on the other hand, seemed to fear him. Leif didn't know if that was because of what he'd done to Stone or if it was because he was wyntonan, but she was always walking on egg shells around him, jumping when he spoke to her. He'd tried to draw her out in casual conversation, but other than short, single syllable answers to his questions, she didn't say much.

The rest of the Marines either ignored him or treaded lightly around him as if he was a rabid dog.

No, that wasn't fair. Kyle Hwei, the corporal who'd invited him for a beer at the club had been very welcoming, and Manu was Manu. He'd even pulled Leif aside to say he'd handled the Stone problem well.

If he could change things, Leif would still be with Kilo. They knew him there, at least, and with Jordan and the others, he wasn't the lone wyntonans in the unit. But he wasn't with Kilo, he was now a part of India. Things weren't always easy in life, and not only Marines, but any a'aden, an adult wyntonan, was expected to just buckle down and get it done.

Leif was going to do just that.

The humans didn't have to like him. They didn't have to be his new best friend. They just had to be fellow Marines. If that was the best he could hope for, then that would be good enough.

Chapter 3

Leif's scanpad buzzed in his pocket, snapping him awake. He shook his head and tried to look alert, wondering what had just been passed by the G2 major briefing the battalion on possibly threats out in the great beyond.

Nothing the major was saying was new, and nothing pointed to immediate action, but with the battalion assuming the divisions alert status again, every Marine and sailor had to sit through a number of briefs that the brass thought vital, but rarely resonated with the troops.

This was the third time 3/6 had assumed the alert battalion since Leif had joined it. The first time, they'd seen action on Torayama's World, then immediately deployed aboard the *Cape Town*, making a landing on Omeyocan and taking down the slaver in the Peitriov System. The second time they'd gone on the alert, nothing happened, just as nothing happened on their subsequent cruise on the *Melbourne*.

Leif looked over to where Kilo was sitting. If Lori was sending him a message, she was sure hiding it well, her attention focused on the major.

If not Lori, then who?

He should forget it for now. The brief would be over soon enough, and he'd get chance to look, but Leif received few enough messages from anyone other than Lori that he was curious.

The major was discussing some unrest on a planet Leif had never heard of, and so far out of the sector that if things did blow up, then the Fifth Marine Division would react, not the Second. His scanpad vibrated again, and he couldn't help himself. He slowly put his hand into his cargo pocket and brought out the stick until he could see the end. The green message light was slowly flashing along with the turquoise light of an attachment.

It was from Home, probably Hope Hollow. No one else would be sending him an attachment.

Up on the stage, the major was droning on. Sitting directly in front of Leif was Lance Corporal Jack Kanakana, a heavyworlder. His broad back served pretty well to block Leif's hands from the front.

He looked forward with his most attentive expression as he pulled out his scanpad. Feeling along the tubed body, he thumbed the preview. The tiny screen popped up and unfolded.

Sitting beside him, Kyle nudged him with his elbow, but said nothing. Leif knew they were supposed to have turned off their scanpads, but he ignored his fellow corporal and took a quick look at the small preview screen that had unfolded at the tip of the pad.

He couldn't get a close look, but he could see a beaming Sorun standing over a batch of what looked to be spice, Grannie Oriano standing next to her.

"By the Mother," he whispered aloud, excited for his paired.

Soran was way too young to be making spice, but there she was, with Grannie Oriano. This was an honor, nothing less.

He felt a rush of pride and a twinge of . . . something else. There was a musth-like aspect to it, albeit just a touch. It was new to him, and he couldn't describe it.

Is this what it's like to be bonded?

The thought scared him. He retracted the preview screen and slid the scanpad back into his pocket, locking his eyes on the major . . . but he couldn't get the thought of Soran out of his mind.

Soran—then Sora—had always been his best friend, and when he'd gone back to Hope Hollow two years ago to go through his first estrous/musth with his tri-year, no one had been surprised that the two had paired.

Images of their unbridled passion flitted through his memories, making his pale white skin heat up, and he was sure turning him pink. But a First Pairing did not make a bonding. Those generally started to form after the Third Pairing, although sometimes after the second.

He reached down and patted the sheath on his leg, under his trou. Soran had already made her intents known. First pairings were explorations, of experiencing the cycle. It was not for the exchange of *haspe*, something that had no equivalent in Standard. A *haspe* was not a promise, but a sign of intent, but she'd pushed it to the limit. Somehow, she'd managed to scrounge up enough to hire one of the few master weapons makers left on Home to make him a *vic*, the old weapon presented to proven *serta*—warrior knights—much like human military medals. A short, triangular blade, never used for the mundane such as peeling fruit or cutting wood, it was designed for only one reason, and that was to punch through an opponent's armor and kill.

He had always assumed he and Soran might bond, but that was before he'd decided to reenlist. By presenting him with his *vic*, she was telling him she accepted his service, even after only their first pairing.

Leif was honored and touched, but he was not as confident. The Marine Corps was bad enough in accommodating human marriages, and the stresses caused many divorces, but it took nothing into account about the biological imperatives of the wyntonans. All they did was shoot up every wyntonan with inhibitors to keep the females from estrous and the males from musth. No one knew how the prolonged use of the inhibitors would affect them.

A simple image of Soran had just made him long for her—not in a physical way, but from an emotional perspective. True, she was standing over the spice as if she'd made it, which linked her to the bedrock of wyntonan culture, but he shouldn't be feeling anything, especially with the inhibitors coursing through his veins.

Are they failing? he wondered, pride for Soran replaced by fear.

Leif, and all wyntonans, were serving only because of the inhibitors. Without them, their biological imperatives, even occurring every three years, would create a huge problem for both the Corps and for the wyntonan Marines. If Leif was developing some sort of tolerance, then maybe he was not fit to be a Marine after all. Humans like Stone might be right, even if they were wrong about the reason.

He attempted to clear his mind, but try as he might, he couldn't focus on the major. All he could think about was that his biology might get him kicked out of the Corps.

Chapter 4

"Is this for real?" Sousa asked nervously as she grabbed her pack.

"No, Harper, we're going out on libbo," Stone said. "Play some snooker at the Blue Cigar."

"I mean, are we going to fight? With our weapons?"

"Better your eighty-eight than a snooker cue, huh?"

Win just rolled his eyes and shook his head.

"Just get out on the parade deck, Sousa," Leif said. "We'll find out what's going on soon enough."

He'd been through enough drills in his short career so far that he knew this could be just one more, but his warrior sense told him no, this was the real deal. And he was excited.

Everyone gave lip service to peace. When they assumed the alert status, the new CO, Lieutenant Colonel König, had said that they should hope for a peaceful tour. But the reality was that Marines, with a few exceptions like Sousa, wanted to mix it up. They wanted to prove themselves in battle. In this way, there was no difference between humans and wyntonans.

The humans, however, had a long history of elevating warriors. For the wyntonans, after centuries of war had decimated their planet, they had managed to overcome their base proclivities for fighting and pushed war into the closet. Their DNA, however, was not easily changed, and for those wyntonans in the Marines, they were able to throw off the shackles. It might not be "civilized," it might not be "moral," but that was how they were built.

"We're in Stick 18," Sergeant Zoran told him as they reached the front hatch. "Get your Marines in place and sit. I'll be there in a few mikes."

The quad was a mass of confusion, or at least, it appeared to be so. But everyone knew what they had to do and where they had to go. It might be chaos, but it was organized chaos as Marines rushed to their places. The alert had sounded eight minutes ago. In seven more minutes, they needed to be ready to move out.

Leif got his team to Stick 18, then sat them down with six minutes to spare. For the grunts, it was easy. They just had to get themselves to the right place. For some of the other MOS's—Military Occupational Specialties—there was much more that had to be done. The crypto geeks, for example, had to get to their safes and draw their gear. They couldn't fall in on staged weapons at the shuttle port like grunts could.

Somehow, it all seemed to come together. It looked like most of the battalion was staged and ready in time. Other units reinforcing the battalion would be staging in their own areas, reporting back to Lieutenant Frasier, the embark officer.

After the rush, to no one's surprise, they waited . . . and waited. There were many moving parts to getting a reinforced battalion to another planet, and while the 15-minute time-line was codified in the regulations, the reality was that it almost always took longer than that. It was better to take a little bit longer to task-organize the battalion for the specifics of a mission than to rush out without what was needed to accomplish it.

The good thing was that the longer they waited, the more likely that this was a real mission. Sousa, as a boot newbie, sitting on her pack, was calming down as nothing happened. Leif, with his four years experience, was getting more excited.

Twenty-six minutes after they formed in the sticks, the squad leaders were called into the CP. Forty-four minutes after that, they came streaming back out to where the battalion was formed.

"We've got a mission," Sergeant Zoran said when she rejoined them. "Han'ie!"

HAN'IE

Chapter 5

"One more thing," Lieutenant Foster Nazari said before dismissing the platoon. "We went over the ROEs, but I really want to stress this. We're here as peacekeepers. The Krocs are citizens, but that doesn't make the Leaguers our enemy. We're here to stop the fighting so that the negotiators can defuse the situation. We do not, I repeat, *do not* want a fight to break out. If someone throws a rock at us, a bottle, we will not overreact. If a crowd blocks our way, we will not overreact. No matter what happens, we will not overreact. Does everyone understand?"

There were some nods, but no one said anything.

"I'm asking you, does everyone understand?"

"Yes, sir!" the platoon chorused.

The battalion was on a peacekeeping mission, but when tempers were flaring, things had a habit of breaking down. No one here should be stupid enough to take on a reinforced Marine battalion, but there are a lot of stupid people in the galaxy whose balls were too big for their brains.

Leif understood the lieutenant's orders, and he intended to obey them, but the ROE was the ROE. They Rules of Engagement authorized them to fire in defense of life, either theirs or the civilians'. If his fire team became threatened, Leif was not going to let that threat stand.

"OK, then, let's get ready. We're leaving the wire in," he paused to glance at his wristcomp, "exactly twenty-nine minutes.

"Make your last head-calls, because we won't be back for more than eight hours."

The battalion had landed on Hull, the nominal capital and largest city of Han'ei. With over five million people, they could overwhelm the battalion if they so wanted. The hope was that they wouldn't want to, however. The Marines were not the enemy—and they hoped the people knew it.

Han'ei was a rich world with a couple of billion people. The bulk of the planet's manufacturing and finances was controlled by the Kurokodairu Clan, one of the more powerful clans in the empire. They owned the charter of the planet and had leased settlement rights to the Humber League, an independent entity with close ties to the empire. The majority of the planet's two billion were Humber Leaguers, a large number of whom worked in the Kroc factories.

After more than two centuries of relatively peaceful coexistence, protests had broken out when the Krocs had raised the license fees—basically, they'd raised the rent, and the tenants were not happy about it. The protests had turned violent, and people on both sides had been killed.

The imperial governor had called for peaceful negotiations, but he was in a tough position. While the planet belonged to the empire, the bulk of the population were not citizens, so he could not order the Leaguers to stand down. And with the Kroc security forces outnumbered, but known for a nasty streak of ruthlessness, he felt things could break down quickly unless there was an imperial force there to keep the warring sides apart.

Enter Third Battalion, Sixth Marines.

There were undoubtedly far more moving parts and perspectives to the situation, but this was how Leif and the rest of the Marines had been briefed. They were to interject themselves into the line of fire, yet not provoke anyone on either side.

Leif hoped the officers had figured out a way to do that. At the grunt level, if they became targets, they'd fire back.

****

Leif stopped, and when Sousa reached him, looking up in confusion, he said, "Take your finger out of the trigger guard. I'm not going to tell you again."

"Oh, yeah. Sorry," she said as he stepped back to his position.

The patrol had been long, and Leif was ready to get back to the camp they'd set up at the shuttleport. The mission had been to show the flag, to let the locals know the Marines were here and had things well in hand. There had been no overt protests to their presence. In the Kroc enclave, in fact, they'd been welcomed. Back in the League areas, however, things were a little tenser, but the Marines had received nothing more threatening than some glares.

Now, on their way back, all he needed was for Sousa to trip over her own feet and accidentally fire off some rounds, either into his backside with him being right in front of her in the column, or off into the buildings on either side of them.

Leif was not comfortable in the artificial canyons. He was a village boy from out in the sticks, and as a Marine, he'd lived either at Camp Navarro or Camp Martelle, both with huge tracts of empty land. Here, in the warrens of Hull, the towering buildings seemed to be closing in on the column of Marines. He could feel thousands of sets of eyes on him, and if Sousa accidentally fired off a burst, she'd probably hit someone.

I guess it's better if she does shoot me in the ass instead of some Leaguer.

He was tempted to take out her magazine and pocket it, but if the shit broke, he couldn't leave her defenseless. A Marine without a weapon was just a target.

They reached a small park, and Leif felt a weight lift off his shoulders. He knew more eyes were now on them, but at least he had a little breathing room. A dozen small children were playing in the grass with a handful of adults watching over them. If they were concerned to see a squad of combat Marines appear among them, they didn't show it.

The lieutenant called for a halt, raising his hand to his helmet to block off outside noise. He'd be reporting their position or getting feedback from the hundreds of microdrones that were birddogging their route. Leif pulled up the patrol route. Another klick-and-a-half, and they'd be back. Just two blocks to the north, Second Squad was paralleling their route, and Third Squad and Staff Sergeant Antoine were another two blocks beyond them. If any one of the patrols got into the shit, the other two could come to their support within minutes.

A few of the children walked up to the Marines, eyes wide.

"Steady, Sousa," Leif passed on the 1P.

The only thing worse than accidentally hitting a local would be to purposely shoot a child.

With all the innocence of the very young, two of the little ones looked up wide-eyed at the Marines. A woman sat on a bench near them, seemingly at ease, but Leif could see the tension in her body. Just as Leif would protect his fire team, he knew she was ready to protect the two children.

One of the little ones, a girl with pale skin and blonde hair, caught his eyes. Leif smiled, and the little girl raised her hand and pointed at him, turning her head to say something to the woman. The woman jumped up and pushed the girl's hand down, then picked her up. Grabbing the boy by the hand, she turned and rushed away.

"Hell, Leif. What did you do, bare your teeth at her?" Kyle asked over the 1P.

Leif didn't have a rejoinder, and he was saved from trying to come up with one by the lieutenant ordering the patrol to move out. He took a last glance at the retreating woman and two kids before shrugging and starting off.

He didn't know what the little girl had said, but from the woman's reaction, he could guess. He'd joined the Marines because when he was a child, he'd been rescued from a very short life as a slave by the Imperial Marines. He wanted to be that guy, the one who saved the others. And now, he'd just been reminded that even among the young, humans did not really accept his kind as equals.

"Let's look sharp as we bring it in," the lieutenant passed on over the platoon net so all three patrols could hear. "Remember why we're here."

Leif straightened up his posture. He couldn't control others, but he could control himself. Whether he was accepted by the people he was sent to protect or not, he would do his duty to the best of his ability.

That's what Marines did.

Chapter 6

"You're not an honest broker," the League spokesman said as he stood, leaning forward with both hands on the table.

"I can assure you, Mr. Jones, that we are not taking sides here. My Marines are here to keep the peace, period. It's up to you and Mz. Ito to work out your current differences . . . with the governor's assistance, of course," Lieutenant Colonel König said, nodding to indicate the governor sitting beside him.

"Wykoff? He's in Kurokodairu's pocket," Jones said dismissively. "I don't think you're here to do the Clan's bidding. They've got their kenpeitai, after all. But you are imperial troops, after all, sent to do the emperor's bidding."

"Yes, we are here on imperial orders. This is an imperial planet. But the emperor has taken great pains to be inclusive of all people, of all races, and that includes tenants."

As the CO said "races," several sets of eyes glanced up at Leif and Jordan. Leif stared ahead, not meeting anyone's eyes.

It had been pretty obvious why Leif was part of the security/honor guard in the room. Kilo's Second Squad, First Platoon, where Jordan was a team leader, had been assigned the task, but Leif had been added to the roster. Having two wyntonans present presented a better picture of an all-inclusive, fair-minded empire. It was showmanship, pure and simple.

But Leif had no problem with it. If his presence could help convince the Leaguers to come to the negotiating table in good faith, then he was happy to be part of the effort.

Truth be told, it felt good to be singled out for something positive based on his race. It made him feel valued. He stood still, trying to look as professional as possible.

He understood the League representative's point, though. They were imperial troops, so it was logical that they were on the planet to protect imperial citizens and assets. The CO had briefed the battalion that they were not to take sides in the conflict, and Leif didn't think that was simply lip-service. The spokesman wouldn't know that, however.

"Think logically, sir. Han'ei produces many products that are needed in the empire—"

"Made in Kurokodairu factories."

"Yes, Kurokodairu factories, and with mostly Humber League workers. If violence escalates, not only will people from both camps suffer, but the empire will suffer. It is in our best interests to see a peaceful resolution to your differences. A large part of that is for humanitarian reasons. If you don't want to believe that, then how about purely self-serving reasons? We don't want a disruption to the economy. Doesn't that make sense?"

This was the first time Leif and been close to the CO for any extended period, but as he'd listened over the last 20 minutes, he was impressed. He was showing another side to being a Marine lieutenant colonel than simply leading his battalion in combat.

"Yes, that makes sense, but since when has the empire always made sense? What about Densiter?"

The CO hesitated, but he didn't avoid the question. "That was under Gregory IV, and it was a horrible mistake."

"Yeah, you can call it a mistake. A two-hundred-thousand-person mistake," the spokesman said.

Densiter was far more than a "mistake," Leif knew. It was a permanent black-eye against the empire and Corps. Leif had heard about it while growing up—every sentient being in human space knew of it. At Camp Navarro, the recruits had spent an entire afternoon on the history lesson.

Seventy-two years ago, while Gregory II sat on the Granite Throne, the workers on the factory planet Densiter had gone on a general strike. "Workers" was a genteel term for what they were. "Indentured servants" was more accurate. The local security forces went on a rampage during the strike, killing over 400 of the strikers during a march. The workers struck back, overwhelming a company of security and stringing the bodies up on display.

Gregory immediately sent in the Marines purportedly to quell the violence. "Purportedly" because his real orders to the hand-picked colonel and Navy captain in charge of the task force were to break the strike and get them back to work, using whatever force was required.

Colonel Hank Torres embraced the orders, but whether out of loyalty to the emperor or because of a perverse love of violence was still a subject of debate. What was not subject to debate was that his rampage was the biggest black eye given to the Corps in its otherwise gloried history.

Captain Alicia Gary and the *Torrey Creek* actually slaughtered more civilians with the ship's naval guns, but it was the Marines, who were recorded on a multitude of holocams during their rampage, that incensed the populace.

More than 140,000 civilians were killed over a 12-hour period, 98% by naval gunfire. The death toll would have been greater had not Lieutenant Colonel Winfred Lee refused to escalate the initial clash, initially pulling his Marines back, then when the *Torrey Creek* started her bombardment, thrusting his Marines forward to act as human shields.

Marine casualties were heavy, with 812 KIA: six in the initial clash with the strikers, and 806 by "friendly fire," both from the *Torrey Creek* and from Marine artillery strikes ordered by Colonel Torres.

The aftermath was brutal. Colonel Torres and Captain Gary were court-martialed and executed. The Wan Clan lost their charter for the planet, and it was turned over to the twelve-million workers. And when information was leaked that proved the emperor was a minority holder of the Wan Clan's operations on Densiter, he was forced to abdicate, the only emperor in the history of the Granite Throne to do so.

Lieutenant Colonel Lee was the saving grace for the Corps. He was killed when he insisted on standing among the strikers being targeted. A very few Marines were actually part of the colonel's plan. The battery commander was not, and when she found out what her tubes had done, she killed herself. There were demands that the Corps be disbanded, but the strikers, now owners of Densiter, objected. Lieutenant

Colonel Lee and the other 811 Marines were considered heroes, and in the end, they kept the Corps alive.

"Never again," was an unofficial motto of the Corps.

The League spokesman brought up Densiter to argue against the battalion's presence. Leif thought the argument was working against him. If anything, Densiter was a guarantee that the Marines were there to keep the peace, not break it.

Lieutenant Colonel König didn't say a word for a long moment, then repeated, "Yes, as I said, a mistake. One from which we all have learned. But Gregory II is not on the throne now. Forsyth III is—"

"He's a child, controlled by the clans," the spokesman said dismissively.

"He's our emperor, to whom every Marine and sailor in this battalion has sworn their allegiance," the CO said, steel in his voice. "I'll have you remember that. And the emperor is dedicated to stomping out the kind of injustices that made Densiter possible. If you wish to reject his imperial concern, that is your choice.

"I'll also have you remember that you and all of your people are here under an imperial grant. You may have paid the Kurokodairu for the license, but the underlying grant is imperial. While the emperor has no control of you as individuals, he can revoke your right to be here."

He turned to look at the governor, and asked, "Have I explained that correctly, sir?"

"Yes . . . yes, that is legally correct."

"I would suggest that when you return to your president and the rest of your leadership that you remind him of that little fact."

The spokesman stood stock still for a long, long moment, then said, "You wouldn't dare."

"You're right, sir. I wouldn't dare, but I don't have that authority. I'm just a mere Marine doing my best to keep you from killing each other. But the emperor might, and he does have the power.

"Now, are you ready to sit down and talk?"

There was another long pause as the spokesman stared at the Marine CO.

"I think I will end this . . . *discussion* for the moment for further consultation. If you will excuse us?"

"I have no authority over you, sir. You may do as you will."

The spokesman nodded at his team, and they stood up and filed out of the conference room. No one said a word until the door closed behind the last one.

"I'm sorry, sir," the CO said to the governor. "I realize that wasn't my place."

The governor was all smiles as he said, "Oh, no, Colonel, that was well done. Well done!"

The Kurokodairu team leader, Mz. Ito, stood up, her grin almost splitting her face in two. She walked over to the CO and clamped him on the shoulder with a healthy blow.

"Come on, David. 'Well done?' That's all you can say? The colonel was superb, simply superb," she said to the governor before turning to the Marine CO. "You put that slimy piece of garbage in his place, Colonel. He'll be shitting himself as he tries to figure out what he's going to say to the president. You've done Kurokodairu good, son."

The CO looked at the offending hand still on his shoulder before he took it in his and removed it, letting it drop free.

"Mz. Ito, I have not done anything, nor will I do anything, to help the Kurokodairu Clan. I told you that we are here as a peacekeeping force, and we will do whatever we can to further the process along. We will not be taking sides. None of us will, by direct order of the emperor."

He gave the governor a pointed stare as he said the last, and Leif had to wonder if there was anything to the League spokesman's accusation against the governor. It was certainly possible. It was standing knowledge that the corruption was rife among the imperial bureaucracy.

"Yes, yes, we know. You are neutral, and if anyone from the press asks, that's what I'll say," Mz. Ito said as if in on the joke.

"I'm not sure you're taking that to heart, ma'am. When I say the Marines are to be neutral, that is what I mean."

Ito looked surprised, but the CO was making no bones about it—he was serious.

"But we're citizens," she said, sounding confused. "They aren't."

"And they are imperial tenants, and as such, under the emperor's protection. So, you might want to tell your directors that. We will protect the Humber League citizens to the best of our abilities." He stepped closer, leaned in, and said, "And we have tremendous abilities, ma'am."

He straightened and said, "Lieutenant Shymaster, we're done here. Get your Marines back to camp. XO, gather the principal staff and commanders. I want them in the briefing tent at fifteen-hundred."

He looked back to the governor and simply said, "Sir."

The Kilo platoon leader gathered his Second Squad and Leif, and they filed out of the room for the march back to camp.

All of this had been way above Leif's paygrade, and it gave him an insight to things he never knew happened. The enlisted Marines tended to think the officers had it cush with the grunts doing all the work, but if this was indicative, then there was a lot more to it.

Suddenly, he was glad he was an NCO. Point him to the enemy and tell him to kill. He could handle that. This high-level political stuff was just so much shit.

Chapter 7

The bottle arched up, sparks trailing as it reached out to the Marines.

"Incoming" several voices yelled, but it was obvious the bottle was going to come up short. It hit the ground a good 15 meters in front of the memory wire—the flammable liquid splashed forward another five meters, flames billowing upwards.

"Hold your fire," the lieutenant passed over the platoon net, just as he'd done at least nine times before since First Platoon and assumed the perimeter.

The last two days since the meeting with the League spokesman had been a series of low-grade conflicts. No shots had been fired at the Marines, but there had been rocks, stinkers, and now Molotov Cocktails. Some of the rocks had hit Marines, doing little, if any damage. The stinkers were more of a nuisance, one that barely bothered the wyntonans, but the humans hated. A Molotov Cocktail could hurt a Marine, even kill one, and the bad guys could certainly range them, but for the moment, it looked like they were simply warnings to keep within the wire and not patrol out in the city.

Not that the CO was going to let anyone dictate to the Marines. Two platoon-sized patrols from Kilo were now out there.

No one was even sure who was doing the throwing. Drones caught images of almost all of them, but with their faces covered by balaclavas, the recognition software was next to useless. Leif had assumed it was the Leaguers, but that was only until Sergeant Zoran said that it could be the Krocs trying to nudge the Marines into a more active conflict. Thinking back to the meeting he'd observed, he had to admit to the possibility.

Whether it was Leaguers or Krocs didn't matter too much to Leif. If they were trying to hurt Marines, that was good enough to warrant action, as far as he was concerned. Let the governor and the negotiators worry about who was being the aggressors here. He fingered the trigger of his M88. It was on safe, checked three times by Sergeant Zoran, the platoon sergeant, and the lieutenant, but he had a magazine with 240 rounds, and if he needed to engage, all it would take would be to thumb the safety off.

A media drone dove down to get a closeup of the flames that were already dying out. The emperor had pushed for a return of a free press, and while they seemed wary of an imperial about-face, they were beginning to stretch their journalistic legs, none-the-less.

"Hey, do you think the media could be instigating all of this?" he asked Kyle over the 1P as he turned to where the Third Team Leader was standing 40 meters away.

"I wouldn't have thought so, but it does make it kind of convenient, now that you mention it, Leif. Look at the drone getting the close-ups. JBS will probably crop that to make it look like the whole area is under flames."

JBS, or the Joint Broadcasting System, was a human-sassares media corporation. Their stated goal was to promote galaxy-peace, but its reputation was as an organ of the sassares triumvate. Held in check by the previous emperor, the new open policy of Forsythe III gave it more access to human space.

Leif didn't know if that was a good idea, not that anyone cared what he thought. The drone circled the flames, and Leif realized that it could now record both the flames and the Marines inside the wire—and he was right in the field of view. He turned around, averting his face.

Marines were not created to just sit. They were an offensive organization, built to close with and destroy the enemy. This was excruciatingly boring, but he couldn't afford to relax his guard. The next cocktail might just have more legs on it.

Just three more hours, Leefen, three more and we're done until our patrol this afternoon.

Chapter 8

Leif stood at the door to the non-descript office building in Kenjii Park, the Kroc admin center in Hull. It was also just a few hundred meters from the Saint James, a Leaguer apartment village. He wasn't sure what normally went on in the office, but for now, it was going to host yet another low-level negotiating session. More specifically, the two sides were going to negotiate just how to set up the real negotiations.

The Leaguers were already inside, having arrived over twenty minutes ago. Leif turned around and looked through the glass door. They didn't look happy. He wasn't sure about human diplomatic protocol, but it had to be a slap in the face of the Leaguers that the Krocs were keeping them waiting, in what was technically Kroc territory.

"If this is how it's going to be, this might be a long mission," Lance Corporal Stone said.

Leif tried to hold in his surprise. Stone had not crossed the line into insubordination since his "counseling session," and he'd done everything Leif had told him to do, but he hadn't ever offered small-talk or anything outside official communications.

"I don't think the Leaguers are going to stay around long," Leif said. "They look about ready to bolt."

"I'd bolt, too, if the fucking Krocs kept me waiting."

This time, Leif couldn't keep the surprise from his face.

"What, Corporal, you think I like the Krocs?" he said, the sneer back as he turned away.

To Leif, humans were humans, which was just as bad as the humans thinking all wyntonans were alike. Of course, there were different factions with humanity, but Leif didn't understand the schisms.

Which probably wasn't smart. Here he was, on a planet with two opposing sides, with a mission to keep the peace, and he didn't even know much about them. Stone evidently had a bad opinion of the Krocs, and Leif didn't know if that opinion was widespread, or if it was something personal to the lance corporal. He made a mental note to look up what he could to get a better understanding of the overall situation.

Chapter 9

Staff Sergeant Makayla Antoine raised a closed fist, bringing the patrol to a halt. Leif stopped and turned outboard. Normal SOP would be to take a knee, but the platoon was on display just as much as it was on an operational patrol, so he stood, trying to portray an image of the professional, don't-mess-with-me Marine.

The platoon sergeant fascinated Leif. A heavyworlder, she was broad across the shoulders, almost as big as Manu. Her skin was as black as Leif's was white, far beyond the normal color palette of humans, and with her shaved head, she was an imposing figure.

Leif hadn't had much contact with her on a one-on-one basis, but she spoke in a quiet tone that could fool someone into thinking she was easy-going. She wasn't. In a way, she was more demanding than Sergeant Zoran, and when a Marine didn't measure up, she erupted into a demon from the bitter cold of hell.

This was her first time out with the platoon as the patrol leader since they'd arrived. Lieutenant Nazari had been called back aboard the *Ouachita Parish* for a meeting when the mission came in, and with the platoon on call as the reaction force, the mission was theirs.

So far, the patrol had been like any of the other nine patrols Leif had been on, either platoon or squad-sized. People watched as they passed by with varying expressions, and other than a few shouts, they were left alone. Leif wasn't sure why the rock-throwing and other violence was restricted to the area around the battalion compound when they were far more vulnerable out in the city.

Not that he was complaining.

He'd gotten used to the tall buildings crowding him. He'd never settle in a city like this, but he was no longer bordering on claustrophobia. Still, if he was going to fight, he'd rather it be where he could see who was coming.

"Listen up," the staff sergeant passed over the patrol net with her strong Wainscott accent. "We've got more detailed intel. There are three teams acting as lookouts, located as you can see."

Three yellow triangles popped upon Leif's helmet display. Their target was a non-descript two-story shop located across from a school. Two lookouts were positioned at either end of the block, and one was behind the shop on the roof of an adjacent building. There were gaps in their coverage that no Marine would have accepted, but then again, these were factory workers, not military men and women.

"I'm adjusting the plan."

Leif wasn't surprised. Most plans failed to survive first contact. This plan hadn't even gotten to first contact, but the placement of the lookouts just offered too many vulnerabilities that they could exploit. What they did not want was to conduct a frontal assault, and given what was supposedly inside the shop, the Leaguers might think it worth a fight.

"Second and Third, you're now the support element, and you're going to advance along this axis."

A broad arrow appeared across Leif's display. It led along their present route, then kept across the square and on to the other side of the school.

"First, you're going to peel off at the alley here. I think you can hug the north side of the alley and stay out of sight of Lookout Number 3 until almost up to the objective."

"We can't stay out of sight of everyone," Sergeant Zoran interjected. "We're kind of hard to miss."

"You don't have to. I'm betting that none of the locals have comms into the objective. If someone jumps out and runs to warn them, well, you can run, too."

"And if they are warned, Staff Sergeant?"

"If they are, you're a Marine rifle squad. They're half-a-dozen factory workers."

"Roger that."

"As soon as First initiates entry, I want the assault element to push across the pitchball field and seal off the objective. No one gets out."

The staff sergeant threw up some more symbols, but in reality, it was a pretty elegant and simple adjustment. By remaining on the main thoroughfare and then in the open near the school, they were giving the Leaguers at the target something on which to focus while the assault element—First Squad—made the breach into the shop.

All the other parts of the plan remained the same. Leif reached to his hip where ten zipcuffs hung. Ten was probably too many, and both Kyle and Manu each had ten more, but better safe than sorry.

"Let's move out," the staff sergeant said. "Be ready for anything."

Leif felt a familiar uptick of adrenaline as First Squad, which was the second in the patrol column, approached the alley. It was difficult for a Marine in full battle rattle to remain unobtrusive when eyes were undoubtedly on them, but they did the best they could, slipping out of the column and hugging the north side of the alley as they hurried forward. They had 70 meters until the alley bent to the right and the target would be within sight.

No one said a word as they moved. At this stage of the game, it all came down to the hours they'd trained together far more than the plan itself. Each of the Marines knew how to clear and seize a building, so it was up to them to put their knowledge and abilities into action.

Lance Corporal Qaan, the point man for the squad, held up a moment just short of the bend. On his display, Leif could see the first Marines from Second Squad crossing the square. They would be in full view of anyone at their objective now. Hopefully, anyone inside as well as the lookouts would be locked onto them.

The squad bunched together—normally a tactical no-no—ready to move at Sergeant Zoran's command. Leif slowed his breathing, pushing back the excitement of imminent combat.

The sergeant waited until Third started across the square, then said, "Now! Go, go, go!"

With Third Fire Team leading, the 13 Marines and one Navy corpsman rushed forward at the double-time, covering the remaining 60 meters in 15 seconds.

"Breaching charge!" Leif yelled at Lance Corporal Stone.

The Marines had many ways to breach a building. With the pressed filament prefabs used in this neighborhood of Hull, a simple DER—a Dynamic Entry Ram—would probably do the trick, but it might take more than a single swing. But with what was reported to be inside, they didn't want to use anything too powerful such as the pyroplast Lori had used on the slaver, which could set off secondary explosions. So, instead of blowing the wall, they were going to cut it with lavastrips.

Stone slung his 85, pulled out the strips and outlined a large opening.

"Ready!" he said after nine seconds, well within his allotted fifteen.

They had to wait for Lance Corporal Cennet with First Fire Team, but within a few moments, he shouted out "Ready" as well.

"On three . . . two . . . one . . . go!" Sergeant Zoran shouted out.

The two sets of outlines lit up with a painfully white glare that his faceshield momentarily struggled to dim. Smoke rose, and the flare went out. Stone and Cennet kicked in the middles, which fell to the inside.

"Going in left!" Private Win shouted, pushing past Stone.

"Going in right!" Leif shouted, right on Win's ass.

Four civilians were scrambling to their feet from a card game, two knocking chairs over in their haste. Stacked alongside the right wall were twenty to thirty cases of the type often used to transport weapons. Those weren't Second Fire Team's concern, though. First Fire Team was pouring in through the other opening, and they would secure those. Second had the bodies.

"Freeze!" Leif shouted, rushing forward, M88 at his shoulder and pointing at the closest civilian.

Stone rushed up beside him, and with Win, the three advanced, all the time screaming out at first for them to freeze, then to get down on their bellies. One of the men hesitated, looking to where a hunting rifle of some sort was leaning against the wall.

"Don't even try me," Stone shouted, stopping two meters short of the man, the barrel of his big M85 not wavering an iota. "Get the fuck down on your face."

The man gave one more glance at the big rifle, then slowly went down to his belly.

"Sousa, up!" Leif shouted, holding out his zip-ties.

The PFC, who'd been hanging back, handed Win her 88, took the zip-ties, and approached the four civilians.

"Bottom deck clear!" Kyle shouted.

With that, Third Fire Team came in through First's breach and moved quickly to the stairwell to clear the top floor.

"Hands behind your back," Sousa screeched out, her voice breaking.

She was nervous, Leif knew, but he had to get her blooded. If she couldn't handle this, then he'd have to bring up the matter with Sergeant Zoran.

"I said hands behind your back," she yelled again, kicking the side of the closet civilian.

It wasn't much of a kick, but the man said, "Don't shoot!" and tried to get his hand behind his portly figure. Sousa took one hand, kneeled on his back, and then pulled the other closer, slapping the zip-ties on the man's wrists.

Zip-ties automatically wrapped around and locked, but they had to be slapped at the right angle. Sousa had spent the hour before they moved out practicing first on a tent support, then on Win, over and over. It paid off. The zip-locks wrapped around and connected with an audible click, the green LED indicating a good lock.

"Good job, Sousa," Leif said. "Now get the others."

He could hear Third Fire Team, along with the sergeant, clearing the upper floor as Sousa zip-tied the other three Leaguers. At one point, he heard "Get on the ground, face down!" He wanted to ask what was going on, but he needed to focus on the job at hand. Sousa had given up her weapon so it couldn't be grabbed and used against her or the others, but still, an aggressive Leaguer could attempt to subdue and try to use her as a shield or hostage to affect an escape. This was a common trope in holovids—it wouldn't work so well against the Marines.

First, any one of them could shoot one of the Leaguers even if they were holding Sousa up as a shield. Second, Sousa, despite her nervousness, was a tough cookie in the MCCCP pit. Third, Sousa wasn't going to be dragged off anywhere. The imperial standard practice was to consider the hostage dead, so the Marines would risk her getting shot if that meant keeping her with them and not as a hostage.

Leif needn't have worried. The one who'd looked at the rifle kept glaring at them, but he didn't try anything as Sousa zip-tied him. The other three, two men and a woman, were obviously scared out of their minds. One of the men had pissed himself.

He didn't look around until all four were secured and Sousa had retrieved her M88. The crates were proof that Intel had been right. This was a makeshift armory, and this had been a righteous mission. It wasn't over yet, though.

"Manu, you doing OK? You need any help?" he asked over the 1P.

He knew Sergeant Zoran would call him up if needed, but he thought he'd offer assistance to his fellow team leader.

"No, we've got two hummers who were sleeping— together, if you know what I mean. Not in the act, but not too long after. We're letting them get dressed, then we'll bring them down and turn them over to you."

"Roger that."

Leif turned back to the captives, but along with the other three Marines, his eyes kept momentarily straying to First Team and their prizes.

"Is there anything in those cases?" Win asked.

That was the burning question. They had to have something inside, but what? It wasn't up to Second Fire Team or any of the Marines to find out, though. They had to ignore what the humans called the "elephant in the room," a phrase of which Leif was rather fond, and one he tried to interject into conversation as often as possible.

"Coming in from the front!" Staff Sergeant Antoine passed over the patrol net.

A moment later, she entered through the front door, along with Sergeant Foster from the armory and an EOD corporal who Leif hadn't met yet.

"Top floor clear," Manu passed on the squad net, which was followed by Sergeant Zoran passing "Objective secure," on the patrol net. She came down the stairs and joined the platoon sergeant as they looked at
the cases.

The EOD corporal asked something of the sergeant, who pointed at Leif. The corporal walked over and started to ask something before seemingly noticing that Leif was not human.

He gaped for a second, stepped back and looked around, then took a step towards Stone and asked, "Can I talk to the hummers?"

Stone looked to Leif who simply nodded.

There were eleven wyntonans in the battalion, and the corporal had been attached to them for two weeks now. He had to know that they were there, but he'd seemed totally surprised to see Leif's white face behind his faceshield.

The EOD corporal knelt in front of the heavy human, his face close, and asked, "Are those cases booby-trapped in any way?" The human said no, and he said, "I'm going to open them, and if something happens, you're going to be charged with that, understand? You're not EPWs, you know, protected. You're just civilian criminals. So I'm asking you again, are they booby-trapped?"

The man shook his head and told him no, they were not booby-trapped.

Leif wasn't sure if the corporal was correct in that the Leaguers were not protected as EPWs. He'd had the regular law classes as boot camp, but he wasn't all that caught up in wyntonan law, much less human law. He figured it was better to just treat everyone as EPWs and under the protection of the Pretoria Compact.

The corporal stared at the man intently, then stood up. He started to thank Stone, but he caught himself and stood in front of Leif for a moment and thanked him before going back to the cases.

Leif didn't think the corporal was being discriminatory when he ignored him and asked Stone if he could approach the Leaguers. He was just surprised and had been taken off guard. After he'd had a moment, he had thanked Leif.

And in some ways, that was worse, in his opinion. Stone was racist, pure and simple. The corporal might not have been, but it surprised him to see a wyntonan in a position of authority. Leif could deal with assholes, but there was still an inherent bias that seemed to run through most humans, whether they could see it or not.

The Marine Corps was race-blind, by order of the emperor, and for the most part, it seemed that way to him. But humans were humans, and sometimes their true feelings became known.

It doesn't matter, Leefen. Just do your job.

His job, though, at least for the moment, was to simply stand around. The Leaguers were secure, his four and the two Manu brought from upstairs. The other two squads were providing security. Leif couldn't help but watch as the EOD corporal opened the first case—which did not blow up, to the great and obvious relief of the fat human. He might have said the cases were not booby-trapped, but evidently, he hadn't been positive about that.

The corporal and Sergeant Foster started going through the cases, snapping holos that were being sent back to Division. Sergeant Foster didn't seem surprised at the types of weapons, explosives, and electronics, but he was surprised at the sheer volume in the shop.

When the first armored vehicle lorry arrived, it was obvious that it was too small, and two more were ordered up. Second Squad came in to help load the cases on the first vehicle, but then they all had to wait another 40 minutes until the second two arrived.

The original plan was for the Leaguer insurgents to be loaded aboard the lorry to be taken back to the camp and turned over to the small imperial security detachment on the planet. When the last case was loaded, Sergeant DuPont, the Second Squad leader told Staff Sergeant Antoine that the lorry was completely full, no room for pax.

The staff sergeant contacted battalion—probably Captain Filliard, the battalion assistant operations officer, who would have been monitoring the patrol with the major at the meeting aboard the *Ouachita Parish*—then announced, "They're coming in with us. Corporal Hollow, get them to their feet. Sergeant Zoran, I want another fire team on them as well.

"Two minutes, Marines. Two minutes and we're moving out."

"On your feet," Leif told the six Leaguers. "Now."

The humans started to get up, all except the heavy guy, who with his hands zip-tied behind him, was having problems.

Leif turned to Sousa just as the evil-eyed Leaguer said, "Help him, you fucking jarhead piece of shit."

The man was staring murder at him, anger evident in every molecule of his being.

"Fucking jarhead piece of shit?" Not "casper" or anything else? By the Mother, we're making progress.

He returned the stare, then told the heavy guy, "Stop." Still looking at Evil-eye, he called Sousa forward, hand out for her M88. "Help the gentleman up."

He nonchalantly stood there, a bemused smile on his face as he watched Evil-eye. It wasn't fake. He felt . . . well, good. He'd just been insulted by the man, but the key word he'd used was "jarhead." Evil-eye could see he wasn't human, but the most important fact—a bad thing in his mind—was that Leif was a Marine.

With a few grunts and groans, Sousa managed to get the heavy Leaguer to his feet, all the while Leif stared at Evil-eye. He handed Sousa back her 88, then made the slightest of nods to the still glaring human.

"Get them in a line, Stone," he said.

"Are we under arrest?" the man who'd pissed himself asked, his crotch a dark stain that stood out from the light tan of his slacks. "What's going to happen to us?"

Are you kidding me? You've got tons of weapons, and you're asking me if you're under arrest?

Except technically, they weren't under arrest, he acknowledged to himself. The Marines did not have arrest authority over civilians. They could take warfighters as prisoners, and they could take temporary custody of civilians to protect life and limb, but they had to either release civilians within 48 hours or turn them over to someone with powers of arrest. In this case, the battalion had an Imperial Investigative Service constable attached to it.

Leif wasn't going to go into the subtleties of the situation, however, so he said, "What's going to happen to you is that you're going to get in a single file and march with us back to our camp. What you won't do is open your mouths and speak. Understood? No, I told you not to speak," he said as Piss Guy opened his mouth. "Just nod your heads if you understand me."

Five of them nodded vigorously. Evil-eye deliberately waited a few moments, then gave a single, curt nod.

I'm beginning to like this guy.

Leif had no idea if the weapons this human had been guarding were intended to harm Marines, but the guy had some backbone, at least. If nothing else, that deserved a little respect.

"Put them in a file, Lance Corporal Stone. I want this guy in the lead," he said, pointing to the overweight man.

Stone kept his M85 as he took each person by the shoulder and lined them up. By SOP, he should have given up his weapon before getting that close, but they'd been zip-tied with their hands behind them, so Leif chose to ignore that.

SOP was *Standard* Operating Procedure, but sometimes, the reality on the ground allowed, even required, adjustments to it.

Sergeant Zoran walked up, took a quick look at the prisoners, then gave Leif his marching orders. The platoon was going to march back in a split column of twos, Second

Squad leading, then First, and then Third bringing up the rear. Leif and the Leaguers were to march between the two columns, with First and Third fire teams flanking them.

"Sergeant DuPont, move out!" Staff Sergeant Antoine shouted out, eschewing the comms.

"You heard her," the sergeant said to Leif. "Get them moving. If anything happens, you make sure you protect them. They're your charges."

Leif fought to withhold a grimace. He hadn't thought about that, but he should have and not had to have the sergeant remind him. His job was to get the Leaguers back whole and unharmed. They might be prisoners—*detainees*—but they were not the enemy despite the weapons cache.

"Roger that, Sergeant. We've got it."

"Let's go, First. Fall in trace behind Second Squad," she shouted out.

"Lance Corporal Stone, you lead. Sousa, you've got the left flank, Win the right. I'll pull up the rear."

As he took his position behind Piss Guy, he had a flashback, of himself, back in Hope Hollow, with the slavers taking them into the ship.

No, it's not like that at all! We're the good guys!

He shook his head, trying to get the image out of his mind. These were criminals, not peaceful villagers gathered for a Spice Day celebration. Whatever waited for them after they were turned over was undoubtedly better than the short life of a slave Leif had faced. Still, part of him understood the depression and fear that Piss Guy and the rest were probably feeling.

The patrol moved out and onto the main thoroughfare, Anlaby Road, which they would take up to Chanterlands Ave before turning down the A31, Beverley Avenue, to the camp. This route stuck to the wider roads, bypassing the narrower shortcuts . It would add an extra 700 meters to their route, but it would give them greater visibility and safety.

"Corporal Hollow," Staff Sergeant Antoine passed on the 1P, "keep me informed if the detainees are having problems keeping up. I'll adjust our speed of march if necessary."

"Aye-aye, Staff Sergeant."

They'd barely moved 100 meters, and the pace was slow as of yet, so no one was having problems. But as with all column formations, there tended to be some accordioning, more pronounced the farther back in the column. A Marine might be almost standing still one moment, then sprinting to keep up the next.

Anlaby Road was a wide, four-lane thoroughfare with a planted median. With the Marines on the move, most of the hovers were being diverted by their drivers down other streets, but a few drivers tried to proceed. Sergeant DuPont and Second Squad were bypassing the controls of the self-driven hovers, powering them down at the side of the road, and directing the drivers of manual hovers to park and power down, then exit the vehicles. A family of three leaned up against the side of their Hyundai Impressa, watching the patrol pass by. The man and child had passive expressions, but the woman kept switching her view from the detainees to the four Marines guarding them.

On the way to the objective, most of the civilians remained out of sight, but the six detainees seemed to be a magnet. More and more people started to either lean out of windows to get a better look or come out to line the road.

"Who are you?" a young woman shouted out.

"Horatio Mycroft. Tell my wife Analisa I'm being held prisoner," Evil-eye yelled out.

"No talking," Win said, stepping up to the man, weapon not quite pointed at him, but obviously ready to use.

Evil-eye—Mycroft—merely smirked at Win, his message already out.

"If anyone else wants to try that, I suggest you rethink that," Leif said. "Your names will be released to the Imperial Cross as soon as you're processed."

He wasn't quite sure what to do, however, if they all started yelling out. Just how far could he go? Suddenly, he wasn't quite as confident as he'd been a moment before.

The patrol reached Chanterlands and turned left. Leif was on edge. If something was going to happen, here, or where they turned onto the A31, would be natural chokepoints.

Marines at the rear of the column could not support those at the front and vice-versa. To his relief, the entire patrol made the turn, and for a klick, they would all be within sight of each other.

The staff sergeant was keeping the pace slow, so accordioning was minimized. Still, there was some. It wasn't the heavy guy who had problems, though, as he trudged along. It was Piss Guy, who kept slowing down and had to be prodded. Leif put Sousa beside him to make sure he kept up the pace.

They reached the A31 and made the turn intact. Now they had a straight, 1.7 klick shot to the camp.

"Some fun, huh?" Manu asked from alongside him.

"Yeah, you just have to march. I've got to worry about Piss Guy up there not being able to keep up."

"Piss Guy?"

"Yeah, he pissed his pants when we burst in."

Manu gave a deep, guttural laugh, then said, "No shit?"

"No, not shit—piss."

"'No shit' is just . . ." Manu started to explain, then caught himself and gave a chuckle. "Not bad, you almost got me."

Leif smiled. Humor was something that didn't always mesh between humans and wyntonans, and he enjoyed it when he could "yank someone's chain."

"Platoon, hold up," the staff sergeant passed.

Leif looked ahead, past Second Squad. People were beginning to come from out of the buildings or possibly side streets and filling the road a couple of hundred meters ahead of them. There looked to be close to a hundred of them milling about.

"Stand steady," the staff sergeant passed.

The crowd started to move forward, approaching the patrol. Second Squad immediately moved to block the road, taking a defensive position, weapons at the ready.

"Bring it in tighter," Staff Sergeant Antoine ordered.

Leif took a quick glance behind him to where Third Squad was bringing up the rear. The patrol stretched out for almost 200 meters, which was standard for a platoon in a column of twos. It did expose the flanks somewhat, however, and the platoon sergeant wanted to present a more compact front to face the approaching crowd. She had to be careful, though. Too compact, and they'd be an easier target for Molotov Cocktails and the like.

"Put the detainees into two columns," Leif told his team.

He debated for a moment zip-tying them in pairs, but Sergeant Zoran's reminder that he was supposed to protect them gave him pause. He didn't know what the crowd wanted, and if they wanted to attack, then zip-tying them into pairs would put them at a greater risk.

He moved the group forward, stopping 30 meters behind Second Squad's line. Behind him, Sergeant t'Bell and Third crowded forward.

"Stop right there," Staff Sergeant Antoine told the crowd, her amplified voice making some of the crowd wince and cover their ears.

They all stopped, though.

"I am Staff Sergeant Makayla Antoine, Imperial Marines, and we are heading back to our camp. Why are you impeding us?" she asked, her volume turned down a bit.

Several of the civilians looked around at each other before one stepped forward two paces and said, "We have no beef with you, Staff Sergeant. But you are not going to take six of our people anywhere. You release them, and we'll be happy to leave you alone."

"I'm afraid that's not going to happen, sir. These detainees were caught in the possession of weapons of war, which is against this planet's charter. They are going back to Camp Mixen for processing within the Imperial and Han'ei legal systems."

"And I'm afraid that's not going to happen. I don't care what you think those six have done. We're not going to let you hand them over to the Kroc kenpeitai," the man said.

"The detainees are currently in imperial custody, not the Kurokodairu's."

"Same damned thing," the man said while another few voices rang out with "Lackeys!"

"You do realize that you're facing a Marine platoon, don't you sir? And I don't see any weapons among you."

Leif couldn't see any weapons from his vantage point, either, but that didn't mean there weren't any. But her point was valid. Two-hundred, even three-hundred, unarmed civilians didn't stand much chance against a combat-ready Marine platoon.

As if to buttress her statement, one of the Basilisk combat drones swooped in to hover 20 meters above her head, its dart-thrower sweeping over the crowd. With 3,000 mini-darts in its magazine, it alone could wreak havoc among the crowd.

The crowd stirred, and more than a few of them backed away, but most remained firm.

"So, what are you going to do? Shoot us? I'm sure that's going to look good," the spokesman said, pointing over his shoulder where two JBS drones approached. "And there's more than just those two.

"Are you sure that's what you want, Staff Sergeant? A massacre of innocent civilians?"

"Civilians who are interfering with a legal process, I might add," she answered, but for the first time, not sounding quite as confident.

"Hell, you ruggers could blow right through them," Leif told Manu.

"What did you say?" Manu asked, but this time over the 1P.

"I said, you ruggers could blow right through them. What are they? Five deep? And a lot of them are already nervous about the Basilisk."

"Hell, Leif, how did you come up with that?" he said, cutting the 1P circuit.

Leif looked over at his friend, confused. He hadn't been serious, so why the weird reaction?

Manu, like many of the heavyworlders, loved rugby, especially Impact Rugby Union, which entailed much more of bodies slamming each other than traditional, 15-man rugby, to say nothing of the fast-moving sevens. Not as many regs played, but some did, and Leif had even got in a few pick-up matches. It was good, exhilarating fun.

Minta humans, he thought, once again reminded of how different the two races were.

He turned his attention back to the front, but for the moment, the staff sergeant wasn't saying anything. The spokesperson stood silently as well, but with a look of satisfaction on his face.

Slowly, Staff Sergeant Antoine turned around, caught Manu's eyes, and nodded.

"Come on, Leif."

"Come on where?"

"Where? It was your freaking idea. We're going wedging."

It took him a moment to understand what Manu had said. "Wedging" was an IRU term, where one team would form a shoulder-to-shoulder wedge, then charged forward, clearing the way for the lone ball-carrier to score a try. Of course, the other team would try to break the wedge, but that was all part of the game.

A familiar sense of excitement began to rise, embers turning into flames.

"But, I'm not a rugger," he protested half-heartedly.

Manu turned to look at him, then said, "We've only got four of us in the platoon who're ruggers, but you've played a bit. Besides, I was there at Camp Navarro for the pugil stick tournament. You kicked my ever-loving ass."

Staff Sergeant Antoine was already on the platoon net, getting the Marines ready. It was a simple plan. The wedge would break through the line of civilians, and the rest of the platoon would follow on their heels. They had half-a-klick to the gates, and no one was going to stop until they reached it.

"Stone, you've got the team. Don't lose any of the detainees, and protect them."

"I've got it," the lance corporal replied, not asking why.

"Sergeant Zoran—"

"I just heard. Kick some ass, Corporal."

Leif followed Manu up to the platoon sergeant, joined by the platoon's two other heavyworlders, Sergeant t'Bell,

Corporal Benny Taiko, and Private First Class "Red" Hornsby, a hulking, 2.4-meter-tall Marine. Neither Benny nor Red had played Rugby, but they were big, bruising guys.

Staff Sergeant Antoine asked Manu, "Are you sure about this?"

"Easy-peasy."

"You'll have to surrender your weapons. We can't have them snatched."

That took Leif aback. What the staff sergeant said went against everything the Corps taught. You never left a Marine without a weapon on the field of battle.

"We are the weapons, Staff Sergeant," Manu said.

The other six nodded their agreement.

She looked back over her shoulder at the crowd where the spokesman had lost some of his confidence, replaced with an expression of curiosity on his face.

"Do it, before they can gain any more confidence," she said. "The reaction force is being deployed, and they'll secure the last hundred meters."

Leif handed his M88 to one of the Second Squad Marines, feeling naked, but surprisingly not concerned. If the spokesperson looked curious before, that had just increased ten-fold.

Leif's *musapha* started to stir within him, which he suppressed. They just wanted to break through the crowd, not kill them. Then he looked at the other six of them. An IRU wedge normally consisted of 13 ruggers. They had seven, and they were facing a hundred civilians. Their assists, the nanos imbedded in their utilities and combat armor, would give them more than naked strength, but a hundred humans certainly outmassed them.

Leif let his *musapha* simmer, just under the surface. This could all go to the frigid depths of hell quickly if they didn't break through, and Leif didn't want to think of any of them being taken and held prisoner. The staff sergeant wouldn't let that happen, even if she had to order the platoon to open fire on the civilians, which contravened what they were trying to do on the planet. He had to make sure they broke through the people without loss of life, and if he had to, he'd let his mistress take over. Hopefully, he could control her.

The seven of them stood shoulder-to-shoulder just in front of the staff sergeant.

"As I said, we are not going to give up the detainees. We're going to proceed to our camp. It's up to you if you're going to attempt to impede us."

The Basilisk moved forward ten meters, and a good third of the crowd flinched.

"Come on! They won't dare do anything," the spokesman yelled to those behind him before he turned and started moving forward.

"Now!" the staff sergeant said.

"*Ki runga i te rangi*," burst forth from four throats in the ancient rugger cry, Leif shouting out "For the Mother" in Uzboss, while the other two simply screamed as they started their rush.

Leif was barely aware of the platoon moving behind him. He focused on the crowd. The spokesman didn't hesitate, and he gave a wide smile as the two forces closed together. Behind him, some people hesitated, but most turned to face the Marines.

The spokesman might have smiled, but he was sent flying when Manu and Leif hit him in unison. A moment later, the two masses crashed together. Bodies flew as the stronger Marines, aided by their assists, cut through the mass of humans. Hands reached for them, and Leif swung armored fists as he forced himself forward, forgetting the niceties of MCCCP training to revert to simply pummeling whoever was in front of him. He felt his fist smash noses, chests, and anything else within his reach. With Manu on his left and Red on his right, they were unstoppable. And within a moment, they were through, clear of the crowd.

Leif turned around in time to see Benny trip over a body. His momentum lost, people grabbed at him and started to pull the struggling Marine away. With a primeval shout, Leif let the mistress flow into his body. He leaped forward and started to pull bodies away, flinging them meters in every direction. Civilians scattered before his rage like *grazbin* before a *wasilla*. The four humans dragging Benny didn't see him until too late. He crashed into them, knocking all to the ground. Two were out cold while the other two were feebly trying to crawl away. He stood over them for a moment, ready to stomp them into red jelly, wanting to crush them, when what was left of his mind whispered for him to stop, reminding him of his duty. His mission was to get the detainees back, not kill the civilians.

It took a huge effort of will, but somehow, he was able to force his *musapha* back. The mistress fought him, not wanting to lose her freedom to rent and tear, but little by little, back she went into the recesses of his mind until he was able to close a mental door, locking her in. He picked up the dazed Benny and started to back away when the rest of the platoon pushed through the broken crowd.

Some humans stumbled and fell, to be trampled by Marines, but most scattered, their will to fight broken. Two Marines grabbed Benny from him as they surged forward.

"Come on," they yelled at him. "Move it."

Leif stood for a moment, taking in the scene. He was breathing hard. *Musapha* took a lot out of a person, but he'd only been under the mistress' grip for a few moments.

A few moments!

Normally, once it came forth, *musapha* stayed until it petered out on its own accord. Leif not only called it forth on demand, he'd controlled it, making it relinquish its hold on him.

He hadn't even known that was possible.

He lifted his head and screamed into the heavens before he joined the platoon as it double-timed to the front gate, where the reaction force was already emerging to escort them inside.

Chapter 10

"That was quick thinking, Corporal Savea," the CO said after Staff Sergeant Antoine had given her report.

The platoon had to wait for five hours until the colonel and his staff returned from the *Ouachita Parish*. They'd been pumped up as they rushed through the gate, proud of completing the mission without killing a single civilian, the best they could tell. Messed some up righteously, but there'd been no claims of any deaths on the footage already released by the Leaguers of the incident.

After cooling off, the aches and pains started to surface. Leif was already dragging from his brief spurt of *musapha,* but he also ached from the bruises that covered his body. His left eye was swollen shut, the skin around it a deep purple. It could have been worse. He'd been slashed with a monoblade, his utilities shredded, but the super-sharp blade had been turned by his body armor. He hadn't even been aware of getting hit, and even after watching the recordings, he still couldn't figure out who'd done the slashing.

And there were plenty of recordings, both from Marine drones, the *Ouachita Parish,* and the JBS recordings which had been immediately released by the news organization. If they had thought that would tarnish the reputation of the Marines, that had been a gross miscalculation. Prior to the CO returning, the Navy public affairs officer had told them that galaxy-wide sentiment was running 67 percent in their favor. The law-and-order crowd liked that the criminals had been apprehended and confined, and the societal rights crowd appreciated that there was no loss of life. Sports-minded folk simply liked the spectacle.

"Thank you, sir, but it wasn't my idea," Manu told the CO.

"It wasn't? I thought Staff Sergeant Antoine said that you were the one who brought the idea up to her."

"That's true, sir, but it was Corporal Hollow's idea first. He suggested it to me."

Leif snapped his head up.

What?

"Well, if that was the case, then you did well, too, Corporal Hollow. You and Corporal Savea, taking initiative in the best of Marine Corps tradition. You were faced with an untenable position, but like all good NCO's, you didn't let that phase you. Both of you came up with a plan, got it approved by your platoon sergeant, then implemented it."

He stopped for a moment, then in a more casual voice, remarked, "And boy did you implement it! Did you see their spokesman? I bet he flew ten meters when you hit him," he said as the rest of the Marines laughed. "I don't think he'll be getting in the way of Imperial Marines anytime soon in the future."

The CO went on for several more minutes, reminding them all that it wasn't up to him, it wasn't up to the officers to make sure the mission was carried out. It was up to the enlisted grunts, the ones on the lines.

Leif barely listened. He was trying to remember back just how the idea of a rugby wedge came into being. *He* thought it had been Manu. He might have mentioned something along those lines, but he'd been joking. It was his fellow corporal who'd seized on it, then put it all together.

He turned his head to where Manu sat, four Marines away from him. Manu caught his eye and gave him a quick nod.

Manu had been given the credit for the success of the mission by both the staff sergeant and the battalion CO. Heck, even Leif had given him the credit. Yet he'd insisted on making sure Leif's role was noted, even if Leif had been facetious in suggesting it.

Leif knew he'd been instrumental in the success of the wedge, and he might have saved Benny from being dragged away. He was confident of his physical abilities, even without *musapha*, and with the mistress, he knew he held all the advantages. But he was now being given credit not for cracking heads, but for coming up with the concept in the first place.

Maybe that's what being an NCO is about. Not simply being the toughest minta in the fire team, but actually making command decisions.

He was probably—no, undoubtedly—being given too much credit for the idea, thanks to Manu, but it was time he started to try and use his brain, not just his brawn, to get things done.

I just hope I have it in me.

CAMP MARTELLE, NORTHUMBRIA

Chapter 11

"Anyone home?" Kyle said as he rapped on the edge of the hatch.

"Sure, Kyle, come on in. I've cleared your wall locker, so you should have room," Leif said, jumping up from his chair where he'd been assembling his Class A uniform.

"Sorry to intrude on your little empire," Kyle said, sounding embarrassed.

"No, no, I understand. We're junior, right? So, we've got to double up."

"Yeah, but it was sure nice to have our own quarters, as long as that lasted."

Leif was actually relieved. Until he'd hit India Company, he'd never slept alone in his life. Back at Hope Hollow, he'd shared a sleeping platform with his family. At boot camp, he'd been in the barracks with his entire series. In Kilo, he'd been a non-rate, and all non-rates shared quarters. One of the perks, as most Marines considered it, of being an NCO was getting his own quarters, and coupled with missing his friends in Kilo, he hadn't adjusted too well, so he was glad that the attachments had arrived for work-ups, and berthing was at a premium. With corporals being on the bottom rung of the NCO ranks, they'd been forced to double up.

The battalion spent another six weeks on Han'ei after he and Manu had led the rugby wedge through the protestors (which is how the civilians who'd attempted to snatch their detainees were now officially referred.) There had been a few skirmishes with the civilians—once with the kenpetai who had what turned out to have an overly-inflated opinion of their warrior prowess—but the two sides had finally come to the negotiating table. With the battalion's deployment date approaching, they were recalled back to Camp Martelle with a company from First Battalion taking their place.

The mission to Han'ei had been declared a success, but there had been a cost. They'd spent almost nine weeks on the planet, nine weeks of patrolling, but without more comprehensive training. With only two weeks before their scheduled deployment, they hadn't had time for their workups. The decision was finally made to pull the battalion from its scheduled deployment rotation. For the next four months, they'd be back on the extended work-up cycle while 1/8 took their place, including representing the Corps for the Walters' World Arrival Day Celebration, a cross between Carnival, Coronation Day, and the Bacchanal, This was the plum show-the-flag assignment in the entire Corps, and it rotated among each of the divisions, so the Marines were pissed that it was being pulled from them. No one would even be still serving by the time it got back to 3/6 again.

The rescheduling was why Leif and Kyle were doubling-up today. The change in their deployment dates meant that many of the Marines would be due to transfer or EOE—End of Enlistment—out before the battalion would return from the next deployment. That meant 3/6 would be getting an influx of personnel. Those leaving would stick around for the time being, assisting with the work-ups, but that meant the battalion would be manned at levels far beyond the T/O for a few months.

Kyle dumped his seabag in the main compartment of his wall locker, then took a look around the room.

"Just like my old room—except for the hulking wyntonan I've got to share it with."

"And I've got to listen to human snoring," Leif said, giving it back.

"Hey, I don't snore."

"Uh, you forget. I was with you on the *Parish*. You made the bulkheads rattle. The squid damage control team kept coming by to save the ship from the torpedo they thought must have hit."

Kyle's mouth opened as he started to say something, then it closed. His eyebrows scrunched together until he sighed and said, "I've got nothing. You win."

"Damned right I won," Leif said, going back to his Alphas.

"Hey, that's looking good, Leif," Kyle said, coming around to his rack where Leif's Alphas were laid out.

They did look good, Leif had to admit. He'd never yet worn the uniform as an NCO, and he'd only just now had his chevrons attached to the sleeves. He had his marksmanship badges hanging from the pocket, and above the same pocket were his three ribbons: his Golden Lion, his deployment ribbon with three stars, and just presented this morning at formation, his Bronze Achievement. Six Marines in the company had received the minor award. Manu and Leif for the rugby wedge, Doc Josten for saving the life of a wounded kenpetai, Sergeant Weir from Third Platoon, PFC Kata from First, and Lance Corporal Tillerson, also from First.

A Bronze Achievement was the lowest ranking award for meritorious achievement, normally given only to sergeants and below, with the company commander as the awarding authority. Leif didn't care that it was much lower in precedence than his Golden Lion. With three ribbons, he had a full row and was now a "one tier" Marine. This was an entirely unofficial designation, but one that carried weight among their comrades. They were no longer boots.

Kyle, 14 months senior to him, had his deployment ribbon with five stars, but Leif's row trumped that—unofficially, and only as a matter of pride. Officially, Kyle was still the senior of the two.

"I still need to get mine ready," Kyle said.

"Better now than later. If you need chevrons, I took the last set in the uniform shop. You don't want to be missing something when Zoran starts her inspections."

"You've got that right, buddy. I've got my chevrons, but I lost my rifle expert down to sharpshooter. I need to get one of them."

"Or just qualify as expert again. We're on the range again in three weeks."

"Yeah, I guess you've got a point," Kyle said. "But for now, I'm going to see how hard my new rack is. I just got my old one broken in."

"Chow's in an hour," Leif said.

"And now I've got a roomie to wake me up right? Gotta look at the silver lining."

He closed his eyes as Leif went back to preparing his Alphas. Within 30 seconds, snores filled the room.

Leif looked across the desk to Kyle, but instead of a frown, he smiled. This was nothing. He'd slept with no fewer than 15 of his family every night of his life back in Hope Hollow.

It's good to have company again.

Chapter 12

The ground rumbled under his feet, a small earthquake. Leif nervously looked to his right where the SP-14 Pangolin pushed through the scrub and started up the swale's walls, not five meters from his shoulder. The behemoth was the Corps' largest piece of ground equipment, a self-propelled 205mm gun. At 98 tons, it was too large for efficient hover or surface effect travel. With gecko tracks and its two biodiesel engines, it had a range of close to 400 klicks depending on conditions.

The gecko tracks didn't look like much, but they were as technologically advanced in their own way as the newest Navy battleship. Leif knew—sort of—how the tracks worked. The bottoms were covered by tens of thousands of microscopic hairs, or setae, that made use of Van der Waals forces in addition to a secreted "sticky shit," as the gunny giving them the brief had phrased it, to enable the huge beast of a gun to climb almost any incline, sometimes even beyond 90 degrees.

Still, as the Pangolin started climbing, it looked like it simply had to topple over backward. The driver, her head sticking out of the open hatch, looked over, caught his eyes, and gave him a thumbs up.

"Sousa, shift over," he shouted as the PFC started up the wall herself right beside the Pangolin.

The gun could climb anything, but the compacted dirt of the walls could give away, and even in Level 3 armor, 98 tons of gun would crush her flat.

Leif's former fire teammate, Rick Ahlstrom, was fond of the expression "nervous as a long-tail cat in a room full of rocking chairs." Leif finally knew what it meant. Today's combined-arms exercise had him seeing potential dangers on all sides.

The mission statement was fairly simple. India Company was to maneuver along a single axis of advance to a bunker complex at the far end of the range. The assault had already passed the PRP (Platoon Release Point) where the platoon leaders took over the movement of their platoons, and the Marines had just passed the squad release points, so what had been a single maneuvering element was now 33 separate maneuvering units, which raised the ante considerably (but gave the most flexibility to meet threats). What raised the stress level even more was that it wasn't just grunts on the move—there were armor, self-propelled artillery, and an arty battery 30-klicks to the rear while the skies were crowded with drones and attack craft. There was even an old 255 battery simulating naval gunfire.

Oh, yeah. It was a live-fire exercise. The rounds and ordnance were the real deal.

The big self-propelled gun pushed up the dirt wall, then fell forward over the lip with a whump that reverberated up his legs.

"Watch your dispersion, First," Sergeant Zoran passed on the squad net.

Leif had been so concerned with the Pangolin and his team that he'd lost a broader situational awareness. On his display, he could see that First Team had somewhat converged as they started up the other side of the swale.

Kyle was a nice guy, and Leif liked having him as a roomie, but over the last few weeks, it had become apparent to him that Kyle was probably not the most capable NCO in the company. This had been somewhat hidden due to the nature of their mission on Han'ei, but here, back at Martelle where they were going through more and more complex training, his roomie's weaknesses were revealed. Leif had tried to give him some advice—as if he was some sort of NCO star himself—and while Kyle was willing, not much of it seemed to stick with him.

"Aye-aye, Sergeant," Kyle responded.

Leif watched the display as he clambered up the wall himself, his exo-assists having no problem with his 300 kilos of armor, weapons, ordnance, and wyntonan. Like an old *serta* of centuries past, or a knight in armor from human history, the infantry Marines' Level 3 armor gave each Marine a significant degree of protection. Unlike the *sertas* or knights, however, the armor was mostly self-powered. Leif was not lugging the entire weight with his own muscles.

He looked ahead. Nine-hundred meters to his front, the bunker complex spread out over a four-hundred-meter frontage. After years of getting bombarded, the physical remnants of the bunkers were looking rather worse for wear. Each bunker, however, had a fully functional dronebot, an AI-controlled training system that targeted and "fired" a wide variety of simulated weapons at the approaching Marines. Each Marine, vehicle, and missile had sensors that would record the enemy fire and assess battle damage.

The purpose of this exercise was to maneuver with the other units. The dronebots would not "kill" anyone this time—they were there to serve as a goad to make Marines maneuver. If they were hit, alarms would sound. The hits would accumulate and the numbers presented at the debriefs.

They may not be "killed" during the exercise itself, but no one wanted to be maxed out on hits.

As if on cue, Leif's alarms lit off. On his display, Stone, Win, and Heinz and Murata from Third Team's alarms lit off as well.

Leif pulled up his topo overlay on his display when Sergeant Zoran shouted, "Second and Third, shift left now and get down," over the squad circuit.

Leif immediately pushed to his left and hit the deck. The incoming fire alarm cut. He'd stepped down into a slight depression, but one deep enough to put him into defilade. A quick check, and the others were out of the line of fire as well.

And he knew he'd screwed up. He'd only begun to try and figure out what to do *after* he'd been taken under fire. Sergeant Zoran had immediately reacted, which meant she'd been working out contingent plans of action as they advanced. When they'd been taken under fire, she didn't have to figure out what to do, she already *knew* it.

And I should have known it, too, Leif told himself.

Sergeant Zoran called for supporting arms, and one of the M-66 Patras tanks took out the opposing crew-served automatic gun with a single hypervelocity tungsten round off of the mini-rail that paralleled the big main gun.

"Back on your feet," Sergeant Zoran ordered. "Close it up."

Leif waited for the 1P to open up, sure the sergeant was going to get on his case, but it remained silent. He didn't know if that was good or bad. She could simply be waiting until the exercise was over and she could get him for all his screw-ups at once.

The leading edge of the bunker complex was only 850 meters ahead of Leif. With their exo-assists, a Marine could cover that in slightly more than a minute. With the incoming, the company took a long 12 minutes before they reached the complex, then they still had to clear it, relying on mutually supporting fires from every asset, from Marine to (simulated) naval gunfire.

Leif was still nervous. There was an awful lot of ordnance flying through the air, but it was exhilarating just the same. He could feel the concussions of the big 205 rounds as they pummeled the bunkers just 70 meters in front of him.

One of the range safety NCOs, with his bright red armor, stood and sounded his horn. This was a live fire exercise, but the Corps was not going to needlessly risk Marines. When the 205 battery had opened up, the Marines had been kept in place within five designated safe zones, hugging the dirt. With the siren, they were now allowed to maneuver again.

First Platoon's objective was a formation of three bunkers on the right side of the complex. The moment the safety NCO cleared them, Lieutenant Nazari ordered the squad leaders to get moving again, leaving Third Squad down as a base of fire while First and Second used fire and movement, not in an attempt to actually flank the bunkers, which would be nigh-on impossible given the restrictions of the training range, but to minimize the number of Marines subject to the bunkers' interlocking fire. Listening to Sergeant Zoran, Leif got his fire team up and forward 15 meters before hitting the deck again while First and Third fired at the far-right bunker. The four Marines flopped down and opened fire while Manu and his First Fire Team bounded forward, pushing slightly past Second.

"Watch your fire," Leif passed to the other three. First Team was not in their line of fire, but they were forward of the four of them. With First on their bellies and firing, it was time for Third to rush forward.

The entire range was awash with fire. Without his helmet dampeners, his ears would be ringing. The entire company was in the assault, but Leif's battle had narrowed to their target bunker, a low, pock-marked structure now 50 meters in front of him. On the far left side of the bunker, the bright red dronebot peppered the onrushing Marines. Red meant "Do not fire," but as he watched, several supposedly errant rounds pinged off the tough body.

No matter how often the range personnel stressed that dronebots were not to be targets, well, Marines were Marines.

"Second up!" Sergeant Zoran passed.

"Let's go," he yelled as he got to his feet . . . just as they took heavy fire from their right. "Down!"

Leif hit the deck, then scanned the battlefield, isolating the fire. This was something more powerful than the dronebot that had been engaging them. The trace appeared on his display—it was not coming from their objective, but from the next bunker formation, another 120 meters to the right, one of Third Platoon's objectives.

First Platoon's objective might be the formation in front of them, but the enemy didn't care about how the Marines partitioned up the battlefield. The assaulting Marines were all fair game to them, and as Second Fire Team had started moving, they'd lost the protection of the terrain and were in the next bunker complex's line-of-sight.

Another lesson learned.

Lieutenant Nazari was already on the issue, coordinating with Third Platoon—which was the entire purpose of the exercise. Whoever had designed the range had done so to force close combined arms coordination. No one was simply going to assault right up the gut and succeed.

"Scoot back, but kiss the dirt doing it," Leif ordered, using his arms to push back until he had the cover of the slight rise again.

The Marines had passed the FCL, the Final Coordination Line, where supporting arms no longer had free reign due to the potential for friendly fire casualties. The leading edge of the Marines was closing in, and it was now getting to be "Danger close" territory. That meant that arty or naval guns weren't necessarily the first choice, even with a specific call for fire. A better selection would be the direct fire weapons, either the tanks, the Basilisk drones, Marine air, or Taipan missiles. For purposes of the exercise, the attacking force was now limited to the tanks or missiles.

"What are we doing?" Sousa asked, her voice taking on a hint of . . . not panic, but maybe concern.

"Just hold on," Leif passed back to her. "We're going to let the big guns take care of our little problem up there.

"We're shifting to the base of fire," Sergeant Zoran passed. "Third Squad's going into the assault.

Just because Second Team was pinned down didn't mean their mission was on hold. The lieutenant simply reacted to the realities of the ever-changing battlefield.

The new assault overlay was downloaded onto his display. Their fields of fire were clearly laid out along with Second and Third Squad's final assault axes.

"Hey, Corporal, I think I can get a shot on Charley-Three with my Taipan," Stone passed.

Leif centered his display on the lance corporal. Sure enough, he would have a clear shot with the missile if he shifted forward five or six meters and acted before the FEA, the Forward Edge of Advance, moved up another 20 or so meters.

"Will you be clear of the Bravo complex?" Leif asked, referring to Third Platoon's objective that had just taken them under fire.

"Barely, but I think so."

Leif checked the range. A Taipan needed 37 meters to arm. Charley-Three was 72 meters from the lance corporal.

Leif hesitated. The fire team could engage as needed, but the plan had been changed, as all plans did. He wanted to confirm it with the sergeant."

"Lance Corporal Stone can engage Charley-Three with his Taipan—" he started before the squad leader cut him off.

"Don't tell me. You're the team leader. Just do it," she ordered.

"Engage," he told Stone, embarrassed once more that she'd had to tell him to do his job. If he was going to wear the chevrons of a Marine NCO, he had to act the part.

There was a whoosh from where Stone was kneeling, and less than two seconds later, the missile slammed into the bunker, sending chunks of plasticrete into the air.

"Get some Stoney," Win shouted.

A Taipan was a powerful man-packed missile that, depending on the warhead programming, could be used against a number of target types, including a bunker. But the exercise gods were a capricious lot, and the bunker had only lost a relatively small part of its structure. To Leif's relief, the gods were smiling this time and the bunker's avatar went gray. It was officially dead.

"Good thinking, Stone," Leif passed.

The first of the nine bunkers was knocked out. That made each succeeding bunker just a little easier to destroy. Not easy, but *easier*.

Leif took up a sustained rate of fire, watching as Second and Third Squads advanced, ready to order his team to shift or cease fire. He didn't want the sergeant or the range safety NCO who'd approached and was now standing directly behind his team to have to give the order. He couldn't do it too early, though and deprive the other two squads of the support they needed.

He barely noticed the Patras that advanced behind Third Platoon's position to take out the troublesome Bravo-One bunker. His fight was right here with the Charley bunkers.

Bravo-One was taken out of the fight by the Patras, which Leif did note. The bunker had been a threat to his team, after all. The lieutenant didn't switch back to the previous assault plan, however, leaving First Squad as the base of fire.

With two bunkers gone, the rest started falling like dominos. Tanks took out two more, and one of the Pangolins had lumbered up at the Alpha complex, destroying a good quarter of one of the bunkers with its 205mm round.

The two remaining Charley bunkers were taken out by pure Marine power, with the attached weapons team lofting sticky mines that hit and stuck to the bunkers before exploding shape charges that drilled into the bunkers.

"Don't need no freaking combined arms with First Platoon," Manu passed over the squad net. "Grunts get it done."

Surprisingly, Sergeant Zoran didn't jump on his ass.

Within three more minutes, the final bunker in the Alpha formation was knocked out, and the exercise was over. Each Marine froze in place until a Red Armor checked their weapons and released them for the march back to the viewing stands.

Leif looked over to Sergeant Zoran as he slung his M88, wondering how badly he'd messed up. He knew he'd made mistakes—maybe not as many as Kyle had—but the team had taken out one of the bunkers, even had the exercise been actual combat, they would probably have been wiped out by the Bravo-One bunker. All of that would come out in the debrief after Kilo Company completed their assault, where all numbers would be crunched and the exercise staff gave their observations. Leif cared about the results, but he cared more what the sergeant thought of his performance.

He shook his head, then told his team, "That's about it, then. Let's get ready for the hump back. This exercise is in the books.

****

"How was it?" Lori asked as she took a seat beside him.

"A little stressful, I've got to admit," Leif said. "The range is pretty small for so much going on. I had to jump on Sousa too many times."

"How's she doing? I thought you said she'd started to come around on Han'ei."

"She was. But she's still unsure of herself."

"You gonna talk to Zoran about it?"

"No. I'll just continue to work on her. We did knock out a bunker, though. Well, Stone did."

"Yeah, I saw that. It was a righteous kill."

"I don't think we'd have gotten that far, though, had this been the real deal. Bravo-One lit us up with something heavy."

"Yeah, I saw that, too," Lori said, giving Leif a soft punch in the arm. "But it's just an exercise."

"Hey, you coming over here to spy?" Kyle said, taking a seat on the other side of Lori.

"I watched it all on the screen," Lori said, pointing to where feeds from the exercise were displayed to the stands. "I saw what you guys did."

"I hope you didn't see Zoran kicking my ass."

"Oh, the entire battalion did. It was broadcast on Window One."

Kyle's face fell, his face went white, and he managed to blurt out, "It was? Oh shit, shit!"

Window One was the center window on the observations screen, larger than any of the others, and on which the exercise controller displayed the most pertinent feed at the time. Leif looked at Lori, his brows furrowed. That wasn't the type of thing that the controller would display, and he wondered why she'd have done that.

"Yes, shit, Kyle. As in *bullshit*. I'm shitting you. No, no one heard whatever the Z-Master said to you."

Oh, more human humor, Leif thought before saying, "Come on, Kyle. Did you really think that would be in Window One?" as if he'd known Lori was joking all along.

"Hell, don't do that to me," Kyle said. "You about gave me a heart-attack."

"So, she did jump your ass, though?" Lori asked.

"Too many times."

Leif wondered when he was going to get his butt chewed. He hadn't been at his best out there. At least it was over, and now they could sit and watch Lima, who'd already passed the LOD and was in the advance to contact.

"This is not a gabfest, Hollow," Zoran passed over his 1P. "You can talk to your Kilo friend later, but for now, I want you watching Lima. You really need to observe how others anticipate the flow of the battle."

"Aye-aye, Sergeant," Leif responded, then whispering to Lori, "Zoran just told me this isn't a gabfest."

"Sorry about that. We're moving out to the assembly area in a few, anyway. I just wanted to say hello and see if you had any hints."

She stood up, turned to Sergeant Zoran sitting a couple of rows up, and gave her a cocky half-salute.

"Hell, Jankowski, don't do that!" Kyle said in a pleading tone.

"Sucks to be India," she said before moving off to join the rest of her company.

****

Where's Lori?

Leif looked up to the order of battle window on the screen, found his old platoon, and identified Lori's avatar. She was First Squad, Second Platoon's Second Fire Team leader, and the team looked to be moving well. Kilo had already passed the SRP, so Sergeant Juniper was in control as they advanced to their attack position.

He switched back to Third Platoon where Jordan was a team leader. Along with Tessa, Carlton, and Dubois, Jordan was part of the original Kilo Wyntonans. Mark, Moria, Lim, and Alim had reached their end of enlistments, Leif was now in India, Ray had transferred to arty, and Johari had transferred to Intel.

Kaatrn a'Telltell had been killed on Omeyocan, the first of the People to fall as an Imperial Marine.

Leif centered his cursor over Jordan's avatar, then hit the overhead view for a real-time image. As with his own exercise, Jordan's fire team was advancing along with a Pangolin. There were only two of the big guns with each company, and he and Jordan had just been victims of the luck of the draw. The Pangolins were great to have in support, but they were ungainly beasts without the visibility and troop avoidance systems of the Patras or Trieste armored personnel carriers.

They were coming up to the swale where Leif had been nervous. Seen from above, the swale looked far less imposing than it did from the ground. Jordan had his team split on either side of the Pangolin, flanking it. It was a valid course of action, but it made command and control more difficult, and limited the armor driver's options—not that he'd deviate much. Tracks from the armor that had been with India and Lima were highways in the dirt, and the Pangolin rumbled along them.

Groszek's a little close, he noted as he watched. *And too far up.*

PFC Groszek was Jordan's Sousa, well-meaning, but somewhat of a basket case. He was on the left side of the Pangolin, and he'd pushed a few meters forward of the big self-propelled gun. He jogged down the near side of the embankment, pulling a little to his right, just as the Pangolin reached the edge and plunged down.

"Jordan, get Groszek back," he passed in Uzboss on the 1P, forgetting for a moment that all of Lima and Kilo's comms had been turned off for the exercise.

He started to stand up to shout out, but the big beast slammed hard, two meters from the PFC. That was too close, but two meters was two meters. Leif settled back down into his seat, relieved.

Don't get stressed out. Let them do their thing.

Jordan was on the Pangolin's right side, and his view had been at least partially blocked. He should have seen Groszbek's close call on his display, but like many Marines, he tended to trust his own eyes rather than the images on his faceshield. Leif made a mental note to bring what had happened up with his friend—at least if no one else during the debrief did.

He switched over to Lori for a moment. She was moving forward with her team, all in a textbook formation.

Just wait until the exercise gods throw one of their curveballs at you.

She'd probably handle whatever was thrust at her better then he had, he knew. She always did.

He flipped back to Jordan and the big Pangolin. As in India's assault, the driver of the beast had his hatch open. Leif was a little envious as he watched the Marine. He was infantry, and proud of it, but driving such a big vehicle had to be fun. At 2.2 meters, however, he was simply too tall for armor.

You can't even drive a hover, and you're thinking tanks? Get a grip on reality, Leefen.

Still, he watched as the Pangolin crossed the swale. He could imagine the ground rumbling beneath its gecko tracks. Leif had been too concerned with his team's movement when the Pangolin with India had attacked the far side of the swale for him to watch, but this time, he zoomed in, hoping to see the setae in action. The swale walls where the other Pangolins had climbed out had to be 70 degrees, and he wanted to see it climb them.

Contrary to logic, the Pangolin slowed down as it approached instead of speeding up. If it hit the wall at too high a speed, however, the setae would not be able to start grasping.

PFC Groszek was still too close for Leif's comfort, but he'd slowed down as well, probably looking for a spot to climb. Unlike the armor tracks in the dirt, there were no clear paths for ground-pounding Marines.

The Pangolin reached the swale wall and started to climb, while on the near side of it, Private Haley Orator was speeding up as if to take the wall in a single leap—which could expose her to enemy fire.

A Marine was supposed to minimize vulnerability, not hand a target to the enemy on a silver platter.

Jordan, on the near side as well, turned and pointed at her, and the PFC skidded to a stop. Leif wished he could listen in on their net, but he knew Jordan would be blistering her hide. As he should be. In combat, silhouetting herself like that could be a fatal mistake.

"Good catch, *Jordun a'Hottentot*," he muttered under his breath as he shifted his view back to the Pangolin as it climbed almost to the vertical.

It reached the top and started to flop over when the entire face of the wall collapsed. The Pangolin's gecko tracks could climb almost anything—but there had to be something there to grab. The dirt walls broke off, sending the big mobile gun sliding back down. The driver ducked back inside, pulling the hatch closed.

And something caught Leif's eye. His heart jumped to his throat before he even realized what he was seeing.

It was PFC Groszek. For some unknown reason, he'd darted towards the Pangolin, maybe to climb the wall in its tracks. His head was down as he darted to his right, somehow missing the oncoming 98 tons of cerrosteel for a vital few micro-seconds.

Five or six fellow Marines stood along with Leif in the stands as Groszek realized the danger and tried to stop, stumbling as the cascading dirt pushed his feet out from under him a moment before the Pangolin lost its battle with gravity and toppled over, blocking Groszek for the pickup's view.

"*Montik!*" Leif shouted in Uzboss, reverting to his native swearing in the heat of the moment.

Sirens filled the air, red lights started flashing across the range, and a voice shouted "Cease fire, cease fire," over the range safety net.

Please be OK, Leif pleaded, his faceshield on maximum magnification.

He switched his pick-up, trying to get a better angle, but suddenly, his visuals went dark.

"What happened?" Marines on either side of him asked.

"The Pangolin, it fell on someone," a Marine said.

"Who? Is he all right?"

"Garent Groszek. He's in Second Platoon. We went to boot together."

"Fucking armor. They just don't pay attention to where they're going!"

Leif tuned them out. He stood on his seat, trying to see down into the swale. Armor and Marines froze in place while the safety NCOs were running towards the swale. They jumped down and were lost from sight.

One of the range tractors fired up and headed out into the range. All hands watched as it made its way to the swale. Massive and powerful enough to haul any piece of ground gear, it wasn't quick. Hundreds of sets of eyes watched, willing it to go faster.

Captain Juan-Sattler, the battalion training officer, moved to the front of the stands and said, "Marines, hold fast."

"What's happening, sir?" several voices called out.

"We're not sure. There's been an accident, and the range crew is taking care of it."

"Is Groszek OK?" the Marine who'd gone to boot camp with Groszek called out.

"We don't know. Just hold tight," the captain said.

The captain didn't lie well, Leif thought.

A few minutes later, a Carabao flew over the range, landing in the middle of the swale, just in sight of Leif in the stands. Most of Kilo was still frozen in place, but some had gathered at the lip of the swale to watch what was happening. Through his magnification, Leif recognized Captain Tzama, the first sergeant, and the Second Platoon commander. He couldn't see Jordan.

The tractor finally reached the edge, planted its shovels, and extended a crane out over the swale. A crew scrambled down, and after a long five minutes, the tractor began lifting. It took almost a minute before the front of the massive mobile gun was raised high enough for those in the stands to see it.

"Is he OK?" someone asked as the crane stopped.

Somebody scrambled up the wall, and for a moment, Leif felt a surge of relief, but she was in tankers' overalls. Two more scrambled up as well where one of the range officers grabbed and took them aside.

The Carabao's landing lights came on, and once again, Leif felt hope, but the plane took off—with no one being brought on board.

"Listen up," Top Picolli, the training SNCO shouted. "We've got the busses coming up now. As soon as they arrive, I want each company to board."

"What's happening, Top?" Gunny Tohoe from Lima asked.

"We'll all be briefed in the chapel," the Top said.

An almost palpable wave of despair swept over the two rifle companies. The chapel meant one thing.

Private First Class Garent Groszek was dead.

Chapter 13

"Piece of shit casper. He killed Groszek."

Leif skidded to a stop just before rounding the corner.

"They shouldn't be NCOs" another voice said. "I mean, some of them are OK as simple grunts, but they're not leadership material."

Leif recognized the second voice as Corporal Chuck Sylvianstri, one of his old squadmates in Kilo Company.

"Our fearless emperor thinks they are," the first voice said.

"Watch it," Chuck said.

"Don't care about no *les majeste*. It's true. He puts the caspers in the Corps for political reasons, and we pay the fucking price."

"It might be true, but you need to be careful with what you say. The walls have ears."

Leif stepped back, his face turning red. The walls might not have ears, but he did. Not that he'd turn in the first Marine for *les majeste*—the previous emperor might have demanded such fealty, but during the current emperor's reign, prosecutions for demeaning the imperial body had all but disappeared. He was in shock at what he'd just heard. He'd served alongside Chuck, and he thought they'd had a good relationship. Now, he was saying that wyntonans were not leadership material?

He'd heard some oblique references that Jordan was to blame for Groszek's death, but he'd heard the same about Sergeant Holmes, the squad leader, and Lieutenant Shymaster, the platoon commander. This was the first time he'd heard that it was because Jordan was wyntonan.

Part of him wanted to continue around the corner and confront the two Marines. Groszek's death was a terrible accident, largely caused by the PFC himself. Leif was sure of that. And if Jordan had some blame in not supervising the Marine better, well, so did the sergeant and the lieutenant, and they were human. This was not a wyntonan-human issue.

He took a step forward feeling his ire rise, but once again, the words Ferron a'Silverton had hammered into them before they reported to boot camp surfaced: they were not to cause waves with the humans. Anything they did would be magnified, so they had to take whatever was dished out to them. Leif hadn't always done so—the memory of beating the shit out Knut Nilson at boot camp, then Stone six months ago flitted across his mind. But this wasn't one of those times. He couldn't go beating up humans simply because they didn't like the People. All that would do would be to confirm that they should not be Marines.

He'd go around Building 54 on the other side.

Leif started to turn just as a voice cried out, "Leif, wait up!"

Lori, Donk, and Bella Main were coming up the walk. Bella had a steely look in her eyes as she looked at him.

You, too? You think this is because Jordan is of the People?

"Any word yet? We only just now broke away," Lori asked.

"I just got here, too."

"It'll probably take awhile," she said, taking a moment to gaze at the one-story brick building. She shuddered, then said, "This place gives me the creeps."

Building 54 was the Military Justice Center—in other words, the military courthouse for the division. All special and general court-martials took place inside. Marines tended to the superstitious, so they avoided mentioning the name, using "fifty-four" as a last resort and only when absolutely necessary.

Inside the building, Jordan, Sergeant Holmes, and Lieutenant Shymaster were waiting to hear their fate. The three had been referred to an Article 36 hearing as a matter of course. Now that the investigation of Groszek's death had been completed, a military judge would determine if the three would be facing courts martial.

None of the recordings of the incident had been released, but Leif remembered what he'd seen. Groszek had made a concerted move to get behind the Pangolin at exactly the wrong moment. The collapsing wall knocked him off his feet, and the mobile gun had crushed him as it toppled over. It had happened so quickly that there was nothing Jordan could have done to stop the PFC.

At least that was how Leif remembered it. He couldn't' be sure. He'd gone over it time-after-time in his head to the point that he might have adjusted his memory to what he *wanted* to have happened, not what actually happened.

"Well, if you're going to wait it out, you might as well do it with us, Leif," Lori said. "Any more from India?"

"I don't know. I just . . ."

"Yeah, we know," Lori said, slipping her arm through his for a moment. "He's your friend."

She didn't say Jordan was her friend as well, which took him aback a moment. He'd just assumed that . . .

He let the thought trail off as Lori dropped his arm and he followed the three around the corner.

"Hey, Lori," Chuck said as he saw them. "Donk, Bella. Oh, hey Leif," he added.

Leif wanted to yell out, "I know what you said," but he held his tongue. He barely managed to nod as they moved toward the front of Building 54 where 40 or 50 Marines were standing in small groups. Some of them were witnesses, and they were called in by ones and twos over the next hour. The rest seemed to be there for moral support.

He stood beside Lori, not saying much, but he kept coming back to her statement. Back on Home, before the first group of wyntonans had left for Camp Navarro, Ferron a'Silverton had told them that there were humans who would try to initiate sexual relations with them for their rumored sexual prowess as well as the novelty of the experience. Sex was technically feasible from a biological standpoint, but to most of their reliefs, this had never happened. Sure, there were rumors, just as he knew there were unfounded rumors about Lori and him, something neither bothered to deny, but for the most part, this had been a false warning. There were a few others, however, Marines and civilians, who seemed to gravitate to the wyntonans, as if they were adopting wyntonan culture and mannerisms. Some even bleached their skin whiter to look more like them.

It rather freaked Leif out.

So why had Lori's statement surprised him? Had he considered Lori, not so much a wyntonaphile, but someone who liked all of the People? Somehow, he'd assumed that she was close to all of them, at least the corporals. Evidently, that wasn't the case. She didn't consider Jordan a friend.

And that could only mean one thing. She liked Leif for who he was, not what he was. After Chuck's comments, that realization felt good. He felt an urge to step up and hug her, one he managed to suppress.

They waited another hour, milling around like sheep. Some of the Marines left, and a few more joined. Finally, Sergeant Holmes appeared, coming through the front doors, accompanied by a Marine captain. All eyes locked on him, and when he smiled and gave two thumb's up, a muted cheer rose. The captain turned and said something to him. He listened for a moment, then nodded. The captain re-entered the building, and the sergeant walked down the steps to where Marines, mostly sergeants, congratulated him.

Bella, who'd been standing with them, left to go join those with Holmes. When the group left, she left with them.

"I hope that's a good sign," Lori said.

Most of the waiting Marines had gone. About two-dozen were left, all corporals and non-rates. Of course, the officers wouldn't be waiting outside, but there weren't many waiting in support for Jordan. Heck, Jordan's own squad leader had just left.

At least there's some, he thought until he looked behind him where Chuck and the other Marine were still waiting.

And he knew then that not all were there in support of Jordan. They thought they were there in support of Groszek, and that meant seeing Jordan burn. As he looked at the two Marines, the lance corporal caught his eye, and his lip raised in a sneer, something common to both races. Leif had to fight to keep his face expressionless. He stared at the Marine for a long ten seconds, then slowly turned away.

Twenty-nine minutes later, Jordan appeared alone. He was not being escorted by the military police, and his corporal chevrons were still attached to his Alpha's sleeve.

"What happened, Jordan?" Corporal Gondol Morehouse shouted out.

"A letter," Jordan said. "No court."

"Fuck that," the lance corporal said loudly from behind Leif.

A "letter" was a Letter of Reprimand, which would be part of his official record. He'd kept his rank, and he wouldn't be facing a court-martial, brig time, and a dishonorable discharge. A letter was not a good thing, but it could have been worse.

Leif was relieved, even if Jordan looked disappointed. Several of his fellow NCOs gathered around him, Lori, Donk, and Leif among them.

"Are you OK?" he asked in Uzboss.

"I didn't do anything wrong. The records proved it, yet the monkeys still slammed me. They had to pin this on somebody, and they picked one of the People."

Leif wasn't so sure about that. He didn't think Jordan was court-martial guilty, but he should have already corrected Groszek, and not focused on PFC Orator. As far as he was concerned, the letter was nothing.

Of course, that was easy for him to say. He didn't have one.

"Just bear with it for now," he said.

"Hey, caspers, how about speaking standard, not ghost shit," one of the glaring Marines yelled out.

"What did you say?" Jordan shouted back, pushing forward.

Leif grabbed him and held him back.

"That's right. Hold him. He killed Groszek, and he'll kill again."

"Lance Corporal Fellis, that's a Marine NCO you're talking to," Lori said, pushing herself forward into the Marine's face.

"Shit, *Corporal*," he said, drawing out her rank. "He wouldn't be no NCO if the judge there had done her job. But no, that wouldn't be politically correct, now, would it? The fucking casper skated."

There it was, out in the open. There was a moment of stunned silence, then Lori broke that with a tirade on the lance corporal, driving him back with the force of her words.

Jordan tried to join her, but Leif kept a firm grip on him, turning his fellow wyntonan and leading him away.

"It's not worth it, *Jordun a'Hottento*," he said quietly. "Let it go."

"No one has to fight my battles," he protested. "I'm not a *grazbin*, cowering in the weeds."

"No, you are a Marine non-commissioned officer," he said, this time in Standard. "And NCOs do not get into fights with non-rates."

He nodded his head at Porter Janis, another of the Kilo corporals, and Porter joined him on the other side of Jordan, grabbing his left arm. With Leif on his right, the two hustled him off.

Several shouts of "caspers" followed them, but Leif was shutting down the confrontation. Jordan had just been given a lucky break, and he would not receive another if they all got into a fight.

As the two dragged Jordan away, Leif kept thinking about what the other Marine had said about the decision not to refer Jordan to a court-martial had been motivated by politics.

That wasn't true . . . was it?

Chapter 14

"That's it," Leif said, speaking Uzboss. "No reaction. No matter what happens."

"That's yanishit," Felice said, her face wrapped up in a scowl."

Leif looked over to Jordan, who was sitting slouched in the back of the room, not taking part. He'd been withdrawn since the accident, something that had become even more pronounced since the hearing. Leif was worried about his friend.

"It might be yanishit, but those are our orders," Leif said.

He looked over the eight other wyntonan Marines. Jordan, Tessa, Dubois, Carlton, and Leif were the NCOs still in the battalion, while Felice (Felean a'Offer), Rafer (Rafen a'Gold River), and Inga (Ingeen a'First Stop) were privates first class, and Wendi (Winden a'Possto) was a lance corporal. Together, the nine of them made up the wyntonan contingent in the battalion.

Leif had sent a report to Ferron a'Silverton, the official minder of all the wyntonan Marines, detailing the deteriorating condition in the battalion. There wasn't a concerted action being taken against them after the hearing. Many of the human Marines were treating them as always. What was different was that more of the humans were open in their hostility at worse, a belief that the People didn't have what it takes to be Marines at best. This had gone over the boundary of mere talk, however, when Inga had been pushed around in the head the night before. She hadn't been hurt, and she'd managed to control her temper, thank the Mother.

Leif had just read out a'Silverton's instructions, which were, in essence, simply not to react to slights and not to let things escalate.

"So, we just let the *minta* monkeys push us around?" Rafer asked.

"No," Leif said automatically, before he could think out a response. According to their instructions, that was exactly what they were supposed to do.

He can't mean that, though.

"If you have cause to fear for your life, or you're going to get hurt, then you can protect yourself," he amended. "But unless it gets that serious, you are to ignore anything else. Understood?"

He received seven nods, three with dangerously sullen looks. Jordan ignored Leif.

I'm going to have to talk to him later, he realized.

"I guess that's it, then. Go on back to your units. If anything serious happens, though, let me know. We can always ask for mast."

Jordan finally broke his blank face with a snort and look of disgust. Leif chose to ignore him. Mast would be a last ditch action. Formally complaining to a company commander or the battalion commanding officer would almost assuredly alleviate whatever specific incident sparked the request for mast, but it would just as assuredly alienate their fellow Marines. "Squealing" to the officers, to use the human term, was frowned upon. Marines took matters into their own hands.

That was a double-edged sword, however. On one hand, Leif had quelled his issue with Stone by beating the crap out of him in the storage locker—it was highly illegal and punishable by a court-martial, but it had been effective. On the other hand, those Marines who didn't think wyntonans were Marine material, or those who simply hated the thought of serving beside one of the People, might take matters into their own hand as well. It was possible, if improbable, that one of them might be in actual danger.

Which was why he'd told the others to defend themselves, if necessary. Ferron a'Silverton cared about his charges, and he wouldn't want any of them hurt, but he was also looking at the bigger picture. The People needed trained fighters, and becoming Marines had been determined to be the best way to resurrect their warrior past. If that included one of them getting beat up, well, that was a small price to pay in the long run.

Not such a small price to pay if we're the one getting the shit kicked out of us, he thought as the others filed out of the room.

Chapter 15

"Hey, Corporal Hollow, Lieutenant Nazaari wants you in his office now," Lance Corporal Qaan shouted across the front of the armory where he and the rest of the squad, minus the sergeant, were cleaning weapons.

What now? he wondered.

They'd only gotten back from a six-day exercise 20 minutes before, and he was starving for some real food, and that wasn't going to happen until the weapons were turned in, if at all. Noon chow would end in a short 35 minutes.

He looked down at his disassembled M88, the pieces scattered across the work table. Not that there were many pieces, nor was the weapon as dirty as say, Lance Corporal Stone's M85, which used a chemical reaction to throw the larger round downrange. The astringent aroma of cleaning solvent filled the still air outside the armory, a smell that was oddly soothing to him.

He couldn't leave his weapon there on the table, and it wasn't clean yet. Sergeant Willow, the armory NCO on duty, was a hard-ass on accepting weapons back. If they weren't spotless, she wasn't going to let them in her armory. If Gyles Wantonington was on duty, Leif could probably sweet talk him into temporarily taking it in with a promise of getting back as soon as the lieutenant was done with him—and after a quick run through the chow line.

No, can't eat unless the rest of the team is done, too.

"You go see what he wants," Manu said. "I've got this."

Manu wasn't the senior corporal. Kyle was. With Sergeant Zoran who knows where, Kyle was in charge, but he didn't look up from his 88, humming as he wiped down the actuator.

Leif nodded and quickly slapped the disassembled weapon back together, slung it over his shoulder, and told

Stone, "If I'm not back and you three are finished, go get chow."

He stepped out from under the overhead and into the sunshine that beat down onto his head. The weather had been brutally hot over the course of the exercise, and he was frankly a little sick of it. Several of the human Marines had suffered heat stroke and had to be medivaced out of the field. Even more, including Sousa, had been burnt by Northumbria's star, despite sunblock and being in uniform the entire time.

Leif held out his hand, checking it. It was as white as ever. Most of the humans tended to think of the wyntonans as albino humans, with skin that would burn under a flashlight, and there was more than a little truth to that—and that was why they always took precautions. With human-designed nanoblocks, they didn't get sunburnt, even under the current heat wave. Human Marines, though, thought of themselves as tough, and most wouldn't stoop to the nanoblocks, thinking them a sign of weakness—and so they got burnt while the wyntonans didn't. This pride thing was just one more difference between humans and wyntonans, one more thing that said they were not the same.

From the discomfort of those who got burnt, however, Leif was more than happy to accept this differentiation. Unity was good, but not having his skin fried was better.

And things were better, a month after Groszek's death. Not "normal," whatever that was, but better. Leif's friends were still his friends, and most of the rest were ambivalent to him. Things were a little rougher with the rest, with more slurs being flung at them, but Leif was a decorated NCO, and that possibly shielded him from the worst of it.

Actually, most of that was probably due to their operational tempo. Marines barely had a chance to breathe as the battalion went through their pre-deployment modules. Exhausted Marines didn't have the time nor energy to devote to sidebars. Once they were onboard the ships, living in close quarters, things might change. For now, though, there was a cease-fire in humans versus wyntonans.

The armory was in the back of the battalion area, near the motor pool and supply. It took several minutes to reach the battalion area proper, with its manicured parade deck surrounded by huge trees. Leif was decidedly grungy, and he was aware that he reeked. A good thing about an infantry unit, however, was that they didn't care for the niceties that tended to infect the RAMF's (an old term—Rear Area Mother Fuckers—that Leif loved). The battalion quad was pristine, but no one would blink an eye at him as he dropped little pieces of Training Area GA off his utilities as he walked.

He entered Building 1023, which housed the India and Fox Company offices. The India lieutenants were off at the end of the passage to the left. He rapped on the edge of the hatch.

"Sir, you wanted to see me?"

"Come in, Hollow."

Seated behind his desk, still filthy from the field, the lieutenant beckoned him inside. Staff Sergeant Antoine and Sergeant Zoran were sitting on the couch in the back of the small office.

"Stand easy, Hollow," the lieutenant said as Leif started to come to attention in front of the desk. "Take a seat."

Leif sat in the single chair next to the couch.

"Good work this week," the lieutenant said. "You did well."

"Thank you, sir," Leif answered, knowing full well that wasn't the reason he'd been called in. That was just small talk.

What the hell is going on?

"Uh . . . I've decided . . . after consulting with Staff Sergeant Antoine and Sergeant Zoran, of course, that I'm taking PFC Win from you and sending him to Third.

Win? Hell, if you're going to take someone, take Sousa. I need Win.

"You'll be getting one of the new joins, a Private Hkkeka."

"Sir? We're only six weeks out . . ." Leif started to say.

The lieutenant cut him off. "So you don't have much time to snap him in."

"Yes, sir. You're right."

"This is . . . well . . . somewhat unique, Corporal, and we believe you're the best-qualified team leader for this.

What is he talking about? I'm a Marine NCO. Whoever I get, I get.

He was sorry he was losing Win. He'd gotten used to having the cynical Marine around. He might not be gung-ho, but he was capable and did what was needed. That was probably why they were pulling him. The squad's new leader, Sergeant Hua, was evidently having a little trouble, and it made sense that the lieutenant would shift some of the better Marines into the squad.

And it was somewhat of a complement that Leif would be getting this boot, only six weeks before deployment.

"Thank you, sir. I'll do my best."

"I'm sure you will."

Leif stole a glance at Sergeant Zoran, but her face was impassive. He couldn't make anything from her.

The lieutenant called out, "Gunny Frank, you about done with Private Hkkeka?"

The battalion call system routed the call to admin on the other side of the quad.

"Five minutes, Lieutenant, and I'll send him over."

"Thanks, Gunny."

"OK, so we wait," the lieutenant said, drumming his fingers on his desk.

"Staff Sergeant Antoine, did you have a chance to speak with Top Picolli about K202?" he said, sounding like someone trying fill in the time.

"Yes, sir. He can fit us in on the fourteenth."

"OK, I'll tell Captain Jiminez. Let's work this into the training schedule."

Leif didn't know what K202 was. A range, obviously, but not what kind. The two continued to discuss the training schedule, things all above his pay grade, so Leif's thoughts drifted.

Private Hkekka. That was an odd-sounding name to his wyntonan ears despite all the time he'd spent with humans. It didn't sound quite like anything else he'd heard. He wondered if the private was from some small human offshoot, and if so, how that would affect the fire team. He had a hard enough time with the regs' human culture, and he hoped he wouldn't have to learn how to deal with a sub-culture.

What am I thinking about? He's a Marine. That's a sub-culture in and of itself.

It was close to fifteen minutes later when he heard footsteps coming down the corridor. Lance Corporal Ten, the company duty, rapped and said, "Sir, Private Hk . . . Hekakaka is here to report in."

"Are the captain and the first sergeant back yet?"

"No, sir."

"OK, send the private in."

Both Zoran and Antione sat up straight, their eyes locked on the hatch.

Leif's new private marched in and centered himself on the lieutenant's desk, and in a deep voice, said, "Private Hkekka, reporting as ordered, sir."

And Leif knew why the private's last name sounded odd. Private Hkekke, all 1.4 meters of him, was not human, nor was he wyntonan. He was a qiincer.

Chapter 16

Fucking fairies!

Leif'd had about enough of one Private NFN (No First Name) Hkekka, and to be blunt, he had no idea why the qiincer was a Marine. Sure, the Ops O about had an orgasm to have flying Marines organic to the battalion, but when flying, the qiincers could carry very little weight. Hell, they couldn't carry much on the ground, either. Too light by far, their spindly legs could not support the typical 75kg combat load—and that was with their exo-assists.

Coming from a planet with a higher O2 level and denser air—which they needed because of the vast amounts of energy expended to fly—they had limited endurance. The Corps had already ordered them armed with the much lighter M77 carbine, a composite dart thrower that massed a mere 2 kg fully loaded. That was barely more than Leif's sidearm, a Ruger 90. True, it could be devastating in a building and close range, but the qiincers were supposed to be flyers, which would probably mean engaging at a distance, and the M77 had a very limited max effective range.

Recon Marines, with their personal sleds, could fly, and they could do that with a full combat load—and long-range weapons.

But more than their lack of strength and endurance was their attitude—"their" because the other two quiincers assigned to the battalion were just as bad. They had no respect for rank, did what they wanted to do at any given time, and seemed to despise both human and wyntonan alike. They acted so superior to the rest of the Marines, as if only they understood some cosmic joke, that Leif had wanted to smack the constant smirks off their faces.

The emperor wanted full inclusion in the military of all races under his rule, but Leif thought this was a mistake. The qiincers just weren't Marine material.

"Private Hkekka, what did I just tell you to do?" Leif asked as he tried to control his anger.

Over the qiincer's shoulder, Lance Corporal Stone was rolling his eyes, but Leif knew that was almost in commiseration. He knew that Stone wasn't his new found brother, but in Hkekka, they both had a common . . . was *enemy* too strong a term?

"You said to shift to the right."

"So why are you on Sousa's ass?"

"Because what you said was wrong," the private said as if explaining the obvious to a child. "I have no fields of observation to the right.

Leif took three deep breaths. With Hkeeka's height, it was probably true that he couldn't see much at the moment with a fire team in a wedge, but that was only temporary. Formations were used for a reason, and not for individual Marines to simply discard.

"It's not up to you to decide what is right or what it wrong, Private. You just do what I say, understand?"

"It was wrong."

"I don't care if it was wrong," Leif shouted, losing his cool and stepping forward and leaning down into the qiincer's face.

The wings furled on his back began to pump out, but Leif didn't care. He knew how powerful the fragile-looking wings really were—one of the lance corporals in Lima had been knocked out when the company's qiincer "accidentally" hit her with the leading edge of one of the main wings. Unspoken threat or not, he was not going to sit there and take this from a private.

"Hollow, what's taking you?" Sergeant Zoran passed on the 1P.

"Hkekka," was all he said.

"Shit," she said, then, "Just get it done as soon as you can."

Even the mighty Sergeant Zoran, the scourge of incompetence and half-assed efforts, had run up against a brick wall with the qiincer. She knew what he was facing.

"And if you pump out your wings, Hkekka, so help me, I'll lay you out before they get to half-mast," he said, low so no one else could hear.

The private looked up into Leif's eyes, and slowly, his wings rolled up again.

"You're wrong," he said, but he nonchalantly started to drift to the right and in his assigned position.

Leif wanted to shake the crap out of the qiincer, but his team had fallen behind and was in the sergeant's crosshairs. He couldn't take the time now for an on-the-spot attitude adjustment.

"Let's pick it up," he passed to his team. "Guide on Poltrain, Sousa," he ordered, referring to the First Fire Team lance corporal.

This was a routine advance to contact, just a bit of extra rehearsal as they moved to Range R402. The company never simply marched to a range—it was always a tactical movement. That didn't mean that it was routine. If Sergeant Zoran missed a screwup (fat chance of that ever happening), then the gunny or the XO would catch it after they went over the hot-wash. Leif'd already had his ass handed to him three times over the last week, and he could lay the blame squarely on a certain private who evidently didn't give a shit.

Private Hkekka had been with the squad for four weeks now, and Leif didn't know what to do with him. He simply didn't have the physical ability to fill in for Win, for one.

Qiincers were one of the fringe races, sharing less of their DNA than most of the rest. Like the aquatic o*manto in the sasseres sphere, they pushed the boundaries of what it meant to be in the family of sentient beings. The Mother (Proginator, God, Supreme) must have been drunk when she came up with them. With their trifurcated wings that looked like zona arrows back on Home or dragonflies on Earth, they were the only known flying sentient race. Being able to fly carried some heavy penalties, though. They were among those races with the shortest life-spans, and they were among, if not the, smallest of the races. With tiny legs Hkekka barely came up to Leif's naval. His back, however, was broad—it had to be to support the muscles that moved the six individual wings in flight.

The wings were normally rolled into small buds right under what was the scapula in the other races. When it was time to fly, a pseudo-haemolymph was pumped into them, reminding all of the other Marines of a penis becoming turgid. It took about ten seconds for a qiincer to be ready for flight, and once airborne, they could hover, change direction, climb and dive with ease using phase-stroking, synchronized stroking, counter-stroking, and free gliding.

They were quite primitive from a technological perspective when first discovered by humans, living in bands that were in constant war with each other. It had taken some time for the Empire to assimilate them—not because the smaller, less-advanced race could fight off the humans, but because the qiincers simply didn't seem to care about the other races and did what they wanted when they wanted. It wasn't until after the Proclamation of Sentient Rights was enacted that they began to interact with the other races.

Leif hadn't known any of this before. Qiincers could fly, and that was it as far as he was concerned. But with all the problems he was having with Hkekka, he did the research to try and understand how to deal with the private. It hadn't seemed to do much good. It was a continual battle of wills. Leif was winning the battle, but he had the impression that Hkekka thought he was letting Leif win.

Which pissed him off to no end.

In theory, having a flying Marine would be a no-brainer, but in this case, the emperor had it wrong. Qiincers just weren't Marine material.

Chapter 17

"Get this. Today, the fairy accused us of being the humans' pets," Leif said, his blood boiling.

"Pets?" Tessa asked.

"Yeah, pets, like a womper."

Leif looked over at Jordan, waiting for him to respond, but his fellow wyntonan seemed more interested in his scanpad.

"Did you hear me, *Jordun a'Hottentot*?" he asked, trying to draw out a reaction.

"Maybe he's got a point," Jordan said, not looking up.

Leif looked over at Tessa and Carlton, who raised his eyebrows.

Jordan had been withdrawn since his hearing, doing what he had to, but without any enthusiasm. The People called it *kwasti*, or the "shadow." The will to live seemed to leach out of a person, where nothing much seemed to matter. Left untreated, it could end up in death—not from a biological cause, but through simple inattention in a dangerous world, or if that didn't do it, through suicide. The other four wyntonan NCOs had discussed the situation among themselves, and they'd considered notifying Ferron a'Silverton, but if they did that, Jordan's career would be over. They kept hoping he'd snap out of it.

"He doesn't have a point," Leif said. "We aren't pets of anyone."

"So you say. Yet we do what the monkeys tell us to do, and when we're good, they pat us on the head and give us a treat. When we're bad, they swat us across the nose. Seems like a pet to me."

Leif wanted to argue, but Tessa shook her head at him. He bit back his retort.

He'd come to the others for support, and Jordan wasn't giving it. He could have gone to the sergeant over Hkekka, or he could have gone to Lori. He'd done that before, after all. But they were humans, and with Hkekka's accusation, that would have just been too weird.

The qiincer was actually performing better over the last week. Leif was sure that Hkekka wasn't buying into the system, but rather Leif had simply worn him down with his constant attention. He'd felt good about it, though, whatever the reason behind the change in behavior, and had even told the qiincer that he was doing better when he dropped that bombshell on him.

Just because Leif and the others followed orders, that did not make them pets. It was a ridiculous statement.

So why did it bother him so much?

"Are you going to do anything about it?" Tessa asked.

"You mean, take him into the storeroom?"

She shrugged.

Leif would be lying if he said he hadn't considered beating the snot out of the qiincer. But while a few Marines had learned that those wings were not to be messed with, the fact of the matter was that Hkekka was half his size. Taking Stone into the storeroom was one thing. Taking the qiincer was another. It wouldn't do his reputation any favors if that was the only way he could get compliance with the little *minta*.

He was just about to explain that to Tessa when the Condition Alpha alarm went off, both with the sirens and personal comms. Leif's heart jumped to his throat. This was the first time in his career that he'd heard the CA alarm.

"What's going on?" Rafer asked.

"Get to your assembly points," Leif said, bolting for the hatch.

Tessa beat him to it, pushing in front of him as she raced out. Leif looked back, where Jordan was still on his scanpad, despite the flashing yellow that lit up the face.

"Jordan, that's Condition Alpha!"

"I'm coming, as soon as I finished this scene," he said, not looking up.

"Now, Jordan," Leif said, putting steel into his voice.

His friend looked up at him, then rolled his eyes and closed his pad. He didn't rush to his feet, but at least he was moving, and that was better than nothing. Leif waited until Jordan had left the room and was moving in the general direction of Kilo's assembly point before he turned and ran toward India's.

Something had happened, something big.

Chapter 18

Leif watched the feed along with the rest of the Marines in the rec room. Kyle was back in the room, watching the developments on his scanpad, but Leif didn't have a solid background on the Empire's intricate clan system, so he sat in the back, listening in to the comments of the others, hoping to get a better understanding of what was going on without looking like an imbecile.

The reason that the entire division, the entire Corps, for that matter, was on Alpha Alert was that the Navocks had formally announced their secession from the empire.

Not all humans nor other races within the Empire's sphere were citizens of the empire. The Leaguers on Han'ie, for example, were not technically part of the empire, so Leif was not sure how this was different. Sure, the Navocks, with their eight planets in the Uriah Bight represented almost 6% of the empire's GIP, according to the talking heads on the holovid, but didn't imperial citizens have free will?

The New Alignment Group—the Novacks—were tightly controlled by the Fremont Clan, with Ser Perspidian Fremont as the clan head. Fremont had pushed for one of his great-granddaughters to become the empress-in-waiting, losing out to the Jin Long Clan. While the goings on at the imperial and clan levels were so far above Leif and most of his fellow Marines that they might as well be the gods bickering among themselves, the talking heads kept reminding viewers that this had created bad blood between the Fremonts and the Granite Throne.

"Bad blood," Manu said with a snort after yet another mention. "It wasn't just the Fremont debutant not getting her claws latched into the emperor that caused this. It was the flipping clan heir who forgot that he's not above the law."

"And you don't think the emperor is getting payback?" Sergeant Oppie Daltonia asked.

"Fuck that, Sergeant," Manu said. "Don't do the crime if you can't do the time. If he didn't embezzle those funds, then the emperor wouldn't have a reason to arrest him."

Leif didn't know Sergeant Daltonia well, so he didn't know if she was an ardent imperialist or not, but Manu was. Leif had learned long ago that the big Marine would not ignore what he perceived to be slights to the Granite Throne.

He's right, though.

Horatio Fremont was Perspidian's grandson and heir-apparent. From the evidence presented by the IBI, the clan scion had been siphoning off large amounts of imperial funds intended for several projects on Galveston and Sunrise, two Novack worlds. After two warnings—once again, according to the reports—the emperor had had enough, and he issued an imperial summons warrant. While not quite an arrest warrant, it required Fremont to appear before him to answer for his crimes.

When Fremont failed to appear, the emperor had sent an IBI team to "escort" him to Earth. Ser Perspidian had placed the team into "protective custody," and two days later, declared that the New Alignment Group, with all of its holdings, were no longer subject to imperial rule.

None of the Marines knew what was going to happen next. There was a huge Navy base on Sunrise, a base now under total lock-down. The Novacks had large numbers in the Navy and fewer, but still significant numbers of Marines.

Leif looked over at Sergeant DuPont. He was a Novack, from Galveston, one of the planets that was supposed to receive the funds that Horatio had stolen. He was sitting quietly, hands folded. Leif couldn't read what the sergeant might be thinking.

"What are you guys thinking?" Sergeant Hua asked Lief. "Are you with us?"

We are not "you guys," Leif thought, but kept to himself.

Sergeant Hua was a good enough guy, and he was just voicing what others were probably wondering. The wyntonans were relatively new to the empire, and their loyalty to the emperor was suspect to many of the humans. With this new schism, they had to be wondering which way the wyntonans would jump.

Which, of course, was far, far above Leif's station. He would be surprised, however, if this changed anything. The Council of Elders had decided that the People needed to be better connected with the humans, and the emperor still ruled over most of the race.

Still, situations changed which sometimes led to shifts in policy.

"I swore an oath to the emperor," Leif said, leaving it at that.

Sergeant Hua nodded, seemingly reassured by his words.

Leif was not as reassured. He respected the emperor and thought the human's heart was in the right place. But he had a sinking feeling that the Novack's actions would not stop at just this.

Lori had once told him about a famous curse from one of the human sub-cultures that said "May you live in interesting times." Leif hadn't really understood what that meant.

He was beginning to understand it now.

Chapter 19

"Battalion, atten . . . HUT!"

As one, more than 1500 bodies snapped to attention, the entire battalion standing in formation on the parade deck. Across the Corps, identical formations were being held, all for the same reason.

Lieutenant Colonel König marched over to take the formation as the XO returned to his position with the battalion staff.

The commanding officer waited a long moment, as if dreading his next words.

"Personnel to be mustered out, front and center . . . MARCH!" he shouted out.

From the formation, Marines and sailors took a step back, conducted a facing movement, and began to march to form a line in front of the colonel. Sergeant DuPont, Lance Corporal Yerez . . . and Private First Class Ke Win from India's First Platoon.

Leif felt . . . he wasn't sure what he felt. Disappointment, sorrow, anger. Win was no longer in his fire team, moved out to free a position for Hkekka, but Leif had always had a soft spot in his heart for the cynical Marine. And now this.

He stood at attention as the Marines and corpsmen filed forward until they could fall in a long line, facing the commanding officer. Twenty-four Marines stood there with the rest of the battalion as witnesses.

"Detail, present . . . HARMS," First Lieutenant Gloria Baltimore ordered.

The CO returned their salute.

"Adjutant, read the orders," Lieutenant Colonel König said in a normal speaking voice, which was picked up by his throat mic and broadcast over the parade deck.

"Attention to orders," the adjutant shouted out. "Special Order Six-Eighty-One-Point-Seventy-Four.

"From: the Commandant of the Marine Corps.

"To: First Lieutenant Gloria L. Baltimore, Imperial Marine Corps; Gunnery Sergeant John D. Sanders, Imperial Marine Corps; Gunnery Sergeant Leticia R. Weisenhunt, Imperial Marine Corps . . ."

Leif kept his eyes locked to the front as he listened to the adjutant call out 18 more names until he shouted, "Private First Class Ke Win, Imperial Marine Corps." Leif felt a shot to the heart as if he'd been punched. Two more names were announced, completing the addressees.

"As of twenty-three-fifty-nine IST, two May, six-eighty-one, said-named Marines are to be mustered out of the Imperial Marine Corps under Other-Than-Honorable conditions.

"Given under my hand, Altamont D. Rhee, General, Imperial Marine Corps."

As simple as that, it was over.

Lieutenant Colonel König, who'd been facing the 24, performed an about face, presenting his back to the former Marines. The battalion staff, except for the adjutant, followed suit.

"Battalion, about . . . FACE!" he shouted out.

Fifteen-hundred-and-six Marines and sailors spun around, presenting their backs to those being mustered out.

Leif couldn't see them, but he heard ex-First Lieutenant Baltimore give the order to face left, then move out. The 24 marched off the parade deck and into a waiting bus that would take them to the shuttle port where they would join the rest of the Novacks being mustered out and transported back to Galveston and out of the empire.

Chapter 20

"Finally!" Kyle said, rushing back into their room and throwing his Alphas and Blues on his rack. "I had to show them our deployment orders."

"Told you you should have got them done earlier," Leif said as he continued to pack his seabag.

He didn't expect an answer. He'd been reminding his roommate to get his uniforms done for the last two months, but it wasn't until Sergeant Zoran had jumped his ass that he actually went to the uniform shop and got it done. Even then, he'd had to jump the queue by showing his orders.

Leif liked Kyle, but he probably was not NCO material. He had no initiative. He glanced at his own Alphas, hanging on his locker door. They'd been done for months now, never worn, but ready to put on for whatever the occasion.

And now, they were going to get that opportunity. While much of the rest of the Marine Corps would remain on One-Alpha, 3/6 would join two other battalions to represent the Corps at the ceremonies on Earth.

This was one of those proverbial once-in-a-lifetime opportunities. Third Battalion, Sixth Marines, was one of three battalion to represent the Corps for the empress-in-waiting's ascension—and wedding. The chance to observe history in the making was not something to sneer at.

And the chance almost didn't happen, thanks to the Novack secession. The Navy and Marines had remained on One-Alpha for a month, ready if hostilities broke out. And there had been clashes within the Navy's Fourth Fleet. Eleven ships had broken with the empire to join the Novacks. In the process, 76 Navy loyalists and an unknown number of secessionists had been killed.

Nine-hundred-and-three Marines had been mustered out and returned to the Novack capital of Galveston—all without violence. The empire might not recognize the Novack secession, but the commandant had insisted that no Marine wishing to leave would be harmed.

The imperial military was still in Condition One-Alpha, but after what was reported to be intense debate, the long-scheduled wedding and coronation ceremony of the empress-in-waiting was to be held as scheduled. The eleven Novack worlds might be under a blockade, but the emperor wanted to show to the rest of humanity, as well as the other races that might be searching for a crack in humanity that could be exploited, that things were normal within the empire.

The battalion, which had it not been taken out of the deployment rotation after the Han'ei mission, would be out there aboard a ship right now, cutting square circles in space as part of the blockade. Instead, it was slotted in as the division's representative for the ceremonies.

Sometimes, things just worked out.

But it all came with a price. The squad had been inspected by Sergeant Zoran and up to the battalion commander himself. It wasn't going to end there. The division IG was next, conducting a battalion-wide inspection tomorrow, just a day before they left for Earth. Rumor had it that the CG would be there to observe.

Marines existed to fight, but simply looking good and not embarrassing the Corps had taken on the highest priority. With all the attention, Leif almost wished that they were still on One-Alpha and another battalion was going to Earth.

Almost.

This was going to be the ultimate boondoggle, and Leif understood that he'd be observing history.

The cynical part of his mind wondered why 3/6 had been selected. True, the battalion had been pulled out of the deployment cycle, so they were available. But within Second Division, they were the only battalion with the first of the qiincer Marines. Integrating the Corps was one of the emperor's pet projects, so that could have been part of the decision-making process. His gut told him there might be something more to it, however.

"How much time do we have?" Kyle asked, pulling his crumbled-up seabag from his locker.

"About twenty minutes until we've got to be in Delta-Six-Oh-Three for the etiquette class."

"Another fucking etiquette class? I'm the etiquette king!" he said, lifting a leg and letting out a loud fart.

"Sure you are, your majesty. But you still better get your seabag packed. We stage them right after the IG inspection."

It didn't make sense to Leif, staging the seabags a full day before they embarked for the trip. All their uniforms but the set on their backs were to be sealed until after they arrived and just before the wedding, so they'd be in the same utilities for Mother knows how long. Adding another day in that one set would give them one more day to get riper with human, qiincer, and wyntonan sweat. If they were supposed to make a good impression as they arrived, this wasn't going to do it.

But the ways of the Corps often defied logic. Undoubtedly, some staff weenie thought this was the best way to ensure their dress uniforms went from the IG's eyes directly to the wedding. That same staff weenie probably forgot that the Marines had to go about their daily schedule until then.

Oh, well, two more days and we're aboard the ship, and all this BS will be over.

RS PENANG

Chapter 21

"Are you sure, Corporal?" Private Hkekka asked, his ever-present smirk curling the corners of his mouth.

"Yes, you heard me. Unfurl . . . unroll them."

The private flexed his shoulders forward slightly before Leif shouted out, "Wait! Take a step back, first."

Is he disappointed? Leif wondered, trying to read the private's body language. He'd just remembered how strong the diminutive qiincer's wings can be when they unrolled, and knowing Hkekka, he'd probably enjoy smacking the shit out of Sousa standing next to him.

He didn't argue, though, and stepped back before with a loud snap, he unrolled and pumped out his wings.

So now what am I supposed to be looking for? he wondered.

He'd naively thought that the BS would have ended as they got into the confines of the ship. He should have known better. If anything, the BS had increased. And now, standing in the main corridor outside berthing, he was conducting a personal hygiene inspection—which again was BS. Not only were they in the same utilities since before boarding, the ship's heads in the troop berthing were on the fritz. The Marines were limited to 30-second sonics in the Navy berthing spaces once a day.

With Sousa and Stone, he'd been around humans enough to know what to look for. Fingernails were a key indicator—if they were clean, the human was probably clean as well. But a qiincer? Sergeant Zoran had specifically told him to check Hkekka's wings. He didn't know how, but the sergeant would be conducting her hygiene inspection next, and she'd probably researched enough to know what to look for.

He stepped up for a closer look, leaning over the shorter Marine. He'd seen the private's wings before, but not like this. They looked frail, with iridescent translucent sections, but he knew better than that. They were extremely strong, both in their own rigidity as well as with the corded muscles across the qiincer's back that powered them. A qiincer could knock out a human with a well-placed blow.

Each wing was separated into three parts. Leif thought a qiincer had six wings, since they were controlled separately, but the qiincers insisted that there were two. The front two lobes could beat in unison for speed flight, but more often beat in opposition to each other. The back lobe could rotate 360 degrees, and they gave a qiincer extreme maneuverability. A qinncer could dart around quickly, but they couldn't carry much with them in flight.

Flying was a valuable ability, but Leif wasn't sure the tradeoffs were worth it. Evidently, the Mother thought so, too. She'd only given one race the ability to fly.

Looking closely, Leif could see the pseudo-haemolymph pulsing through the translucent wings.

"Huh," he mumbled as he leaned even closer.

"What, Corporal?" Hkekka asked.

"Nothing, Private."

"No, you made a noise. What's the matter?"

Leif leaned back and looked down at the Marine. There was the tiniest bit of stress in his voice, Leif thought. But why?

"Nothing's the matter."

A small vibration ran up all six lobes in a rippling effect. *What does that mean?*

Hkekka was his Marine, and even if he was a total dick, Leif was responsible for him. Yet he really hadn't researched much about qiincers. Sergeant Zoran undoubtedly had, just as she knew about wyntonans.

It didn't look like the private accepted his answer, but he couldn't figure out why not.

"OK, you all look fine. Stand easy. Sergeant Zoran will be here in five."

"Hey, Stone, give me a quick look," he said, remembering that the sergeant would inspect him as well.

The BS never stops, he told himself as Stone gave him the once over. *Just one more day, though, one more day and we're on Earth. Maybe then they'll get off our asses.*

EARTH

Chapter 22

"Look at that," Lori said. "Isn't it beautiful?"

Leif looked up from his scanpad at the display at the front of the shuttle. Earth was pretty, he'd agree, with the blues, browns, and whites, but no more so than other planets.

Lori, like most of the other humans, was brimming over with excitement. She had never been on the planet, and there were tears in her eyes as the shuttle left the *IS Penang* to descend to the surface. Leif was curious as to the home that spawned humanity, but he didn't feel the same visceral attachment to the planet as the human Marines.

The shuttle shook as it entered the thermosphere. Technically, they were now "on" Earth, and Lori and most of the other Marines broke out into applause and shouts.

Across the aisle, Hkekka nudged Bamort, one of the other qiincers, and rolled his eyes, with that ever-present smirk of superiority, no sign of whatever had bothered him yesterday when Leif inspected him. Leif might have been thinking the humans' reactions were overdone, but he'd never show that to others. He knew he needed to have another talk with the qiincer. Forsythe the Third might be the emperor of all of them, but this was really a time for human celebration, and the qiincers and wyntonans needed to play nice in the background.

For the next 20 minutes, almost all of the humans were glued to the display, which showed a real-time image of their descent. Oohs and ahs filled the compartment when they broke through the high-level clouds and Mount Kilimanjaro came into view. Somewhere down there, humans had first stepped out of the trees and started their journey. Not the

People, though, so to Leif, it was just one more mountain, not as impressive as Old Man Time back in the Silver Range on Home.

In a way, Leif envied Lori and the human Marines. Leif missed Home, but for the People, they'd never left their mother planet. When he'd returned two years before, it wasn't so much exciting as comfortable, like slipping into an old pair of shoes or a favorite chair. For the humans, it was different. The vast majority of humans had never set foot on their planet of origin, so to return to their roots had almost a religious aspect to it. Looking at Lori, she was beaming.

She caught his stare and grabbed his hand, squeezing it. To be that enthused about anything was something special.

With Lake Victoria in the far distance, the shuttle came into Hanni Imperial Spaceport, which was really just an annex of the Nairobi Imperial Spaceport complex, settling down for a landing with nary a bump. Cheers and high-fives broke out again as the shuttle powered down.

"Welcome to Hanni Imperial Airport, Gateway to the Imperial City," a canned voice said. "If you are a resident, welcome home. If you are a visitor, we hope you enjoy your stay. In a moment, you will be asked to debark the shuttle where you will be taken to processing. Citizens of the empire, please proceed to the red stations. Non-citizens, please proceed to the blue stations for entry.

"Your luggage will arrive at carousel fifteen."

"Stay in your seats!" a gunny Leif didn't know shouted out as soon as the announcement was finished. "We've got ground transportation coming."

It took another 15 minutes before the gunny told them to grab their carry-ons and debark the shuttle—not through the gangway, but down a portable stair and onto the tarmac.

"First Squad, on me," Sergeant Zoran said as Leif reached the tarmac. "We've got luggage duty."

"Hell, why is it always us?" Stone asked.

"Just lucky," Leif said.

A flatbed hover was already there, ready to take the bags. After a few minutes, a ground robot trundled up, positioned its belt, and opened the luggage compartment. The working party formed a chain between the bottom of the belt and the flatbed. Within moments, the first bundle of bags started down the belt.

"Let's do it," Leif said, taking the first bag off the belt and handing it to Sousa, who then handed it down the line until PFC "Red" Hornsby, who'd been part of the rugby wedge on Han'ei and was the biggest Marine in the squad, hefted it into the hover.

Hkekka had taken his place in the line, but he'd been bypassed in the chain by the other Marines. Leif could see the cloud of anger beginning to form on his face.

"Private Hkekka, get on the hover and make sure the bags are lined up," he told the Marine to get him involved.

The rest of the NCOs and non-rates from India and Kilo were loading the first of three buses that were lined up and waiting for them.

"Be careful with my bags! I don't want anything broken!" Corporal Roan from Kilo shouted to the laughs of the others.

Manu gave him the finger before he had to grab the next bag and pass it on. They emptied the first compartment, then had to wait as the cargo robot moved onto the aft compartment. Leif took the brief break to look around. The snow-capped Kilimanjaro monopolized the horizon, some 40 klicks away. Parts of the Nairobi megopolis were visible around the side of the terminal off to the north, huge buildings rising from the summer haze like an oasis. To the west was the famous Serengeti, leading to the Imperial City on the shores of Lake Victoria.

"Heads up!" Sergeant Zoran shouted. "We're back in business."

The first bag was already coming down the belt, and once again, the Marine chain loaded the bags onto the flatbed. It didn't take long, but as Red lifted the last bag up, the third and last bus was pulling away.

"Hey, stop!" Kyle shouted.

"Leave it, Corporal," the sergeant said.

"But—"

"Load up on the flatbed."

"That's what I'm talking about, Lance Corporal Stone said as he clambered up.

Leif had to agree. After being cooped up on the ship, then the shuttle, sitting out in the open on the back of a hover was preferable to loading a bus. He hopped up, sat on a bag next to Manu, and settled in for the ride.

The hover was on autodrive, its destination already entered. As it pulled away from the shuttle, Manu pointed at the next shuttle which was parked about a hundred meters away. A group of the battalion's lieutenants had stripped off their blouses and were unloading their shuttle's luggage. Three bags had fallen off the end of the belt while the junior officers struggled to keep up.

"That's what happens when you segregate the shuttles," Manu said. "Someone's got to do the dirty work."

"Should we stop to help them?" Private Wonstat, Manu's newest team member, asked.

"Can't, Wonstat. This here hover's not programmed to stop," Manu said.

The flatbed cut under the terminal, emerging on the other side, then left the spaceport. The area around the spaceport had been kept on the wild side, and Leif craned his head, hoping to spot a lion.

Leif had killed a *wasilla* for his a'aden hunt, armed with nothing more than a spear. A lion was the Earth equivalent to a *wasilla,* and the younger generation sometimes even referred to *wasillas* as "lions," much to the chagrin of the elders, and he was anxious to see one. All he saw on the drive, however, were some scrawny dogs and a long-legged bird with a huge bill.

He wasn't the only one disappointed. Several of the humans had wanted to see one as well.

The flatbed pulled into a modest-looking compound, well outside of town. A line of shops, shacks, really, were on the road outside the compound, but there were none of the famed East African night spots. There was none of anything, really, except for grass and bushes.

The flatbed had beat the busses to the compound. Master Sergeant Watanabe stood waiting, hands behind his back, as it came to a halt.

"Welcome to the Golden Cheetah, Marines. This is going to be your home for the next four days."

"Shit, we're going to be held prisoner until after the wedding," Manu said.

Just to the north somewhere, Nairobi beckoned, but Manu was right. The powers that be didn't want anything to cast a shadow on the ceremonies. Drunk Marines in the seedy areas of the megopolis were a recipe for trouble.

"Hey, who are you guys?" a voice shouted from an open window above them.

"Three-six!" PFC Rose shouted.

"Two-twenty-three!" the Marine shouted back.

"Close the window," the Top Watanabe shouted up to the 2/23 Marine. "You'll have more than enough time to get acquainted."

He turned back to First Squad and said, "Those bags aren't going to get staged by themselves. Sergeant Zoran, get to it."

Leif snorted. Here they were, at the cradle of humanity, and all they were was a working party.

Some things never changed.

Chapter 23

"Battalion, atten . . . HUT!" the CO himself called out.

As one, every Marine and sailor snapped to, eyes locked to the front.

The command was repeated down the line until each of the three battalions was at the position of attention.

From out of Leif's field of view, the general, in a reedy voice that was almost too quiet to hear, shouted out, "Detail, present . . . HARMS!"

The Marines had practiced the simple pass in review a dozen times over the last two days, and each time, the general's voice sounded worse and worse, but she'd refused to use a throat mic to amplify it.

Not that it really mattered except for appearances to the thousands of spectators lining the route. The CO for 1/9 repeated the order, and Leif could hear the snap of 1500 rifles coming to present arms.

"Battalion, present . . . HARMS," Lieutenant Colonel König shouted out, his voice penetrating the hot, muggy morning air.

Leif brought up his M88 (without rounds), holding it vertically in front of his chest. The rest of the battalions came to present arms one after the other. The crowd around them murmured and some broke out into applause . . . all for a simple present arms.

Most of the humans had probably never seen Marines in the flesh before, so maybe their reaction was understandable. The Navy, sure. The Navy had their base on the Earth's moon, and sailors were often on Earth itself. Except for the Marine Band and those staff and officers assigned to governmental shore billets, combat Marines were limited to the vast Killdeer Station farther out in the solar plane, and that was only one battalion. It was only on special occasions, and backed by imperial decree, that Marine units were allowed on Earth soil.

A rolling cheer crescendoed as the imperial party drove down the Granite Way. No matter what was happening with the Novacks, no matter how the Granite Throne might have lost favor, here on Earth, at least, the emperor—and his new wife—were as popular as ever. With his eyes locked to the front, Leif couldn't spot the emperor and still empress-in-waiting (for another hour), but he could judge their approach by the cheers.

With his peripheral vision, he saw the muzzle of Private Hkekka's M88 waver. The 88 was not a heavy weapon, coming in at just 4kg without the magazine, but for the smaller qiincer, that was more of a load than it was for the larger humans or wyntonans.

"Steady," he whispered out of the side of his mouth. "Just gut it out."

And then the emperor and his new wife were driving past, both waving from the back seat of the purple Soffrey convertible. Leif had a two-second glimpse of them as their hover whisked them to the Grand Hall for the empress's ascension and coronation.

Weeks and weeks of rehearsals and travel for two seconds.

That wasn't true, though. There might or might not be the review of troops. The Marines had rehearsed that as well, but the imperial party had not indicated if that was going to be a go or not. Evidently, it depended on the empress herself, and after everything that was going on today, reviewing thousands of Marines and an almost equal number of sailors might be well down the list of priorities.

With the imperial party past, the general called out to the battalion commanding officer to order arms. When the CO gave the command, Hkekka let out an audible sigh of relief. Leif wasn't going to say anything about that, however. The private had kept the position without faltering, and he'd earned that sigh.

Her voice almost completely shot, the general ordered the commanders to march their units to the plaza and take their positions. Leif was already sweating in his blues, the collar digging into his neck. Just marching to the plaza would take an hour, and then they'd wait under the hot African sun for several more hours until after the coronation, all probably for nothing.

The thought of tonight, when they were finally released on liberty and he could get out of his throat-choker and down a cold beer, was beginning to sound like the best thing that would happen to him today.

****

"If you need to fall out, that's OK," Leif whispered.

"Get off my case, Corporal. I'm fine," Private Hkekka answered.

Just trying to help, minta.

No matter what Hkekka said, he wasn't "fine." Qiincers took the sun and heat even worse than the wyntonans, and today was brutally hot. Without a breeze coming off the lake, the plaza was sweltering, and the Marines had been out in the sun and on their feet and without water for going on five hours now. Humans in the crowd were dropping like flies, and even a few Marines had been carted off before the review of troops. Leif should have dropped Hkekka then, but the qiincer had insisted that he was OK. Now, the private was trembling as he stood at attention next to him, holding—for the sake of uniformity—the heavier M88 rather than the normal M77 carbine the qiincers had been issued as their personal weapons.

"Battalion, atten . . . HUT!" the 1/9 battalion commander shouted out.

Next to 3/6, First Battalion, Ninth Marines snapped to attention—maybe not quite as crisply as they'd done earlier in the day.

"Present . . . Harms!"

Leif was standing at parade rest, his eyes locked to the front, but he could hear murmuring as the emperor was greeted by the 1/9 CO and escorted to the right side of the battalion formation

A review of troops was not an inspection. The emperor would not be walking the ranks, but merely walking along the battalion frontage. Most bigwigs didn't even walk but rather sat in a vehicle and rode past the troops. On the one hand, Leif appreciated the fact that the emperor and empress were walking, but on the other hand, it took a lot longer, all the time with the Marines cooking in the sun.

Behind him, Leif heard a Marine collapse. He hoped there wouldn't be more.

"Stand by," Gunny Westinghouse hissed from the rear of the company.

The battalion was formed four companies deep, each platoon on line. India Company was in the front rank, and that meant each platoon's First squad occupied the first rank of the company's frontage. That meant each First Squad would be in full view of the imperial couple. At the front of the battalion, the CO was standing in before his headquarters, which was centered between India's Second and Third Platoons. His staff faced forward, but he was facing towards the battalion—and where he could watch the emperor and empress.

He came to attention, then shouted out, "Battalion, atten . . . HUT!"

It was a relief to move again, to change position, as the battalion came to attention.

The CO did an about face, then a moment after the 1/9 CO gave his order arms, he shouted out, "Present . . . HARMS!"

With a clear view to the front, Leif watched the emperor, in an understated white uniform with imperial gray trim that set off his black skin, sword at his side, walk to Lieutenant Colonel König. Stride-for-stride next to him was the new empress, in a striking gray uniform, her red hair tied up in a bun, the sun glinting off the simple platinum band that had just been placed on her head during the coronation. Five steps behind, the general followed. That was all. No other entourage.

The emperor reached the battalion commander who saluted. The emperor returned it before shaking his hand, then introduced the empress. And then they were walking over to the right side of the formation . . . and India's First Platoon.

Normally, the company commander would be standing in front of the company, the platoon commanders in front of the platoons. For the review of troops, however, Captain Jiminez and Lieutenant Nazari stood side by side, in line with and just to the right of Sergeant Zoran. The emperor went right to the captain, shook his hand, then started walking the line. He passed First Team, nodding as he walked, then spotted Leif.

"*Corporal* a'Hope Hollow, the roads are long, but they eventually meet, Mother willing," he said in Uzboss, but using the Standard word "corporal."

Leif's mouth dropped open in shock, both at hearing the wyntonan greeting and that the emperor knew his name.

"Mother willing," he stammered out.

"I'd like to hear about that, sometime," he said, pointing at the Golden Lion on Leif's chest. "I read the citation, of course, but I'd like your perspective."

Leif didn't know what to say, but he was saved from speaking as the emperor had already stepped off, stopping in front of Hkekka.

"*Tast deozkeo oklamano*," the emperor said—at least that's what is sounded like to Leif.

"*Tast deozkeo, kostomo. Et Hkekka*," Hkekka said.

"I'm afraid that's about the extent of my *Qiiantor*," the emperor said. "So, Private Hkekka, how are you coping—"

"Forsythe . . ." the empress said, putting her hand on his arm.

"Yes?"

"These Marines have been out in the sun all day. We don't need to keep them standing here, holding their weapons up like this, while you chat."

"Ah!" the emperor said. "Of course, you're right. Of course."

"I'd like to talk to you and the other *qiiana* sometime, Private Hkekka."

He turned to continue his review. The Empress Jenifer, standing in front of Leif, caught his eye and winked before she followed. As she stepped in front of Sousa, she leaned in to say something, but even with his hearing, he couldn't make out what she said.

With the empress pushing him, the imperial party took only a few minutes to review 3/6 before moving on to the final battalion and the CO could give the order arms and then to parade rest. This time, Leif had to bite back his own sigh. His arms were aching, and he was feeling a little faint.

Leif had seen the emperor three times now, and each time, the human had gone out of his way to speak a few words of Uzboss, something Leif appreciated. And now, he'd evidently done the same with qiincer. He insisted that he was the emperor for all his citizens, not just humans, and he seemed to be making the effort to live up to that claim.

Chapter 24

"There we go," Leif said as Kyle brought back three pitchers of Dynx. "That's better then this . . ." he paused to see if any locals were in hearing range, "this Tusker stuff."

It wasn't that the local Tusker beer was bad. It was actually decent, and the Marines had fulfilled their duty to sample the local cuisine—beer counted as cuisine, right?—but when there was serious drinking to be done, Dynx was the only answer.

The People had their own beer, which seemed to be a staple in most of the sentient races. Some said beer was simple parallel development, but Leif tended to the train of thought that the Mother (Proginator, Jehova, Supreme) gave beer to all the races as a token of her love. As much as he was proud of his wyntonan heritage and culture, he had to give credit where credit was due. Dynx put all wyntonan beer to shame.

Jordan downed the rest of his Tusker, then without saying a word, grabbed one of the pitchers from Kyle's hand before he could place them on the table. He filled his stein, then downed half of it in one long gulp.

Leif held back the frown that tried to form on his face. Jordan seemed to be in a better place, but every once in awhile, he did little things like that, things a pre-hearing Jordan wouldn't have done.

Kyle didn't seem to take offense, however. Kyle rarely seemed to take offense at anything.

"Thanks, Kyle," Leif said, taking one of the pitchers and filling the other corporal's stein first, then Lori's, before filling his own.

He took a long swallow, and the heat and sweat of the day faded even further from his memories. Not just today. All of the practices and rehearsals. What was past was past, though, and now it was time for some fun. There had been a line of buses ready to take the Marines into Nairobi, and in record time, they'd returned their weapons to the armory boxes, showered, changed, and made it to the buses. They had Cinderella liberty—all Marines had to check into one of the returning buses by midnight—which rather sucked, but for the moment, it was good enough.

Nairobi supposedly had three wyntonan restaurants with authentic food, and Leif, Jordan, and Tessa were supposed to meet up with some of the other wyntonans at one of them later on in the evening, but for now, the beer was hitting the spot.

"To a job well done!" Manu said, lifting his stein.

"Not that we had to do much, though," Jorge Stikklestein said as he lifted his beer.

"What do you mean? I was sweating like a dog, standing out there like a damned statue."

"Dogs don't sweat," Jordan said matter-of-factly before pouring himself another beer.

"What?"

"Dogs don't sweat," Jordan said again. "They pant with their tongues out."

Leif looked at his friend in surprise, first that he bothered to correct Manu, and second, that he knew that about the Earth animal.

"Well, la-dee-dah," Manu said. "How about this, then? Like a fat man porking a fat woman in a Siberian sauna. Do they sweat, Jordan?"

The rest broke out into laughter as Jordan nodded.

"You OK?" Leif asked quietly as Manu and the rest continued the debate on whether their duty had been difficult or not.

"Sure, why do you ask?" he said in Uzboss. "Kwasti?"

"You said it, not me," Leif said.

"Just mind your own business," he said again before draining his stein, switching to Standard and shouting out, "Hey, how about that beer? Let's keep it flowing!"

Wildman slid over a half-empty pitcher, seemingly not noticing the edge in Jordan's voice.

Leif noticed it, though, and it worried him.

Chapter 25

"They're not so big," Sergeant Weir said. "How about it? Would you two rather face one of your wassilla-things or one of those?"

Leif looked out of the tour wagon at the six lions lounging under a lone tree, ignoring the line of wagons that had invaded their territory. It was big, bulkier than a wasilla, but as the big black-maned male yawned, it didn't have the look of a wasilla's feral intelligence.

Several of the human Marines turned to see his answer. Not all—in fact, only a small minority—of the People had actually faced a wasilla for their a'aden ceremony. Both he and Jordan had, though, something well-known by the rest of the Marines.

"I'll take on the lion," Leif said after only a moment's consideration to a chorus of disappointed sounding "bullshits" from the humans.

"What about you, Jordan?" Benny Taiko asked.

He gave the lions a cursory glance, then said, "Makes no difference."

"That's right, Corporal," Lance Corporal Honus "Jester" Pannington, one of Jordan's Marines, said. "A lion's just as tough as one of your wasillas."

"So, you about ready to go face either one, Jester?" Lance Corporal Amy Slythe asked.

"Hell fucking yeah! Give me my M85, and I'll drop either one," he shouted, aiming an imaginary rifle at the big cats. "Bam, bam!"

"Bam, bam my mother-loving ass," Amy said. "With a fucking spear in your hand, like Corporal Hollow there."

Jester flexed his biceps and kissed each one in turn, then said, "Don't need no spear. Just these guns."

Someone from the front of the wagon threw a half-full bottle of water that bounced off his chest.

"What an idiot," Lori said as Jester gave the finger towards the Marines in the front.

Leif understood the lance corporal, however. Wyntonan males weren't continually pounding their chests like human males—they saved it for when they were in musth, and then they took it to another level. But still, it was basically the same thing. The two races weren't all that different.

Not like the fairies, he told himself, glancing back to the two qiincers at the back of the bus, both engrossed in their scanpads.

Here they were, surrounded by alien animals, and they couldn't bother to look out and see them. If this wasn't a required evolution, Leif was sure they'd just as soon remain back at the Golden Cheetah. Leif just didn't understand them.

He held out his scanpad to take a selfie with the lions in the background. Even if they weren't wasillas, they were impressive, and he wanted to send the shot back to Hope Hollow. For all his success as one of the first wyntonans in the Imperial Marines, he knew his extended family would be more impressed with him sitting safe in a wagon with the almost mystical beasts outside and under the tree.

"If you look ahead and to your right, you'll see a magnificent marabou stork," the driver/guide said.

A large, particularly ugly bird was stalking through the grass, eyes intent on whatever small creatures it might find. The black and white plumage was OK—not that Leif thought Earth birds, with their big feathers, were as pretty as wyntonan *kons*—but the head was naked mottled skin, as if it was diseased.

Other than the lions, none of the other animals he'd seen so far impressed him. He didn't care much about the grass-eating "gazebos" or "wild-the-beasts," or whatever the guide had called them (and weren't they all "wild beasts" here? That was a stupid name, he thought). The crocodiles sunning on the banks of the lake had been impressive, even if they hadn't moved a millimeter while the Marines watched. Leif had seen a holo of a crocodile playing tug-of-war with several lions over the body of one of the grass-eaters. The grass-eater was still alive, bleating in panic while the alpha-creatures fought over its body. It was alive until the crocodile won the battle, that is, and disappeared beneath the surface of the water, the lions pacing and watching for it to reappear. Something like that would have been cool to watch, but with the lions sitting in the shade a klick away from the motionless crocodiles, he didn't think that was in the cards for today.

India and Kilo Companies were among the last of the Marines to go on the safari, and the others who'd already gone had come back with tales of rhinos, elephants, and many more animals with which Leif was unfamiliar. Along with the crocodile-lion tug-of-war, the holo had shown a huge rhinoceros, attacking one of the safari wagons, slamming its head into the side of the much larger vehicle. That had resonated with him. He often felt like he was futilely banging his head against the big green machine that was the Corps. He'd seen the lions, so he could check that off, but he really wanted to see a rhino, too.

And have it charge the wagon.

He'd record that and send it back to Soran. She'd get a kick out of it.

"Hey, did you see Womby?" Kyle asked, leaning over the back of their seat.

Lori gave a quick glance to Leif and rolled her eyes. Womby was one of the most popular newsfeeds, but it was "low-brow," to use her terminology, pandering to the "lowest common denominator." Leif couldn't really tell much difference between any of the feeds, but he wasn't about to tell her that.

"No, what now?" she said as if humoring him.

"The empress. Her dad is asking the emperor to pardon Horatio Fremont. Says with the wedding and ascension and all, that the emperor needs to extend good will to the Novacks."

"No shit? Let me see that," she said, grabbing his scanpad. She read for a few moments, said, "Bullshit," and unrolled hers, snapping it rigid, and undoubtedly wanting to read from a "real" news syndicate.

Leif shook his head and looked back at the lions. They didn't care about the humans and their political games. For hundreds of thousands of years, they just went on with their lives.

"No way he's going to do it," Lori said, but sounding unsure of herself.

"I don't know. It's the empress' father doing the asking, the head of the Jin Longs. How's Forsythe gonna say no to his new empress?" Kyle asked. "Especially as he's already commuted the sentences of all those other prisoners in the Empress Jenifer's name?"

"'Cause that asshole Fremont's still on the run, so how can he pardon him? And the Novacks seceded from the empire, that's why. They killed Imperial citizens. Hell, Kyle, didn't we all just hit One-Alpha for the last two months? And you think he's going to give in just because the Jin Longs ask him?"

"A Jin Long's the empress. He can't risk that alliance, not if he wants to keep the empire intact," Benny, sitting beside Kyle, said.

"They're traitors, too, just looking for an excuse," Lori said, her face creased in a scowl.

"Hey, watch it. The empress . . ."

"Calm down, Lori," Leif said, nudging her with his arm.

It wasn't that long ago that people had to be careful of what they said about the imperial family, unless they wanted to be dragged off during the night and "disappeared." *Lese Majeste* was still on the books, and while it had not normally been invoked under Forsythe's reign so far, it wouldn't take much to get it going again.

"He's not going to give in," she muttered, unwilling to let anyone else get in the last word before she turned back around.

Leif didn't care much about human intrigue. Let them play their political games. He'd just keep quiet and do his job.

So why am I disappointed?

He knew why. He didn't know the empress, of course, but for some reason, the thought of her, side-by-side with the emperor, fighting injustice wherever it reared its ugly head . . .

Yeah, right, Leefen. Grow up. That's not the way the universe works.

Leif admired the emperor, and he'd hoped the empress would measure up to him, to compliment him. He'd sworn loyalty to the emperor, and now the empress, and he wouldn't break that oath, but it would be easier if he respected both of them. And if Her Imperial Majesty Jenifer the First was merely a tool of the Jin Long Clan, well, then why was he oath-bound to the imperial couple? To whom was he loyal?

The Corps. Your fellow Marines. That's all you need to know.

"Take a last look at the Canyon Pride," their guide announced. "We're going to head to the Njenga Bowl right now. I've got reports that one of the elephant herds is heading over, and we should be able to catch them there."

As the wagon lurched forward, Leif looked back at the six lions. None of them bothered to take notice of the Marines' departure.

Chapter 26

"Well, I told you," Lori said as they crowded into the resort's bar, a note of vindication in her voice.

They'd returned from the safari, hot and dusty, just in time to catch the emperor addressing his subjects. His decision was firm and final. Horatio Fremont, scion and heir to the Fremont Clan, was still charged and would be arrested at the earliest opportunity.

There were more than a few ooh-rahs and cheers when he said it, but many, if not most of the Marines, were silent, wondering what his decision might portend. The Jin Long Clan was one of the most powerful clans in the empire, with their fingers everywhere. At least ten of the Marines in the bar were from the clan's planets, and where before they were bursting with pride that "their" empress was now on the throne, they now had that same shell-shocked look as the Novack Marines had when the New Alignment Group had declared independence.

Just behind the emperor, the empress silently stood, her face impassive by what was obviously a force of will. Her right hand visibly trembled as the emperor announced his decision.

He never mentioned the empress' family, but he didn't have to. This was a direct rebuke not only to the Fremonts, but also to the Jin Longs. And to the empress' father in particular.

The main feed was on the emperor, but one of the sidebar shots was focused right on August Chen, the empress's father. Anger clouded his carefully sculpted looks while he absorbed the rebuke. If he thought he'd just become the kingmaker, this had to be a rude awakening. He turned and whispered something to a man sitting beside him, then spun about, his entourage scrambling to keep up as he stormed out of the room. The empress's mother took one quick look over her shoulder at her daughter before following her husband and clan head out.

The emperor didn't seem to notice as he stressed that this was a simple legal matter, that he didn't hold anyone else in the New Alignment Group accountable for Horatio Fremont's crimes. He said he was ready for talks to bring the empire back together again.

Over his shoulder, tears formed in the empress's eyes.

Chapter 27

"Hey, I was just coming to see you," Lori said, walking down the hall as Leif closed the door. "You want to take me to the pool?"

She was in a pink bikini bottom, sandals, and a light lime-colored top, towel in hand and an eager look on her face. He knew why she was asking. The degree of modesty among the humans varied, with some of them wearing full bodysuits at the pool while others went naked. Lori went topless. She was also considered quite attractive by human standards, and while most of the 3/6 Marines had long quit hitting on her, there were two more battalions at the resort. With Leif there as camouflage, she garnered less overt attention.

He'd given in and been her pool "date" twice now, willing to help out a friend. He just didn't understand what fascinated humans with swimming. Some of the People could swim—it was a logical survival trait. But Leif wasn't aware of any who went swimming for fun. The Mother had only created one water-borne sentient race for a reason.

Besides, the African sun was rough on wyntonan eyes and skin. All of the human worlds were too hot and too bright, and Earth was even worse than some. Ever since leaving Home, he'd had to apply the nanoblock each week. In this, at least, both wyntonan and qiincer agreed, even if the qiincers, in their half-dusk homeworld, found coping more difficult than Leif and the rest. There was no way a qiincer would lounge around a pool in the noonday sun just for fun. No way most wyntonans, either, except that he had twice.

"I . . . I promised some of the others to join them in sticks," he said, trying not to make it sound like a lame excuse.

Her brows furrowed a bit, and she said, "I swear, I don't know what you guys see in that. It doesn't make any sense."

I don't know what you see in swimming. Now that doesn't make any sense. No one's going to drown in a round of sticks.

"I know, but I promised. Can I take a rain check?"

"Oh, sure. I mean, it's not like there's much else to do. But if your game ends, come take a look to see if I'm still sunning, OK?"

"Sure, I'll check it out. Have fun," he said, turning and walking down to one of the resort card rooms.

She was right about having time, though. The Marines were not officially in an alert status . . . but the planned individual leave period for their last week on Earth had been cancelled. Except for a few group events, like hiking the base of Kilimanjaro or the boat cruises on Lake Victoria, the Marines were restricted to the resort grounds. Leif and some of the others had planned on visiting Cairo, but he wasn't too upset by the restriction. Some of the humans, however, had made extensive plans, and they weren't too happy. Unhappy Marines, kept together in close contact, was not a very good mix, and several fights had broken out.

All the more reason to get away from the humans for a short time. He pushed open the door to the Jomo Kenyatta room.

"*Daya! Leefen a'Hope Hollow,*" several voices shouted out in Uzboss.

"*Daya, daya,*" he said before adding "Hi, Thurston," in Standard to the only human, a lance corporal from Lima who seemed to embrace all things wyntonan.

"*Daya,*" he said in passable Uzboss.

Leif smiled, but he was disappointed to see the human there. Thurston was a nice enough guy—a little too nice, to tell the truth. But for an afternoon, Leif wanted to forget about humans, he wanted not to have to listen their reedy voices. He loved some humans as individuals: Lori for sure, Manu, maybe even Kyle. But as a whole, sometimes they grated on him. Not badly, but enough so that he just wanted to kick back and relax with his own kind.

Well, hell. He's almost a wyntonan, he thought. *He thinks he is, at least.*

With fourteen of them, from Jordan as the senior-most corporal to Norm from 1/9 as the junior corporal, they could forget rank, forget the Corps, forget humans for the afternoon and simply enjoy each other's company and a good game of sticks.

And eat. An enticing smell wafted over to him from a plate on the side table. As expected, it was a heaping mound of yakisoba, but with the heady bite of spice.

"Whose is it?" he asked, his mouth already watering. Leif had been out of last year's spice mix for a month now. He'd gotten used to the bland human food, but that didn't mean he liked it.

Inga raised her hand. She was from the Cloudy Peninsula, which was well-known for its cuisine. If Leif couldn't have Granny Oriano's latest mix, Inga's would do fine.

He grabbed a plate of the human noodles with wyntonan spice, then took a seat at the big table. Thurston pushed the cup to him. As the latest to arrive, the throw was his.

"OK, OK, who's going to climb the tree?" he asked in his best thrower's taunt. "Tapers high, tips low," he added before throwing the sticks.

"Thanks, oh good friend of mine," Jordan said in a disgusted voice as the sticks fell into their positions. "That minta there is killing us."

"This minta is just lucky," Thurston said as he took the cup out of Leif's hands. "You know better than that, Corporal. Us monkeys can always *climb trees.*"

The wyntonans laughed, even Leif.

OK, that was funny. But that's all for you. It's time to get serious.

He leaned forward and prayed to the capricious god of the sticks to give him a better lay.

****

Three hours, a couple of hundred throws, and lots of conversation later, the game was still going on. Leif had won some, lost some, ending up at about the middle of the pack. Thurston's early streak of luck had abandoned him, but his mood never lessened.

Leif felt a little guilty over his initial wish that the human wasn't there. He really was a good-natured guy, and his Uzboss was passable. As far as Leif knew, he was the only Marine in the battalion who could say more than a few words. Even his good friend Lori probably had a vocabulary of only 20 words or so.

He leaned back in his chair and looked at the plate that used to sport yakisoba. All that was left now were a few tiny scraps. He'd never admit it to Granny Oriano, nor to anyone here, but Inga's village's spice mix was among the best he'd had. It had turned the edible human dish into something amazing. He let out a satisfied burp.

The room filled with alarms beeping like mad. Marines looked wide-eyed at each other for a moment before pulling out scanpads or looking at wristcomps.

"Formation out in front. Now." Leif said needlessly. Everyone could read as well as he could.

There was a scramble as chairs were pushed back and they rushed the door. Out in the hallway, Marines were appearing, some looking confused, others rushing for the entrance.

"Hkekka, are you on your way?" Leif passed to his rifleman.

"I got the recall, Corporal."

Leif tried to pull up a news feed as he ran, but the net was down—probably on purpose.

The main entrance was a mass of Marines, all pushing to get outside. With the pool directly in back of the lobby, a good portion of them were in various stages of undress. He caught Lori's eyes as the groups merged. She gave him a questioning look, to which he shrugged. He didn't know what was going on any more than she did. He lost sight of her as he forced his way out, looking for where 3/6 was forming.

"Marines, fall in. Three-Six to the right facing the building, facing in. One-Nine in the middle facing the resort, and Three-Twenty-Three to the left facing in," a voice thundered across the large grassy area in front of the resort.

Several SNCOs took over, herding the Marines as ordered. It took four or five moments before Leif saw Lance Corporal Anttante, the India Company guide, standing beside the first sergeant as the senior enlisted Marine harangued the company members to get moving and fall in. Leif quickly took his place, wondering what was going on. He took a quick look up, half expecting to see military craft landing. The sky was a deep blue, but empty. Nothing in sight.

It took several more minutes, but finally, over 3000 Marines and sailors were in a rough formation. They were a ragtag lot, very few in uniform. There was a low rumbling as they as asked each other for the scoop.

"At ease!" the voice filled the area.

Three-thousand-plus voices quieted as one.

A major from 1/9, in uniform, was standing in front of the giant box formation. He spoke to a master sergeant, also in uniform for a moment, then the top took off back inside.

To Leif's surprise, the major reached up to his collar and turned off his loudspeaker.

"At ease!" he yelled out, not nearly as loud, but in the front rank of 3/6, Leif had no problem listening.

He just didn't know why the major, who was probably the duty officer, was using voice power.

"Listen up. We are now in a comms blackout. No one will attempt to call out or receive calls until the blackout is lifted."

Which explains the net being down.

"We are now in One-Alpha. All hands will report in full battle rattle to your company armory boxes and draw your weapons before reporting to designated issue-points for ammunition draws."

There was a low murmur of surprised voices. Military combat forces were prohibited by charter to be armed on Earth soil. The unloaded weapons used in the ceremonies were there by imperial dispensation. As far as Leif knew, the special task force didn't have any ammo with them.

"Quiet," the major yelled, his voice cracking. He took a deep breath, then shouted, "At this moment, the sassares, in what looks to be in a coordinated effort with the Novacks and Jin Longs, have mobilized and are moving on imperial forces."

Dead silence swept over the formation as if 3000 hearts stopped beating. In the distance the cry of a hawk reached out to them.

Chapter 28

"With the sassares lurking outside every major military installation, we can't expect any reinforcements. They have effectively frozen the Navy in place," Lieutenant Nazari told them.

Leif sat deep in the overstuffed faux-leather chair. The lieutenant had taken over the Ebony Room, an old-fashioned library straight out of Earth's 19th Century. The walls were covered with shelves full of paper books and framed prints. There wasn't a net terminal in sight. No one seemed to think it incongruous that 37 Marines and a Navy corpsman, all in full battle rattle, were sitting in rapt attention in the ever-so-proper room as they listened to the brief.

This wasn't a normal situation—not that the Marine Corps really had a "normal." But this was somewhat beyond the pale. Not somewhat—*way* beyond the pale. Six hours ago, Leif had been playing sticks with his fellow wyntonans. Five hours ago, the general and the senior officers had returned from their retreat. Four hours ago, shuttles started landing, bringing ammunition and weapons from the *RS Penang*—which was against the imperial charter, but Marines were not going to face possible combat unarmed. The general and the *Penang's* captain had decided to act first and ask permission later.

Not that Leif thought the emperor would mind. The Corps was loyal. There was the question concerning 143 Marines from Jin Long Worlds. Forty remained with their units, loyal to the emperor, and one-hundred-and-three had taken residence in the Mashujaa Wetu Wing of the resort, not under arrest, but without their weapons. A captain from 2/23, the senior Marine among those, had promised to remain out of any possible conflict, and his group had been granted parole.

The threat was not with the Jin Longs, nor the Novacks. What was left of the Imperial Navy and Marines would be more than enough to overcome the combined forces of the two clans, even with another four clans yet to declare. The threat to the empire was from the sasseres. Analysts had long assured the public that the Navy and Marine Corps could beat back sassares aggression. A weakened military, with at least two clans on the other side? Leif wasn't so sure.

No new fighting had broken out. Forces were in a show-down, one where the slightest miscue could result in out-and-out war. And that was why the emperor had agreed to a meeting with Boris Chen, the empress's brother and clan heir-apparent. The situation had to be defused.

And that was why the Marines were about to leave the resort for the palace. The Imperial Guard was tasked with security for the imperial family, but neither they nor the capital security forces were military. If there was an attack, then they could not adequately defend against it.

There was a regiment of Marines on Ganymede, but with the three battalions not 50 klicks from the palace, they got the call. Not to fight, but as a show of force.

"Lieutenant, your busses are inbound, five minutes," a sergeant said, sticking his head into the library.

"Well, I guess this is it. I've given you what I know, and yeah, it isn't much. Just remember, we are not going there to start a fight. No one will even think of firing their weapon unless we're fired upon first, and even then, only if the emperor is in danger. Understand?"

"Ooh-rah," came out of 37 throats.

"OK, Staff Sergeant Antoine, let's load 'em up."

****

Leif stood at a modified position of port arms, feet shoulder width apart, and staring intently at the party standing and chatting with each other in the middle of the White Hall.

Boris Chen was a younger copy of the Jin Long Clan head. Leif sometimes had problems recognizing the difference in some humans, but even he could see the similarities here. He wondered if that was genetics or if the younger version had a little help from the body sculptors.

Along the walls, behind the line of Marines, stood about fifty men and women: the imperial staff. They stood silently, waiting for the emperor.

If Chen was pissed at having to wait, he wasn't showing it. He laughed at something one of his party said, clapping her on the shoulder. Leif had a sudden desire to march over there and slap the human across his face.

Leif liked the emperor well enough. He respected the human. But he wasn't blindly infatuated with the man. That wasn't important to him, however. What was important was that he'd sworn an oath to the emperor. If a person—wyntonan, human, qiincer, whatever—did not abide by their oath, then they didn't deserve to steal oxygen from the rest of them.

Unlike the masses of humans in the empire, that man there, as the heir-apparent to one of the clans, had personally sworn an oath to the emperor. And now it looked like that oath meant nothing.

From behind the throne, two lines of Imperial Guards, in their red hussar tunics, white jodpurs, and silver helmets , marched out, forming a half circle. To Leif's surprise, two of them were wyntonan.

How didn't I know that?

He tried to catch the nearer one's eyes, but the guard ignored him.

The emperor kept pushing that all of his subjects were the same. But it was one thing to have wyntonans and qiincers in the military, to have tokits, alindamirs, hissers, and tost'el'tzy in the government. But the Imperial Guard was kept at close quarters, always armed. These were the most trusted humans . . . and evidently wyntonans . . . in the empire.

The two lines of guards met, closing the half-circle. Chen smirked at them as if in on some cosmic joke.

"His Imperial Majesty, Forsythe the Third, Protector of the Empire and Servant of the People, and Her Imperial Majesty, Jenifer the First, Keeper of the Flame and Servant of the People," the herald announced.

There was a stir as the two appeared from behind the throne dais, the emperor's arm bent at a 90-degree angle, the empress's hand resting lightly on his forearm. They slowly walked around, mounted the steps, and sat in their matching thrones.

The young emperor looked down upon the Jin Long party for a long moment, then said, "Brother-in-law, I trust you are well."

"Well enough, brother-in-law, well enough."

There were gasps from the crowd. In a formal setting like this, such familiarity to the emperor was a huge breach of etiquette.

The emperor waved his hand, and the people quieted. "So, you said you had a message that had to be delivered to me, face-to-face?"

"May I?" he asked, pointing to the IGs, the same smirk on his face.

The emperor flicked his fingers, and the front guards parted, leaving a clear path to the throne. Chen nodded, then marched up alone, leaving his entourage behind. He stopped ten meters out, giving another slight nod.

"So, what is the message from my father-in-law?" he asked.

"It's not for you, I'm afraid. It's for the empress." There were more gasps, but he conducted a reasonable bow, sweeping one hand low.

"Your Majesty, I am here to escort you home."

This time people broke out into whispers. Leif snapped his attention from the Jin Long heir to glance at the empress. She was tight-lipped, her face white.

With a full company of Marines inside the hall and three battalions outside, they could keep the empress from leaving. But would the emperor order that? Or would he let her walk?

The heir looked around at the people in the hall, then in loud, well-trained voice, said, "We do not want war with your empire, but we will not allow one of ours to be kidnapped and held against her will."

Leif had expected another gasp in the hall, but it was deathly quiet. Evidently, others had noted the empress's demeanor, too.

Is he keeping her against her will?

Leif had sworn allegiance to both of them. If they were at odds with each other, to whom was he to follow? By law, it was the emperor, who had ascended to the throne first. But that hadn't stopped a divided empire before. Over two hundred years before, during the Fog Uprising, the emperor had tried to depose the empress, assume primacy, and raise his mistress to the Granite Throne. Almost half of the old Imperial Guard had followed him, abandoning their oath to the empress. The revolt was suppressed within a day, but with tremendous loss of life.

The imperial couple were just within Leif's peripheral vision, but he shifted his head slightly to get a better view. He knew he should be watching the heir's party, but he couldn't help himself.

The emperor, slowly looked at his empress, then nodded. She was white as a . . . well, as a wyntonan. A "casper." She took a deep breath and slowly stood, then walked gracefully down the steps of the dais. Taking two long strides, she stopped five meters from her brother.

"You will bow to your empress, Horatio Chen," she said, her voice catching ever so slightly.

Her brother's eyebrows raised for a moment before he nodded, his smile breaking out even further. He conducted a long bow, one hand sweeping the ground in his best court manner.

"Now, *Empress* Jenifer," he said, shifting his gaze from her to the motionless emperor still sitting on the throne. "If you will come with me, we will escort you out of your bondage. You no longer have reason to fear for your safety."

"I did not give you leave to talk," she snapped. "But now you may. What is this 'bondage' to which you refer?"

For once, the self-assured expression on his face seemed to falter. "I . . . the emperor," he said, raising a hand to point at him and causing several of the imperial guard to take a step forward, hands on their weapons. He didn't seem to notice that. "He has insulted your clan, refusing to take heed of father's sage advice, advice that would keep the empire from fracturing."

"My clan?" the empress said, anger evident in her voice. "Were you not at my ascension? Did you not hear my words when I renounced clan and all other loyalties to pledge my life to the citizens, all the citizens, of the Empire?"

"Well . . . well, yes. But father, Jenny—"

"I am not 'Jenny' any longer, Horatio Chen. I am Empress Jenifer, and I can assure you, I am not being held here against my will. I gave my very being to the empire six days ago, and I have not forgotten that oath. Unlike others, it seems," she said pointedly.

By the Mother, she's loyal!

All of this was so far above his head that it shouldn't make much difference to him, what political games the humans played, but he felt a warm rush flood his body, almost like a serene form of musapha. He was surprised at how relieved he was that this human woman was not going to abandon her position.

The Jin Long heir took half a step back, then looked at his party as if seeking support. That seemed to straighten his spine, and he turned back, saying, "Make sure you mean what you say, *sister*. If you turn away from the clan, nothing I can do will save you."

A dozen imperial guards stepped forward before the empress lifted a hand to stop them.

"And in deference to my prior life, *brother*, I will offer this advice. Remember your oaths, and to whom they were given. I owe my existence to your clan, and I wish it prosperity and a long, distinguished existence, but if you move against the throne, then you move against the empire. You move against *me*!

"It is not too late to rectify this. It is not too late to sever ties with . . . with entities not of the empire."

The sassares. She's calling them out.

"Go back to your clan head and assure him that I am not being held here against my will. I am here because this is my position in life. I have freely given this oath to serve our people. If he," her voice gave a slight hitch at "he," "if he chooses this path forward, then I will do everything in my power to crush him."

She spun around and walked back to the throne, her steps clacking loudly in the dead silent hall. The Jin Long heir watched her for a moment before his self-assured smirk returned.

"You're making a mistake. You let your position, which father gave you, get to your head. I'm sorry about that. I really am. But you always were a hothead."

He turned back and returned to his entourage while the empress sat back down. The emperor held out a hand, which she took as she watched her brother leave the White Hall. She held her face impassive, but there was the glint of a tear in her eye.

"Holy shit," Stone whispered beside Leif.

Holy shit indeed. What happens now?

Chapter 29

It didn't take long to find out. Eighteen minutes after the Jin Long heir left the palace, after the imperial couple and Imperial Guard had left, and while the White Hall was still being cleared, the *RSS Han Awakening*, the official Jin Long flagship, opened fire on the *RS Penang*, disabling its main drive. At the same moment, Novack, Jin Long, and militias from four other clans moved to confront Imperial Navy and Marine forces. Backing them up was a significant portion of the sassares Navy.

The *RSS Han Awakening* was one of the most expensive ships in human space, but still, it should not have been able to cripple a Navy capital ship. No one knew exactly what they'd used—or at least, if they did know, they weren't promulgating that down to the Marines on Earth.

Immediately after crippling the *Penang*, shuttles began to debark clan militia, to join the 20,000 Jin Long citizens who'd arrived as tourists to celebrate the empress's ascension, but who had already donned uniforms and taken up weapons that had been smuggled in.

This wasn't something that had simply gotten out of hand. This had been planned. August Chen might have been taken by surprise at the empress's refusal to join him, but that didn't affect his long-term plans.

Which were? Leif didn't know for sure. Some Marines thought it was to break up the empire, but after watching the heir, Leif thought the Jin Long clan head wanted to start a new imperial dynasty.

With imminent engagements throughout the empire, the bulk of the imperial military had to remain in place. Half of the Navy division at Ganymede Station, along with the Marine regiment, were scrambling to reach Earth, but at intersystem speeds, that would take at least fifteen hours.

In those fifteen hours, the 3000-plus Marines had received orders to protect the imperial city. The Imperial Guard would defend the imperial family with their lives, but they were not set up for combat. One of the guards, who'd ditched her dress uniform in favor of a dark red and gray combat overall, was deep in conversation with Captain Jiminez. She kept gesturing back into the palace.

"Eyes front, Hollow," Sergeant Zoran passed to him on the 1P. "The skipper can handle that. You worry about your team."

Leif grimaced and swung back to the square in front of the palace. She was right, as usual. The guard would take care of the palace. The Marines were to keep anyone from getting inside.

Three-thousand Marines was a pretty sizable force, even if the three battalions had never trained together. Being in the defense helped—there was not nearly as much interunit coordination necessary. But unless this was a feint, they could be facing 20-30,000 militia. Some of those militia might have very well served in the Corps.

He felt a little twinge, his musapha beginning to stir. He had to force it back down. Now was not the time nor place for him to draw upon it. If things went to shit, then he might call it forth, but now would just be a waste of energy. It scared him, too. He was ever more aware of it, treading just beneath his conscious thoughts as if waiting for the opportunity to pounce and take over.

He couldn't let that happen. Musapha was a tool, nothing more, but one he had to control. Anything else was unacceptable.

"Sousa, you OK?" he asked, both for her sake and to get his mind on a better path.

"Sure, Corporal," she said with bluster. Then, in a quieter voice, "Do you think they're gonna come?"

"Don't know. They might. And if they do, we'll be ready, right?"

"But . . . I mean, they're citizens. And not just any citizens. You know, Jin Longs."

"Who're in open revolt, just like the Novacks. If they come, they're asking for it, right?"

"I suppose so," she said, not sounding convinced.

"Look, Harper," he said, reverting to her first name. "You want to see Ira again, right?"

Ira was her nephew, son of her younger sister. For the last eight months, everyone in the platoon had been subject to holo after holo of Ira's first words, his first steps, the family puppy licking his face. All she could do was to exclaim how special he was, how smart he was.

"Well, yes, of course."

"Then get this straight. If they come, they will try to kill you, right? And if they do that, you'll never see Ira again. You won't be there to take care of him. Do you want that? Do you want him to follow his mother's path?"

Ira's mother—Sousa's sister—had left what Leif had gathered was a comfortable life to join a local gang and was now out of the picture. Sousa was not going to reenlist, instead going back to Mojave to take care of her nephew.

"No," she said hesitantly.

"And the empress, we just swore our oath to her. That means something, right."

Anger flared in her eyes, and she blurted out, "Yes! The empress!"

"Then, if they come, you need to kick some ass, right? To get back to Ira, right."

"Yeah," she started, then after a moment, "Yeah, right," with more feeling.

"Give me an ooh-rah, Sousa, and get ready."

"Ooh-rah, Corporal Hollow. Ooh-fucking rah!"

On the other side of her, Lance Corporal Stone had been taking in the conversation. He caught Leif's eye and gave an ever-so-slight nod. Leif looked away, a little embarrassed.

It wasn't that what he'd said was a lie. If the Jin Longs came and fighting broke out, they'd try to overrun the Marines, killing everyone one of them. Sousa would never see her nephew again. She had to fight, not just for herself, but for all of them. And that meant she couldn't have reservations which might make her hesitate. Even the slightest hesitation would be an advantage to the enemy, and with the odds facing them, the Marines couldn't give them any advantage, no matter how small.

Still, he felt guilty. Sousa might not be the brightest flare in the pack, and he'd just played on her emotions.

Hell, it's all for the cause.

He looked away from Stone and caught Hkekka's eyes. He'd evidently been listening in, too. Unlike Stone, he didn't nod, but rolled his eyes and looked back to the front.

Leif knew with no uncertainty that appealing to the qiincer would be useless. After all these months, he still didn't know what motivated the Marine. And now, with combat looming, he wondered how the flying Marine would perform. Like as not, he'd desert the line. He had no respect for the emperor, after all, and obviously thought the Corps was a joke.

Leif reminded himself to keep an eye on the qiincer if they got into the shit.

What a great fucking team leader you are. A racist lance corporal who I had to beat up to do what I said, a stupid PFC who needs to be coaxed into her duty, and a fairy who hates the Corps and the empire. Yeah, Leefen a'Hope Hollow, you're doing your people proud.

Leif knew he was a kick-ass warrior, a fighting Marine. He just wasn't sure he had any leadership potential, and that scared him. If the Sergeant went down, Manu would take over. And if he went down, then Kyle . . . no, not Kyle. It would have to be him, date-of-rank be damned. Could he lead the squad?

He refused to answer himself, afraid of what his subconscious would say.

"First Platoon, get ready to shift right," Staff Sergeant Antoine yelled out to the groans of the Marines.

They'd shifted position three times over the last ten minutes. Leif welcomed the movement, however. Anything to get him away from his pity-party of self-perspective.

****

"Gremlins? You've got to be fucking kidding me," Lance Corporal Stone said as soon as the word was passed. "Those fucking ingrates. I'll kill every last one of them."

Leif was tempted to call out his HG-man. Referring to tokits as "gremlins" was the same as calling the People "caspers" or "ghosts." In this case, though, Leif understood the frustration.

With the *Han Awakening's* shuttles landing just outside of organic anti-air weapons, the Jin Long militia, along with the militias of at least four other clans, were gathering for their advance to "rescue" the empress. The fact that she didn't want to be rescued didn't fit their narrative, so it was conveniently ignored.

Unless the higher-ups could negotiate an agreement, the two forces were going to clash. But now, before that could happen, there were thousands of tokits, armed with kitchen knives and utensils, marching on the Marines.

The tokits were almost a running joke among the other races. They occupied the lowest social rung in the empire. Many were street hustlers, trying to eke out a living however they could. Others made up the vast army of domestics that kept the rich and powerful comfortable. Far cheaper than robots, they cleaned the homes, hotels, and streets of Earth. They cooked for them.

While the People had suffered discrimination at the hands of humans, that had never reached the same levels that the tokits and possibly the hissers suffered. Both were the "dung" in the "dung races." Even the People thought themselves a step above them, as much as no one would admit to that.

And now, all those years were coming home to roost, it seemed. They'd risen up and were marching on the palace.

Not that they could do much except make Marines expend valuable ammunition. The tokits were not a martial race. Leif had never even heard if they'd had wars before the humans subjugated them. And armed with kitchen knives, they'd stand no chance against the three Marine battalions, no matter how many there were.

Whatever happened, they were bringing it down upon themselves. Still, Leif didn't look forward to slaughtering them. They were sentient beings, after all, and as a wyntonan, he knew what it could be like as a subservient race in a human empire.

"What do you think?" he sent to Jordan on the 1P.

After the last shift, Jordan's squad was the right flank of Kilo, and Leif's was the left flank of India's. He could see his friend, 45 meters away, as they waited for whatever was to come.

Jordan looked at him and shrugged. "It's their call."

Leif was still worried about him. He'd seemed somewhat better during the celebrations, willing to at least engage with others. But he still wasn't the same Jordun a'Hottento he'd met on the dirigible from the Silver Range in to the capital to enlist. Things looked like they were going to get hairy—not from the tokits, but from the human militias—and every Marine had to be fighting at max efficiency.

"All hands, you are not cleared to fire until released," Lieutenant Colonel König passed on the battalion net. "NCO's keep on top of that."

The CO rarely passed word himself, going through his commanders and staff. Leif wondered if that was coming directly from the general. Not that he minded. He hoped the tokits would come to their senses and fade away into the city.

"You heard the CO. Your weapons better be on safe," he said, with both Stone and Sousa acknowledging.

"Private Hkekka, I said your weapon better be on safe."

"Since you didn't ask a question, I didn't answer," the smart-ass qiincer said.

"Well is it?"

"Is it what?"

By the Mother . . . Leif thought, giving himself a moment to calm down. He could kick Hkekka's ass after this, if they both made it through, but now wasn't the time.

"Is your weapon on safe?" said through clenched teeth.

"Why yes, Corporal, it is."

The qiincer was playing with him, with that ever-present sense of superiority that they displayed to all the other races, often referring to themselves as angels, after the heavenly creatures prevalent in most human religions. They knew how much that pissed off the humans.

In the near distance, the rumbling coalesced into discernable chants. Leif didn't speak any of the many tokits languages, and he didn't bother to turn on his translator ap. The tone was clear enough. They were chanting to build up courage, to create a unified front.

Stupid gremlins.

"Here they come. Get ready, but remember, don't fire until ordered," Lieutenant Nazari passed on the platoon net.

And the first of the tokit mob passed through Liberty Garden and entered the plaza. Twenty or thirty of them pointed at the Marines facing them, their voices raised in a warbling trill. Leif hadn't known they could do that. More and more poured in, the front ranks edging closer and closer as their compatriots pushed from the back.

Leif flicked his safety off, then back on again. He was ready.

"Hold your fire," came over the net. "The general's going out there."

Leif craned his head to look to his right, to Lima's line. Far down the plaza, almost 700 meters away, a lone figure strode out as if she hadn't a care in the world. Leif knew next to nothing about General Lateesha Womack. He'd seen her at the celebrations, but he'd never met her, nor had he given her much thought. But to see her march out there to face thousands of tokits, well, that was impressive. It would have been far easier, and safer for her, simply to order the Marines to open fire.

She reached the first of the tokits who began to engulf her, amoeba-like. Leif expected to see her fall under a hail of flaying knives, and he kept waiting for the command to open fire.

Instead, to his tremendous surprise, the tokits parted, and the general started back to the Marine lines, a few tokits in tow.

What's going on?

The mass push forward halted, and a few moments later, the mob started retreating.

"I knew they were cowards," Stone said with contempt.

"All Marines, this is General Womack."

If the battalion CO rarely spoke directly over the net, it was unheard of for a general.

"The tokits have demanded to be part of the defense of the imperial family. I have asked them to clear our AO to stay out of our lines of fire, but they have rejected that request, and as imperial citizens, I have no control over that. They will, however, move into the Liberty Garden. So, if we do get into the shit . . ."

A general says "shit?"

". . . please keep in mind that the tokits are our allies in this. Be conscious of friendly fire."

"Well, look at that. The emperor's outreach to all us dung races worked," Jordan passed to Leif. "He's got the gremlins ready to fight for him."

Leif couldn't tell if his friend was being sarcastic or not.

Chapter 30

"Fuck, they're getting slaughtered," Stone mumbled as all eyes were locked on the Liberty Garden some 800 meters away.

You've proven your loyalty. Just get away' Leif pleaded, trying to will the tokits to break contact and flee.

But they fought on, knives and bars to the militia's Haptsteins and FWs. This wasn't some holo-flick, where the badly outgunned underdogs somehow managed to overcome their enemy by simple righteousness of their cause. They were getting mowed down by the militia. At full mag, Leif could see militiamen laughing as they tried to beat each other to the punch in killing the tokits.

Sergeant Minh, one of the battalion's scout snipers, had taken a position behind one of the ornamental columns at the top of the stairs, using the flat base to steady her ASW-52, the Corps go-to sniper weapon. She chuffed out shot after shot. Downrange, militiamen would be falling, but there were only so many snipers in the battalion. For the rest of them, they had to hold their fire for fear of hitting the tokits.

Not that holding our fire is helping them.

He looked over to Sergeant Zoran, who was standing and watching the lieutenant, a racehorse in the gate. Leif could see her eagerness to get into the fight, to try and save the tokits before it was too late. He felt the same way. He'd enlisted in the Corps because once, a lifetime ago, the Marines had saved a non-descript village from slavers, including a very young wyntonan. Now grown up, he wanted to be that savior.

But no matter how distasteful, their orders were clear. Their job was to defend the palace complex. If they rushed forward, that could leave a gap in the lines that could be exploited by the enemy.

There were many ways to conduct a defense, to include multiple maneuvering elements to take advantage of the shifting tides of battle. This was not one of those times. Kilo's Second Platoon had been pulled back as a tactical reserve, ready to plug holes in the line or exploit success, but for this mission, the tactics were basic. Hold the line in place and don't let the militias through.

A round pinged off the column, making Sergeant Minh duck back. The militias had snipers, too, and with fewer and fewer tokits to face, their attention was shifting back to the Marines.

At least there was no arty hitting them. As the lieutenant had said, artillery pieces were a little harder to smuggle onto the planet's surface. Small arms were much easier.

As if in counterpoint to that argument, a rocket shot to the Marine lines, hitting down among Lima Company. Leif hugged the balustrade wall that led up the side of the broad stairs behind him. He'd rather be dug in, but that was a little difficult in the Imperial Plaza. Granite was pretty tough to dig into.

"Well, that's about it," Stone said as a roar of victory washed out over the plaza. The mass of militia started forward again, their killing spree over, and the flush of an easy victory over the tokits goading them on.

The Marines were armed with more than kitchen knives, however, and if the militia wanted a fight, the Marines would make them pay.

The Imperial Plaza was a vast, granite-covered open space, over a klick wide. If the Jin Long militia really wanted to breach the palace, Leif would have advanced through the Empress Lan Garden to the north of the palace where, while not protected from fire, they had cover, at least. One-Nine was oriented to the north, ready for that contingency, but it looked like the bulk of the militia, at least, were willing to advance across the plaza, exposed to fire as if their commander hoped to simply overwhelm the Marines by brute numbers.

The thing was, it might work. Oh, they'd pay a horrible price, but they could afford it. There were only so many Marines to face them. And according to the lieutenant, the eyes of the empire were undoubtedly fixated on the battle, and crossing the plaza would have a much greater visual impact to those watching from what had to be a thousand newsfeeds.

"Weapons free, India, weapons free. Fire at will," Captain Jiminez passed.

Leif straightened up, placed his elbows on the top of the wall, and started firing. The mob of rushing militia was too big of a target to miss, so he just focused on center mass, firing round after round on semi-automatic.

Three steps below him, Stone was firing his M85, the grenades arching out to reach the militia.

When the Marines went into battle, they relied on interlocking layers of arms: naval gunfire, airpower, artillery, mortars, rockets, crew-served weapons, and finally, the individual Marine. With the charter, and now the *Penang* out of action, they had almost none of that. Weapons Company had their mortars, Thirty-Fours, and two beamers, all brought down on one of the shuttles before the *Penang* was hit, but rounds and power cells were limited. One of the four Thirty-Fours opened up, the big .50 caliber rounds chewing holes in the militia advance, but still they came. A rocket reached out before the gun crew could stop, and it followed the disturbance in the air the .50 cal rounds made to backtrack to the gun. There was an explosion, and the Thirty-Four fell silent.

Leif stopped firing for a moment to check his team. Stone was chugging out rounds. He might be a racist asshole, but Leif knew he could count on him to keep his cool.

Sousa surprised him, though. She was standing tall, steadily firing into the mass, her face twisted in anger. Maybe the sight of the tokits getting slaughtered had spurred her into action. He'd have to keep a watch on her, though. She couldn't go berserk on him, rushing out to meet the enemy, when keeping the line intact required all of them.

Hkekka? The qiincer was fingering his M77 trigger, not engaging as he watched the incoming militia.

Leif started to yell at the Marine before checking himself. This was no longer a ceremony of Marines standing tall for the imperial party, so Hkekka had turned in the M88 that had been temporarily issued to him and drew his personal M77.

The M77 was normally a close in, blast-them-all-to-hell carbine, great for combat in a built-up area, but it's range was very limited before the darts lost their punch. The oncoming militia were still out of range of the qiincer, so he was rightfully biding his time instead of wasting his limited ammo.

They're fine. Get back to dropping Jin Longs.

Leif brought up his 88 again, and as the militiamen charged forward, he could begin to make out individuals. His sights kept adjusting as the range narrowed, taking into account the trajectories of his rounds, so he didn't have to take the time to manually adjust them. This wasn't as sophisticated as the mini-computers that made up Sergeant Minh's sniper scope, but it was good enough for government work.

He sighted mid-mass on a large human in the front of the wave and squeezed the trigger. A moment later, the man stumbled and went down, to be trampled by those behind him. Leif didn't know if he'd hit the man—militia were dropping like flies as the Marines took a deadly toll. Him, another Marine—it didn't matter. He shifted his aim and fired again.

An explosion rocked the other side of the wall, shrapnel or granite debris pinging off of his helmet. He instinctively ducked, then raised his head to look over it. Two Marines from Second Squad were down, their bodies too mangled for him to recognize. The low wall might be mere decoration for the steps, but it had been enough to save his ass. Sousa's too—she was just getting back up to her feet from where she'd been knocked flat.

Like the Marines, the militia were not supposed to be well-armed, but they seemed to have more than a few rockets with them. Explosions were erupting up and down the Marine lines.

"You OK, Sousa?" he asked she oriented back on the militia.

"Don't worry about me," she yelled back, starting to fire again.

A drone with JBS emblazoned on the side swept in to focus on the two Second Squad Marines. Leif snarled and fired twice, blowing the stupid thing apart. Two wasted rounds, but he'd do it again in a heartbeat.

The net was alive with orders being passed back and forth, and Sergeant Zoran was everywhere, but his fight was narrowing down to a small section of advancing militia and his three Marines. This was Leif's battle. Whatever was happening with the other platoons, with the other companies, he had no control over that. He just had to keep his team in the fight and killing the enemy. And that was becoming problematic.

The palace grounds were raised from the plaza level, a three-meter wall supporting the foundation. Most of the Marines were prone at the base of the wall with little or no cover. Four wide stairs led up to the palace level and the upper plaza. First Platoon occupied one of the stairs, with First Squad along the right side. That had given them a bit of cover, but the militias were now orienting to these stairs. This canalization was making it easier for the other Marines to target them, but it also put those on the stairs right in their path.

Another militia rocket streaked in, but Leif didn't have time to look as he dropped a mag and inserted a new one. They had to stop the attacking wave.

"How're you doing with ammo, Stone?" he asked.

"Four mags."

"Sousa, give him yours."

The M85 was the heaviest weapon in a fire team. The rounds, which were essentially small grenades, were big, too, which with a flick of the selector, could be fired in indirect or direct mode. Stone had been issued 14 magazines of ammo, but because of their weight, Sousa had taken two and Leif four to spread the load. Stone was still firing in indirect mode, but when the militia closed to within 100 meters—which was going to be any moment now, Leif wanted those rounds blasting holes in the militia as fast as the lance corporal could pull the trigger.

Sousa tossed the two mags to Stone, who didn't bother to put them in his hip pouch but lined them by his knee. He was making his stand right there on the bottom step.

"Hkekka . . ." Leif started to say, but the private had already started firing, measured shot after measured shot. The tiny darts were devastating within 20 meters, but they rapidly lost velocity. Still, even if not necessarily lethal at this range, they could at least take some of the militia out of action.

A round pinged off his chest armor, then another in quick succession. He'd heard it more than felt the strikes. Both left marks, but his armor was still intact—which meant Intel was probably right that the militiamen were armed with Haptsteins. Foolproof and easy to use, the small caliber pellets were effective against unarmored civilians—like knife-wielding tokits—but not so much against armored Marines, even with Level One armor. The pellets could still be deadly, but his torso was pretty well protected.

Not all of them were armed with the Hapts, however. Doc Ben-Ari pushed past Leif, pulling Terry Qaan up against the slight protection of the stairway wall. Terry was unconscious, his armor cracked, and blood was flowing past the bottom edge, staining his utility trousers. Intel thought the militia also had FWs, and with their T-assisted rounds, they gained velocity after firing and could defeat Marine body armor.

Ironically, in a way, the closer the combatants, the less-effective the T-assisted rounds were. The "assist" in T-assist didn't kick in until after a hundred-and-ten meters.

Which the closest of the militia had reached. The only thing keeping them away was the wall of bodies falling as the combined firepower of the battalion, as well as that of 1/9 to the north, was taking its toll.

They looked like a mob, as Leif kept up his fire, but these were trained militiamen. Someone had to be in charge, because a group suddenly broke off and diverted to the Marines at the base of the wall. Within moments, they'd closed the distance, and Third Platoon and on to Lima suddenly had their hands full—which diminished the fire plunging into those trying for the stairs, exactly as the unseen officer had intended.

"Tighten up!" Lieutenant Nazari yelled as he moved to the front, spraying his 88. "Kill the sons-of—"

He pitched forward, his body sliding bonelessly down the last two steps to the plaza base. Staff Sergeant Antoine immediately took over, ordering First to left and Second to slide onto the stairs.

Which made sense. When the militia reached them, the rise of the stairs would divide the platoon, leaving Second Squad out there to dry. That also took away the tiny bit of cover the balustrade offered Leif and his team.

"You heard her. Shift left," Leif shouted.

He grabbed Sousa by the arm, pulling her as she continued to fire. She dropped an empty mag and slammed a new one home.

"Here," he said, eyeing Sergeant Zoran and Manu.

He turned to the others, but Stone and Hkekka were right behind him.

"They keep coming," Stone grunted as he fell into his best kneeling position and started firing again.

Among the Marines, the various militias and security battalions had low reputations for professionalism. Commonly calling them "Gun Clubs," among the less offensive nicknames, they thought militiamen were only in it for the money. Yet at least a couple thousand had to have fallen charging across the plaza, and they still kept pushing into the teeth of the Marines' defense.

Not up to professional standards? Maybe. Cowards? No.

"Give me some support!" Sergeant Hua, the Third Squad leader shouted into the platoon net. "They're on us!"

Leif dropped two militiamen 20 meters in front of him, then risked a quick glance. Third Squad, which had just taken First's position, was in hand-to-hand combat. The militia had reached the bottom of the stairs. Like water rushing for a breach in the dam, others militiamen were flowing in that direction.

"Stone, cover Third," Leif ordered.

He half expected Sergeant Zoran to countermand his order. By shifting Stone's fire, he'd just cut the squad's M85 rounds by a third.

The sergeant didn't intervene, and Stone started pumping round after round into those militiamen who were streaming to join those fighting Third Squad. He couldn't fire into the hand-to-hand combat as his rounds didn't recognize friend or foe, so that was the best he could do.

Sousa stumbled, then straightened back up. Her utilities on her hip, just above the armor edge, were torn. A bright red stain appeared at the rip. She kept fighting, though.

The only reason the platoon hadn't been overrun was that there were just too many militia jammed together at the chokepoint of the stairs. Bodies—some living, many not—clogged the ground, bringing down others who tripped over them. It was only a matter of time, though. It was clear that given the situation, they probably couldn't hold out. The best they could do was to attrite enough of them so that the Imperial Guard could keep the emperor and empress alive until the reinforcements got there.

"Look, a fucking casper! Get it!" a voice reached out from the mob, clear as a bell amid the cacophony of war. Arms pointed at him, and like one, a group detached themselves, stepping over bodies in their desire to reach him.

This is it.

Leif didn't bother to acquire each target. At this range, he couldn't miss. With his 88 at the hip, he fired round after round, dropping one, two, three. Still they came on, and he couldn't fire fast enough to save himself.

A blast took out four of them at once, body parts flying, a red mist filling the air.

What the . . .

"Get back, Corporal Hollow!" Lance Corporal Jeremy Stone shouted, stepping in front of him. He advanced on the mob, pounding away with his M85. Each round blasted a hole in the advance. The militia, willing to advance across the kill zone that was the plaza, hesitated. The possibility of death from far away was different from the sure death of the muzzle of Stone's big M85. Sousa and Hkekka joined Leif and turned their weapons on the threat, and the three were taking a deadly toll. The militia were focused on Stone, though, as if he were the devil incarnate.

Rounds hit the lance corporal, and he stumbled twice as they hit home, but for the most part, his helmet and armor held. He dropped a magazine, and one militia took the opportunity to charge the few meters between them. Before he could reach Stone, the lance corporal slammed home the next magazine and fired, taking the militiaman's head off his shoulders.

Not the next magazine, his last one, Leif realized, seeing the empty mag pouch on his hip.

Stone had 15 rounds left, now 14, and then his M85 would be nothing more than a half-assed club.

"Jeremy, get back. We've got you covered!" he passed on the fire team net.

Stone gave a quick glance back to the other three, then shrugged. "I've still got a mag, and I intend to use it, Corporal."

"Shit, let's go," he yelled to the other two.

He took a single step down before Sergeant Zoran blasted his ear with, "Hold, Hollow. Support with fire only. Do not close with them."

Leif looked wildly around, angry that she was stopping him. His musapha was clamoring to get out, and he was about to grant that wish.

"Our mission is the emperor," she said. "Period."

Leif held out an arm to stop Sousa from running down the ten or so steps to join Stone.

"You heard her," he said. "She's right."

He had no love for Stone. In some ways, he hated the racist asshole. But he was a Marine, and he'd stepped up when Leif was the target.

"Break contact now, Stone. Come back to us. That's an order," he tried one more time.

"I think I told you I wasn't going to take orders from you." He fired his last round, dropped his 85, unslung the 88 from his back, and began to send the smaller rounds into his attackers

Without the threat from the M85, the militia mobbed the lance corporal. They'd be just as dead from an M88, but the lighter weapon did not seem to be as threatening to them. Scores dropped between the combined fire of the four Marines, but there were just too many of them. Lance Corporal Stone disappeared beneath the onslaught.

Leif wanted to let go, to let his musapha take over, and it took a force of will to keep it bay.

Just a little longer, when you can do the most damage, my mistress.

With Stone gone, the militia turned their attention back to the three Marines. Standing 15 meters apart, both sides were firing at each other, like gunfighters in a human western. This wasn't how modern war was fought. Yet, they were doing it. If they simply charged up the steps, they could overrun the three Marines, but for an unfathomable reason, they were willing to trade shots with their better-armored foe. Leif was hit a dozen times, maybe more, but only one found flesh, and that only took out a small chunk of his calf.

A militiaman leveled his FK at him and fired before he could react, striking him dead in the chest, but the round didn't travel far enough for the T-assist. It felt like an Earth mule kicked him, but his armor held. He took out the militiaman with a shot to the throat with his far less powerful M88.

Marines were falling, slowly being pushed up the stairs, step-by-step. The top of the steps was 200 meters from the palace doors, 200 meters where they had to stop the Jin Longs. They would do that, or die trying.

If they even made it that far, which wasn't looking probable. The militia were getting the upper hand, and Leif could feel their optimism in the air. They were getting slaughtered, but they could afford it. The Marines could not.

The platoon was pushed back farther and farther. They reached the top of the stairs, which enabled them to go prone and fire down. They were still exposed, but not as much as the Jin Longs. More were swept aside, but still they came on. They could sense victory. Once they reached the top and could spread out over the upper plaza, the battle would be essentially over.

"Coming from the rear, India!" a voice filled each Marine's helmet.

Hell, Kilo's Second Platoon!

Lost in his team's slice of the battle, he'd forgotten that Second Platoon had been pulled back as a reaction force.

Looking behind him, he could see them charging forward, still out of sight of the nearest militia. Right at the front, running alongside Lieutenant Shymaster, was Jordan, screaming as he ran. The wave of Marines burst through the India Marines and rained death upon the attacking militia. M85's popped, blowing holes in the ranks.

The platoon was only 38 Marines strong, but the surprise gave the militia pause as scores of them fell. The front ranks tried to retreat back down the stairs, but the sheer mass of bodies below them kept them trapped as they were cut down.

A cheer rose from the India Marines. They knew this would be a short-lived respite, but it did them good to see it.

"Fall back, bounding overwatch!" Captain Jiminez passed over the company net. "First Platoon base, then Second, then Third."

Kilo's charge made sense then. It would enable India to break contact. But to what end? There were 200 meters of statues and fountains, then the palace. Leif had read about an old Earth unit, from a country called Spain. He forgot the specifics, but the defenders had been pushed so hard that the backs of their hats had been flattened by the fort's walls, yet they never gave up. Their exploits were honored when Spanish units kept a flattened hat as part of their uniform for centuries after.

Are they expecting that? To back up against the palace wall?

Whatever the plan, Leif didn't have time to wonder about it. Second and Third Platoons, along with Kilo's Second, were already falling back while First was providing the base of fire into the mass of militia below. The enemy was so close that Leif could see his rounds impacting on their bodies. With the fire from only one platoon, the militia were beginning to realize that they could advance. In fits and starts, they began to climb the stairs.

"First Platoon, pull back," Staff Sergeant Antoine ordered.

Leif grabbed Sousa by her harness and lifted her, pulling her back. He'd lost track of Hkekka, though.

"You still with us?" he sent on the 1P as he ran back into the upper plaza.

"Still around," the qiincer said. "Are you?"

What? That makes no sense, Leif thought as he dodged around a statue. *Stupid fairy humor.*

A round hit him hard . . . in the chest!

PFC Renault from Second Platoon raised his hand from around the base of a statue, shouting "Sorry!"

Leif kept running, then slapped the Marine hard on the helmet as he ran past.

After all this shit, getting taken out by friendly fire?

The Marines from First Platoon kept running, passing the prone Second and then Third, who were getting in position to fire. With one platoon firing at a time, they hoped to delay the militia until . . . *until what?* Leif wondered. He still didn't know.

But it wasn't just India. From all sides, Marines were converging. Kilo, Lima, Headquarters . . . and from the looks of it, 1/9 and 2/23 as well.

And up ahead, the vast double doors of the palace were open, about 20 IGs protecting it. A civilian was standing, playing traffic cop as he waved his arms for the Marines to enter.

So, we're going to defend from inside.

It made sense. Kill as many of the Jin Longs as the could as the militiamen crossed the kill zones to approach the palace, then hunker down inside what had to be some stiff defenses.

"First Platoon, stop and provide covering fire," Staff Sergeant Antoine ordered. "We've got a friendly fire casualty in Third Squad, so watch who the hell you're firing at."

Leif and Sousa stopped and went prone behind yet another fountain, their weapons trained downrange as Marines streamed by them. He spotted Hkekka and grabbed the private. For once, the smirk was off his face, replaced by a . . . a smile?

The little bastards enjoying this!

Second Platoon was passing them first. Not enough, though, and five Marines were being helped by others. Sergeant Ramsey was giving the orders.

Where's the lieutenant and Staff Sergeant Gilbert? Leif asked himself, knowing the answer. If Ramsey was in command, neither of the other two had made it.

Fifty meters ahead, Third Platoon was in contact. Leif could get glimpses of them through the statues. Beyond them, the militia were closing in.

He looked back. The doors were still open, but he knew they'd be closed before the first militia arrived. He just didn't know when. A couple of hundred Marines had reached the doors and were hurrying in. The general would want as many as possible, but there was a limit to how long they could wait.

"If you get a clear shot at a Jin Long, take it," he told his two remaining Marines.

Two. Just two. Stone's gone.

It really hadn't hit him yet that he'd lost a Marine. It would later, but just as he kept his musapha at bay, he had to push Stone's loss back. He had to focus on the now.

Kilo Company showed up. He caught a quick glimpse of Lori, and he was relieved to see her. He'd catch up with her later, if he could. Kilo's Second Platoon had joined First Platoon in providing a last line of covering fire, but the rest of the company disappeared inside the palace.

The firing was heavy up ahead. Leif kept watching for Third Platoon to bound back to them, but they held in place despite the mass of militia flooding the upper plaza. Much longer, and they'd get overrun. Leif snapped off a few shots, not knowing if he hit anyone.

"Sergeant Zoran, what's going on with Third Platoon?" he asked, unable to contain himself.

"They said they're staying in place," she said. "Just get ready."

His subconscious knew that, but her words cemented that in his foremind. Third Platoon was going to hold until they were overrun, to give more Marines time to get inside the palace. Leif had friends in the platoon, friends he'd never see again. Inga, for one, whose spice mix he'd enjoyed just two days ago.

"Make them pay," he whispered.

"Third Platoon's staying in place," he told the other two. "By their choice," he added.

Sousa gave a little shake of her head, then gripped her 88, a determined look on her face. Hkekka . . . well, Hkekka was Hkekka, the smile still plastered in place. For the first time, Leif wondered if the fool even understood the gravity of the situation.

"Watch up ahead and to the right. That's Two-Twenty-Three coming in," Sergeant Zoran passed.

Behind him, unfamiliar Marines were moving into the palace. Leif assumed they were 2/23. If some of their Marines were moving to engage the militia, then they were in the same boat as Third Platoon.

Leif was sorely tempted to just let go, to let his musapha wash over him and run to join Third Platoon. It might not make much of a difference, but any delay could save more lives.

"Get back down, Hollow," Sergeant Zoran hissed into his earpiece. "Your place of duty is right here."

To his surprise, Leif had stood and taken a couple of steps toward Third Platoon. Off to his left, the sergeant was standing and glaring at him. He took one more look forward, then reluctantly retook his place.

"What was that all about," Sousa asked him.

"Nothing, I just had to see something."

Hkekka snorted at that. Wyntonans were not good liars, and while Sousa seemed to accept that, the qiincer had evidently seen through him.

Screw you, too, you minta.

And then the militia were in among the Third Platoon Marines. First Platoon and Kilo's Second started firing in support, dropping the militiamen right and left, but it was a foregone conclusion. Within a few minutes, there was no more Third Platoon. Firing kept on to the right for another minute, where the 2/23 unit fought, but it, too, went silent.

Marines had died in a suicide mission, a platoon from India and some from 2/23. In those few minutes, though, at least two hundred more Marines had made it to the safety of the palace. It might be temporary safety, but that was better than nothing.

Behind First Platoon, the big doors started to close.

Leif had expected it, and surprisingly, he wasn't angry. He didn't want to die, not here on a human world, before he could even start a family back on Home. But if this was his fate, then it didn't do any good to rail at the Mother.

"Here they come," someone shouted down the line, as if it needed explanation.

The militiamen were angry. They'd lost so many of their brothers and sisters, and their objective was just ahead of them. Nothing was going to stand in their way.

Two platoons of Marines faced thousands of militia—two platoons who were going to make the assault an expensive proposition.

Fire reached out. There was no reason to husband ammo anymore. The first fusillade was deadly, cutting hundreds of militia almost in two, leaving piles of bodies on what had been pristine and manicured grounds. The advance faltered, and a cheer rose up from the Marines.

As if shamed by the cheer, militia NCOs rallied their troops, and stumbling over the bodies of their comrades, they advanced, 40 meters out, then 30 as more and more fell.

"Harper," Leif shouted out over the din of battle.

"Yeah, Corporal."

"You've done good. You're a helluva Marine."

She smiled, wiped a bloody hand across her face, and said, "You, too, Corporal."

A powerful blast rocked the upper plaza as two of the statues disintegrated in fireballs. As the smoke cleared, blackened body bits littered the ground.

"Hah, so the palace isn't totally unprotected!" Leif told Sousa.

"For the Mother," a voice yelled out in Uzboss, pushed through a shoulder speaker at max power.

"Jordan?" Leif asked, switching to the 1P as his mistress stirred a little more forcibly

Far to his left, a handful of figures were charging the militia, taking advantage of the confusion the blast has caused.

"I feel it, Leefen," he answered in Uzboss. "The mistress. She finally called me!"

"Don't . . ." Leif started to say, but then stopped. Once musapha took over, then nothing was going to dissuade him. Jordan had always resented the fact that he'd never raised musapha, and now, at last, he'd done it, and it was driving him to his death.

His own musapha started to well up, and he stood to join his friend. Carlton, too, who was screaming his own battle cry, he saw, along with a handful of humans. Marines, rushing to meet their fate.

"Fall back, into the palace," Staff Sergeant Antoine shouted into her mic.

Too late for that. We've been left out here, Leif thought as he started to release the beast. He gave a look over his shoulder, but to his surprise, the doors had only been partially closed. The Imperial Guard were at what was now a three-meter-wide opening, almost pushing the last Marine stragglers through.

I'm coming, Jordun, he thought as he turned back toward the enemy.

"Corporal Hollow, help me!" Sousa cried out.

Fear trilled through him, but Sousa was not hit. Kyle was, and Sousa was trying to drag the limp body back to the doors. His musapha was filling him, and he wanted nothing more than to join his friend, his oldest friend in the Corps, but responsibility tugged at him, fighting his mistress.

There was a clear line of sight through the statues to where Jordan, Carlton, and two of the humans crashed into the militia, who already in shock from the blast, recoiled in fright. But they couldn't get away as Jordan and Carlton became god warriors, dealing death with every shot and every blow. Jordan pushed the barrel of his 88 under the chin of one militiaman, pulling the trigger, then swinging it around to crush the head of another who'd stumbled into his range.

I am the strength of the mountain
As I crush your bones
And then drink your souls
I erase you from the Mother's memory . . .

Jordan sang as he fought, the old warrior song of the Silver Range, long banned by the Council of Elders.

"Corporal Hollow, help me!" Sousa repeated.

Hkekka was almost at the doors, and the rest were running pellmell toward it.

"Drink their souls, Jordun a'Hottento," Leif passed as he banished his mistress back into the depths.

He ran over to Sousa. There were body parts of two Marines around him—the upper torso belonged to Poltrain, her face unmarked and looking as if she'd simply fallen asleep. Not so with Kyle. His entire head was covered in blood. No, that wasn't correct. What was left of his head was covered in blood. His helmet was gone, as was a good chunk of what had been the back of his head. His heart LED was a steady green, though, so he was still alive. He picked Kyle up, slinging him over his shoulder, and with Sousa covering him, started running for the palace. The doors started to close, the last of the Marines and the guards slipping in.

Your spirit will not walk, a shadow on the land,
I am the destroy—

Jordan's song cut off.

Leif and Sousa sprinted the last few meters, throwing themselves through the door just as it clanged shut with finality behind them.

Chapter 31

"You holding up OK, Leif?" Sergeant Zoran asked quietly.

"Yeah, I'm fine."

But he wasn't fine. Stone was dead, the first Marine in his charge to die. Leif had sworn to bring back all three of them, and he'd failed. Kyle. His roommate's blood and brain matter were still wet on Leif's shoulder and back from carrying him, the coppery smell making him a little nauseous. And Jordan. *Jordun.* His real name seemed more appropriate now that he was gone. Leif had met him at Crocked Gorge to catch the dirigible to the capital, and they'd been together every step along the way since then.

Jordun had been the gung-ho one, the one who was going to make a name for himself and for the People. He was going to become an officer and rise in the ranks, while Leif was going to let his enlistment expire. Now, Jordun was dead while Leif soldiered on.

Being a Marine was a dangerous calling, and many—too many—had paid the price today. Leif was wracked with guilt. How had he survived when so many others had died? It wasn't just the luck of the draw that had kept him alive, but his own choice of action. Leif realized that he couldn't have changed the course of the battle on his own, but could he have affected his little slice of it? If he'd let musapha take over, could he have saved Stone? Should he have joined Jordun, going out as a warrior should?

"It's hard," the sergeant said, putting her hand on his upper arm. "But we're not done here. I need you with me, OK?"

"But, what if I had—"

"You did what you had to do. Don't second guess yourself now." She hesitated, then said, "Things are going to get hairy. Be ready to . . . well . . . *draw* on your strengths when the time is right."

Leif had been staring at the ground, but he jerked his head up at her words.

"Draw?" Does she know about musapha?

"I . . . I'm not sure what you mean."

"Musapha," she said, mangling the Uzboss, but clear enough.

"You know about that?"

Her brows furrowed in confusion for a moment, and then she said, "You're one of my team leaders. Of course, I'm going to learn what I can about you."

"But not all—"

"I know. Twenty percent, right? But you have it, I'm sure. I saw that on Han'ei with the mob of Leaguers."

While most humans probably thought musapha was a myth, it was not unknown to humans in general. However, Leif had thought he'd hidden his abilities from the humans around him. The other wyntonans knew about it, at least the NCOs, but as not everyone had it, it was considered bad form to discuss it, akin to boasting. With the humans, he'd held back for another reason. He wanted to make it as he was, not with some almost supernatural ability giving him an advantage.

"Why didn't you say anything?" he asked.

She shrugged. "I read that it is considered something personal, so I let it be. But now, we're going to need it, I think. You held back out on the plaza, so you should still have it ready to go." She paused for a moment, then asked, "Why haven't you mentioned it to me, though? I've wondered about that."

"Because . . . because it is just something I was born with. I want to prove myself as who I am, not what the mistress makes me."

"Oh, for the love of God, that's bullshit, Hollow," she said, wrinkling her lip.

Leif recoiled, not expecting that response.

"You are who you are. Hkekka can fly. Manu is a tank. Red is a beast," she said, tapping him hard in the chest with her forefinger. "Should any of them hold back because of their abilities? Should Manu pull his punches because he's stronger than any of us norms?"

"Well . . . no."

"And neither should you. You ca . . . you wyntonans, you've got abilities to bring to the table. I wasn't sure before, but the emperor is right. You, the qiincers, all of us. Together, we make the whole stronger. And if you've got this ability within you that makes you a better fighter, then what the fuck is wrong with that?"

"It's not that . . . "

But it *was* that. Deep inside, he didn't think it was "fair." He'd made a name for himself twice simply because the Mother had picked him to be able to draw forth the mistress.

"Then what the fuck is it, Hollow?"

She stood in front of him, necked craned up, her eyes locked on his. He didn't know what to say.

"I thought so. Look, the battalion is being pulled back to the lower levels to protect the emperor. Two-Twenty-Three and One-Nine are staying here as the first line of defense. That means we have one mission, and that is to protect the Granite Throne, and when the Jin Longs come, and most assuredly they will, we will need to pull out all stops to keep the emperor and empress alive. *All* stops, understand?"

"Yes, Sergeant," he said quietly.

"You keep your mistress, as you call it. Her. You keep her bottled up until all else is lost, then you fucking let her go and wreak havoc on the bastards. Show them what a Marine can do. Got it?"

"Yes, ma'am," he said, reverting to his recruit days.

"Ma'am? I'm not a ma'am, I—"

". . . work for a living," Leif finished the traditional sentence for her.

She looked at him, then for the first time he'd ever witnessed it, broke into a laugh. For such a hard-ass Marines, she giggled like a little girl. Her punch was not like a little girl's though, as she gave him a shot in the arm.

"Yeah, right. Just . . . do your best when the time comes. But until then, you're still a team leader. How're your Marines?"

"Stone . . . well, you know. Sousa's wounded, but she can fight. Hkekka, he never even got touched."

"Go get them ready. We're moving deeper into the palace in twenty."

She gave him another punch, more of a tap, then turned to leave.

"Hey, Sergeant," he called out as she walked away.

She turned her head over her shoulder.

"Thanks," he said.

She nodded once, then continued on her way.

Chapter 32

Twelve minutes later, Hkekka in tow, Leif was at the palace hospital to pick up Sousa. The hospital was probably the best equipped in the entire empire, but it just wasn't equipped to handle the huge inflow of patients. They found Sousa in the passage where the less-serious wounded were being treated by Navy corpsmen.

"Doc says I'll be good as new in a week," she said, showing off the patch of plastiskin that stretched from her hip to her butt through the blood-stained rent in her utilities.

She had already passed that to Leif over the net, but it was good to see that with his own eyes.

"Have you seen Corporal Hwei?" he asked her.

Her face sobered up, and she pointed down the passage, saying, "The serious ones were taken inside."

That was actually good news. If he was taken inside the hospital, then that meant they thought he might be saved. As he and Hkekka had arrived, another corridor was filled with those who were already dead or close to it, chaplains of various faiths giving last rites or other means of comfort.

Leif checked the time. They had another eight minutes, and it would probably take them four to get to the assembly area, which was one floor up.

"Let's go," he said, making his way through the mass of people to reach the main door into the hospital.

Sergeant Zoran was already there, but instead of the fierce warrior, she seemed like a supplicant, begging a civilian nurse for something.

"Kyle Hwei. Corporal. He had a head wound," she said, pulling on the nurse's arm.

"Look, I'm sorry, but I don't have time for this. There's too many of you. You'll just have to wait."

Leif felt a stab of guilt. Just a few short minutes ago, the sergeant was being the strong one, snapping him out of his depressed funk. Leif had lost one of his Marines, but she had lost at least four. He hadn't checked with Manu yet, and he hadn't seen Doc Josten, but Kyle was the only Marine left alive from First Team, and his survival was in doubt.

Used to the beautiful and orderly hospital, treating the high and mighty, the nurse was obviously out of his league, so he couldn't really be blamed, but Leif felt a rush of protectiveness come over him. That was his sergeant there.

He pushed forward, too close, using his height to tower over the human. "Corporal Hwei is the only Marine left alive from his team. You're doing triage, and you've got your scanpad. Just check, and we'll be out of your hair," he growled.

The nurse took an involuntary step back, looking up at the blood-covered Marine. He gulped, then seemed to grow a bit of a backbone.

"Look, you need to leave and let us . . ." he paused, looked beyond Leif, and said, "Your Majesty!" before giving his head a short bow, more of an exaggerated nod.

Leif turned around to see the emperor and empress, flanked by six of the Imperial Guard. He backed off the nurse, ashamed that he'd tried to use his size to intimidate the man, who was only doing his job, after all.

"Mike, isn't it?" the emperor asked.

"Yes, sir. Mike Hammond."

"Is this Marine correct? Can you look up the status of their friend?"

Leif was doubly ashamed now. The emperor had heard the tone of his voice when he tried to push the nurse.

"Yes, sir. I could check it here if he was scanned. A few were just rushed inside before the triage clerk could log them in."

"You're doing a great job, Mike, and we all appreciate it. But these Marines have only a few minutes before they need to deploy into position to keep the Jin Longs out of the palace." He paused a moment, to let the image of rampaging militia sink in. "If you could take a second, I think it would help clear their minds for what's ahead if they knew the status of their friend."

"Yes, Your Majesty. Of course. I'm sorry—"

"No reason to be sorry, Mike. You're all doing a great job here," he said, raising his voice at the last sentence for everyone around to hear.

He nodded his head, then walked into the hospital. As she was about to pass the empress reached out and gave Sousa a squeeze on the shoulder. She leaned in and whispered something to the Marine before she followed her husband.

"What was his name again?" the nurse asked as soon as the imperial couple disappeared inside.

"Hwei, Kyle M.," the sergeant said, stepping up beside him.

The nurse punched in the name, then said, "Class Three, massive head wounds. He's in queue for surgery, but his prognosis is guarded."

Leif vaguely remembered the triage classes from recruit training. Class Five was the worst, with no hope of survival. Those in the corridor they'd passed were Class Five. Class Four was serious, where survival depended on acute medical intervention

So, if Kyle was a Class Three, that's good, right? But what was that last part?

"What does 'guarded prognosis mean?'" he asked.

"He'll probably live, but he may not fully recover. It says here head wound, so I've got to think he's got severe brain damage with that kind of prognosis. Sorry about that.

"But now, really, I've got work to do," he said, stepping over to a Marine lying face down on a gurney.

"Thanks, Mike," the sergeant said before turning to Leif and the other two Marines. "We've only got a few minutes to get up to the assembly point. Let's move it."

"What did the empress say to you?" Leif asked as they made their way through the wounded Marines.

"Nothing."

"Nothing? She's the empress. It wasn't just nothing."

"It's private, OK, Corporal?" she said, almost snapping at him and pulling away.

Leif stopped for a moment, wondering at her overblown reaction—and now curiosity burning at what the empress did say.

"Humans!" Hkekka said, pushing past him as if that answered everything.

For once, Leif agreed with the qiincer. No matter how long he served with humans, he was never going to truly understand them.

With a sigh, he followed the sergeant and his two Marines back to join the rest of the battalion.

Chapter 33

The "rest" of the battalion was much diminished. Out of 1,214 Marines and sailors at the start of the battle, a little over 400 were combat-effective. A few more would probably trickle down from medical treatment, wounded, but able to fight.

The other two battalions had suffered far less, so they were going to be the first line of defense if—when—the Jin Longs breached the palace walls. And they would breach them. The palace had significant defenses, but the enemy was bringing in heavy equipment to tear down the outer walls.

Guides were escorting 3/6 by platoons deep into the bowels of the palace where they'd be the last line of defense. If 2/23 and 1/9 fell, the 400 Marines and sailors, along with about 100 Imperial Guards, would be all that was left to protect the Granite Throne.

Were two people worth it? Lief wondered as he followed Hkekka down a stairwell?

No, he knew. Two people were not worth the loss of life on all sides. But these weren't just two people. They made up the Granite Throne. And if the imperial line was broken and replaced by the Jin Longs, then the empire would change, and not for the better. He'd seen Boris Chen with his own eyes, and if he'd ever been able to take the measure of a human, it was then. If the Jin Long heir was willing to sacrifice the thousands of militia he'd done so far in order to take over the throne, then there was no doubt in Leif's mind that he didn't value the life of his own citizens, much less others. All the advances over the last five years, particularly with regards to the non-human races, would be reversed.

No, Jenifer and Forsythe were not worth the mounting death toll. They were not worth Jordun, Stone, the lieutenant. They were not worth the thousands that had been killed on both sides. But the emperor and empress, they were. The

Granite Throne, and all it represented, was. And it was worth all those left yet to die. If that included him, so be it.

By the Mother, stop being so freaking philosophical, Leefen a'Hope Hollow! You'll fight because you're a Marine. Period.

He shook his head. That was really the bottom line. He was a Marine, and he'd fight because he was ordered to. He'd fight for Sousa, for the sergeant, for Manu. Hell, he'd fight for Hkekka. And the ways things were going, it looked like he'd have to.

He reached the bottom of the stairwell and out the door into a large corridor. Civilians were moving back and forth with purpose. Two Imperial Guards, no longer in the dress uniform, stood at a set of double doors, scanning everyone who entered.

Their guide, an extremely young-looking woman marched up to the guards, flashed her pendant, and escorted the Marines into the room. The guards stared at each Marine as they passed, but said nothing.

Leif looked around in awe as Staff Sergeant Antoine led them to the far left where Captain Jiminez was in deep conversation with one of the Imperial Guard. This was a command center, no doubt about it, but it looked like the set of some science-fiction movie. He'd thought a Marine Corps CP was impressive, but this put any Marine command post to shame. Banks of flat screens covered the far wall, and no less than six holo platforms were interspaced throughout the hall. At least a hundred people—mostly humans, but tokits, alindamires, hissers, and a few qiincers—manned stations.

None of the People, Leif noted, surprisingly disappointed.

But there were four wyntonan Imperial Guards among the humans.

One of the flatscreen monitors displayed the bridge of a ship. Underneath the image, a clock was counting down. At the moment, it read 9 hours, 22 minutes, and 6 seconds. Leif didn't need to ask what that was. If the palace could hold out that long, then maybe they'd get out of this with their skin.

Of course, the Jin Longs would know when the reinforcements would arrive as well. They'd be doing everything they could to seize the palace before then, kill the imperial couple, and install one of their own on the throne. Leif didn't know what would happen after that, whether the military would swear to the usurpers. If that actually became a question, he'd be beyond caring.

Many of the monitors showed the scene outside the palace. Thousands of militia were occupying the upper plaza by now. They were being held in check by the passive security measures of the palace, but other monitors showed a variety of pieces of heavy equipment on their way. Some were already in the main plaza, militiamen cheering them as they made their way forward.

"Squad leaders, I want a full equipment check now. Then redistribute ammo. We need to be ready for whatever the skipper wants," the staff sergeant said before going over to him.

Sergeant Zoran had already done that at the assembly area, so Leif turned to Sousa and asked, "You hanging in there?"

"Still pumped with drugs," she said, slapping her ass, then wincing. "That was stupid, but I'm good."

He was tempted to ask her again what the empress had said to her, but given her reaction, he held back. If they got through this alive, though, he'd find out if he had to drag it out of her.

The rent in her utilities had grown, exposing more of the expansive plastiflesh patch on her ass. The human's medical ability was impressive—and while not as good when treating wyntonans, it was still better than what the wyntonans had for themselves. She'd suffered a serious wound, but here she was, ready to go. But just as the docs could pump up a Marine, the patient could crash hard as the meds gave out. Sousa may be fine now, but that could change in a hurry, and knowing the perversities of war, it would happen at just the wrong time.

"If you need a boost, then we can get Doc Yamata over here," he said. Doc Josten was KIA, so the Second Platoon corpsman was now doing double duty.

"I'm fine, Corporal. Don't worry about me."

"I'm just saying, if you start to feel anything, let Doc or me know."

"Sure thing, Corporal," she said with a slight giggle.

Sousa didn't giggle. Ever. The meds had to be messing with her mind, he knew. According to Marine Corps regulations, he should stand her down, but sometimes, the situation overruled the regs.

A burst of energy, almost palpable, filled the room. All eyes swung up to see the emperor and empress enter the room and stride down to the front. They'd changed into combat utilities. White and grey cammo, which wasn't very practical unless they were on some ice world. Each was wearing a grey Sam Browne belt—a broad belt around the waist and another rising up the back, over the right shoulder, and connecting with the waist belt on the left side. Hanging from the waist belt at the right hip, each had a holster, the butt of a handgun exposed.

Not really tactical, Leif noted, but better than the dress uniforms they'd been wearing.

All the bigwigs, including the general, converged on the imperial couple. Leif wished he was closer so he could hear what was going on.

"Hey, eyes on me, not them," Staff Sergeant Antoine said. "School circle."

With one last look at the emperor, Leif joined the rest as they gathered around their platoon sergeant—no, platoon *commander,* now.

"India is staying here until . . . well, until we're ordered elsewhere. "Third and Weapons are going inside the Bravo Command . . ."

Of course, this isn't going to be the only command post. But if this one falls, then the emperor and empress . . . he let the thought trail off.

". . . while First and Second are staying here. We are not, I repeat *not*, the Imperial Guards, and we're to stay out of their way. But if the shit reaches us, we do what we do best, and that's kill the enemies of the empire. Understand?"

"Ooh-rah," they shouted out in knee-jerk fashion, causing those technicians near them to look up, startled at the outburst.

"Squad leaders, let's try and work out at least a hint of a battle plan."

"And the rest of us?" Manu asked.

"Hydrate and eat. Then you might as well relax and watch the show," she said, pointing at the displays. "We'll see from here when we're on deck."

Chapter 34

The outer wall blew inwards in a cloud of debris. The 2/23 Marines had been warned by the palace command center, so they had pulled back and weren't caught in the blast, and now they streamed forward to meet the threat.

Outside, the militia were too slow to react. Too many deaths, courtesy of hidden palace defenses, had made them overly-cautious, and it took the infantry a few moments to realize the outer wall had finally been breached. Leif watched on one of the feeds as they emerged from temporary cover among the fountains and statues and charged forward . . . to be met with withering fire from the Marines inside. The first two or three ranks of militia were mowed down like spring wheat.

Lance Corporal Heinz pumped his fist in the air, but the rest watched silently. Considerably more than 10,000 militia were still outside the palace, and this was only the first breach of what would be many. The Jin Longs hadn't even bothered trying to knock out or neutralize the cams and scanners as a dozen breaching crews were at the walls. It was as if they were taunting those inside, showing them the tools of their destruction.

It wasn't going to be easy, as the 3/23 Marine showed. But even the most gung-ho Marine knew it was inevitable. They couldn't win. Their only hope was to hold out for another seven hours.

Leif looked at the display: 6 hours, 36 minutes, 4 seconds.

Lieutenant Colonel König and most of his staff had arrived and were huddled up with a handful of civilians and Imperial Guards. Sergeant Major Crawford had been there, too, but when Kilo and Lima were pushed forward to join the first line of defense, he'd gone with them. Leif had spotted him several times on the feeds as he made his rounds, but he hadn't seen Lori. He knew she'd made it inside the palace, so she had to still be alive, but he'd feel better if he caught a glimpse of her.

"Look at them," Sousa whispered. "Get some!"

Leif turned back to the feed from the first breach. The Marines were pouring deadly, disciplined fire, which maximized effect on target while husbanding what had to be dwindling ammunition. A Marine fell right in front of the feed, and the two on either side of her didn't flinch.

There was a flash, and an explosion sent up a cloud of smoke that forced the scan into ultrasonics. Marines were scattered on the ground. A dozen lay still, but the others got slowly got to their feet and started firing as the outside feed showed another mass of militia charging.

The ultrasonics were not as clear as the visuals, but they were clear enough to see the NCOs gather those still alive and form a line to stop the assault. A few were firing, but the most of the remaining Marines held their weapons like clubs.

Leif felt a rush of pride.

This is what we are, the best damned warriors in the galaxy . . . and like a hammer, it hit him. He'd long been proud of being a Marine, proud of his accomplishments, but maybe for the first time in his career, he'd thought of himself simply as a Marine, not a *wyntonan* Marine. He wasn't sure what that meant, but it felt right to him.

The smoke cleared, and the inside feed switched back to visuals just as the two forces clashed. Voices shouted from those watching in the command center, and it took a moment for Leif to realize that one of them was his.

Militia fell, ten, twenty, taken down in hand-to-hand combat, but one by one, the Marines fell as well. It took less than a minute, and the breach was clear. The militiamen streamed in. One soldier looked up at the feed, then gave it the finger before finally shooting it out.

All up and down the outer perimeter of the palace, the militia were blowing holes in the wall, ignoring the entrances. The palace walls were extremely robust, with hidden defenses, but they were not impregnable. There was no longer a viable course of action to keep them out. The only thing the general could do was to maneuver the remaining units into choke points leading to the throne room.

Yes, the throne room, not the command center four stories underground. One of the 1/9 lieutenants had suggested that comms repeaters be set up there, with spoofing to simulate heat signatures. The emperor and others kept using those repeaters to send out fake messages in the hopes of sending the militia to the throne room first, as if the emperor would be waiting there like some king of old. Anything to buy a little more time.

6 hours, 24 minutes, 46 seconds.

"What do you think, Bro?" Manu said, sliding into the seat next to Leif.

The two team leaders hadn't talked much since the first assault. Manu's voice was calm, but his right foot tap, tap, tapped the floor.

"If they go for the throne room, maybe," Leif said. "You heard the staff sergeant. They'll have to cut through five sets of security doors to get there."

"Think they'll go for it?"

"Don't know. Maybe," Leif answered.

That was true enough, but it didn't answer the real question Manu wanted to ask.

Were they going to have to fight again?

Which was odd. Manu was a decorated Marine, fearless in battle. Leif had fought beside his friend. He'd never seen the heavyworlder show any sign of fear.

Leif leaned over and quietly asked, "What's up, Manu? What's going on with you."

Manu leaned back and closed his eyes for a moment, took a deep breath, then straightened up and said, "It's this fucking waiting, Leif. We're like rabbits in a hole waiting to be dug out. I can't take it. Just let's get it over with and kick some ass, you know?"

No, I don't know, Manu.

But maybe he did. Manu was a man of action. When faced with a threat, he reacted. Just sitting here, watching the

Jin Longs advance, he couldn't do a thing about it, and that was preying on his thoughts.

"Do you think, if I asked the staff sergeant, she'd let me go forward?"

"And leave your team?"

He grimaced, then said, "Yeah, you're right. I just . . ."

"The waiting will be over soon enough, Manu. Just think of your duties. You've got Marines counting on you," he said, tilting his head where his friend's three Marines were back by the table getting coffee.

"Yep, you're right," he said, taking an even deeper breath as if that could clear his mind of the little tiny demons that were niggling at him. "I'm OK."

He looked up at the displays were militiamen could be seen flooding in through five breaches.

"Hey, Leif," he said, holding out a closed fist. "We kicked some butt out there, right?"

"That we did, Manu, that we did," Leif answered, bumping fists.

"And we'll do it again," he said, sounding like the old Manu again. "Ooh-fucking-rah!"

He slapped Leif on the shoulder and vaulted over the back of his seat, then swaggered up to his team.

Ooh-fucking-rah, Manu. Ooh-fucking-rah.

****

The Jin Longs didn't take the bait. Or, to be more accurate, not all of them. After a fierce fight with Charlie 1/9, they breached the inner palace. The lead forces headed towards the throne room, with what was Bravo and what was left of Charlie hitting them, then pulling back, trying to sell the ruse.

The problem was that others following them, and those that breached in 2/23's AO, didn't follow suit. They were spread out, slowed by a tenacious defense, but advancing. When a large detachment made their way down to the fourth underground level, it was obvious that the attempt to divert them, while it worked, had not worked well enough.

Leif kept looking at the staff sergeant and the captain, waiting for orders, but they had their heads together with the other officers and SNCOs in deep discussions.

Leif got out of his seat and walked over to Sousa, who was standing by the coffee.

"Stand by. We've got to get orders soon, so make sure your gear is ready. You still with us?"

"Doc Yamata gave me a jolt of happy juice. I'm feeling it, but I'm still here, ready to go. This helps, too," she said, holding up a half-empty cup.

"OK, then," he said, giving her upper arm a soft slap. "Tell Hkekka to get ready, too."

She looked up, then grabbed Leif by the arm and pulled him aside. He turned to see the emperor, empress, the general, and two civilians coming up to get some coffee. They were making a show of just being casual, but Leif could see there was more to their actions. He and Sousa, along with a few other Marines and civilians, moved out of the way.

Not far enough. They were keeping their voices low, but Leif, with his better hearing, was able to hear what they were saying.

"So, you don't see a way to hold out?" the emperor asked the general.

"No, sir. From what Guard Commander Smith told me of the defenses, we can hold out for a few hours, possibly until the reinforcements arrive, but I can't guarantee that."

"There are no guarantees in war," the emperor said. "Your General Akeem said that three hundred years ago during the Sunlight War. But give me a probability."

"Thirty percent, no better."

"Based on what?"

"Based on my gut. And thirty-two years of experience."

The emperor pursed his lips as he took that in.

The general was being optimistic, Leif thought. He'd put their chances at less than 10%. But then again, he didn't know what surprises the palace defenses could spring on the invader.

"We can't bet on that, then," the emperor said, quieter, almost too quiet for Leif to hear.

"Corporal, what do you want—" Sousa started before Leif waved her quiet.

The emperor took a ring off his finger and held it up, turning it as he gazed. Leif realized it was the imperial signet, the symbol of imperial power and the Granite Throne. It was used to mark all imperial proclamations, and imperial power was granted to whoever held it—at least on a symbolic level. Three signets had been lost over the years, and a new one had simply been made each time. But this one was over a couple of hundred years old, and the symbolism was strong.

The emperor closed his fist around the ring, then held it out to the empress.

"No!" she said, loud enough to catch the attention of those around them.

"Yes," he said, taking her right hand with his left, extending it, and placing the signet in her palm. "You have to."

"You come with me," she said.

The emperor took a moment to look up to the displays at the front of the room, displays showing Marines fighting and dying, displays showing Jin Long militia making their way deeper into the palace.

"I can't, Jen. We discussed this."

"Force, please reconsider. Listen to the empress," the older civilian said.

"I thought you were the one to teach me about honor and responsibility, old friend, back when you said I didn't have the strength to assume the throne."

The old man flinched, and once again, Leif had to strain to hear his lowered voice as he said, "We're long past those days, For . . . Your Majesty. You long ago showed me the error of my ways. And that is why I'm begging you to reconsider."

"Listen to the Privy Counsellor," the empress insisted.

"If you were not the man you are, I'd advise you to stay, to pass the primacy to the empress. But because you are who you are, I know the empire needs you. Whatever happens over the next few hours, over the next few days, the empire needs you to pick up the pieces. You and the empress. Otherwise, the Granite Throne will be broken, and I fear what comes next."

The old man looked with hope at the emperor, who in turn looked to General Womack.

"And what do you think," he asked her.

"This is far above my station, Your Majesty. The commandant has ordered me to take my orders directly from you for the duration."

"Hell, I was hoping you'd back me up, General. All that gung-ho and ooh-rah stuff you Marines shout all the time," he said with a chuckle.

None of the others changed their expression one iota.

"OK, bad joke," he said, his face sobering. "But my decision is made. I cannot run away when the empire is threatened, not when others are willing to give their lives for the cause. If I did, how would I rule?"

"And how will I rule if *I* run away? How is that any different?" the empress asked, her voice rising again.

By now, the entire control center knew something pivotal was going on, and the place quieted down as heads turned to the five humans. Leif unconsciously took a step closer.

"It *is* different. You are simply obeying orders, my love, keeping the signet intact."

"I don't care about the signet," she snapped, still holding it in her open palm. "We can make a new one. I care about you!"

"I know you do. But I know you care about the empire, too, about our plans on how to bring it back to prominence as a force of good. That won't happen if your brother takes over. You know that."

He closed her fingers around the imperial signet.

Tears welled in her eyes, then she said, "I'm not accepting this. I'm just holding it until I can give it back to you."

She didn't put it on but slipped it into her pocket as she leaned in to give him a kiss on the cheek.

"Your Majesty—" the privy counselor started before the emperor cut him off.

"It's decided. General, if you will."

General Womack nodded, then raised a hand to the Marine staff, giving a thumbs up. She turned and followed the emperor back down the aisle to the front of the room. The empress didn't move but stared after the emperor.

"What's going on?" Sousa asked as the Marine staff moved into action.

Staff Sergeant Antoine pulled back and walked over to where the rest of the Marines were standing, circling one finger on the air, the signal to gather around her.

"OK, listen up. Eighteen of us are leaving."

"What?" Manu blurted out. "We can't leave when we've got—"

"We've got our orders, and we will leave, Corporal Savea," she snapped, then softened her tone and said, "But we're not bugging out. Along with 20 Imperial Guards, we're going to make sure the Empress Jenifer reaches a secret hangar where she's going to take off to meet the fleet. There's a back way out of the palace, where a Carabao will fly us to the hangar. They'll probably spot us as we take off, so our mission is to hold the hangar until the empress takes off."

"One Caribou?" Leif asked.

"Just one."

Which explained the 18-person limit. A Caribou could carry 40 pax, and that was in emergency mode. With 20 Imperial Guards, then meant the empress and one other filled the plane.

"The escape craft will take the empress and three others off the planet to rendezvous with the incoming fleet."

"And then what do we do?" Manu asked. "Just sit on our asses?"

"Once the empress is off the planet, I intend to ask the Carabao pilot to bring us back here. As far as I'm concerned, the mission isn't over until every fucking Jin Long asshole is dead!"

A chorus of ohh-rahs filled the control center, causing heads to swivel in their direction.

All but one. The empress still stood motionless, eyes on her husband.

Chapter 35

"We ready?" Major Jespers, the battalion XO asked.

Leif was somewhat surprised that the second-senior Marine in the battalion was accompanying what was essentially a platoon (minus), but with the lieutenant KIA, evidently the powers-that-be didn't trust a staff sergeant to lead the Marines. Even as a major, however, he wasn't in charge of the mission—the head of the empress's personal guard was. The Marines were only there to give support, nothing more.

"Yes, sir," Staff Sergeant Antoine answered for the platoon.

"We're moving out in less than two," he added.

Four people were applying body armor to the empress, who stood still, hands raised above her head. Marine armor was high-tech, but what she was getting was almost supernatural. As three of her orderlies held up what looked to be hard white plates on different parts of her body, the fourth activated a small control, and the plates seemed to come alive, molding themselves over her curves and joints. As the last leg section was applied, she was beginning to look like some fantasy heroine, an elf queen.

But it wasn't finished. With a twist of the control, the entire thing flared with a blue light that focused on the joints between the plates.

"Max thunder," Private Wonstat said.

"Just pray that it works as good as it looks," Manu answered, thumping on his own chest armor.

"Major, are you ready to move out?" the guard commander—Leif didn't know the ranks in the Imperial Guard—asked.

"Roger that."

"Fromsky, Delbert, let's move," the commander said to the two guards who were going to lead the movement.

"Wait, Guard Commander," the empress said before she broke off to hurry down the aisle to where the emperor was walking up.

That armor isn't slowing her down, Leif noted with professional detachment.

The empress broke into a run over the last few steps, throwing herself into the emperor's arms. They just hugged for a few moments, saying nothing.

"Your Majesty," an aide said, pointing to the displays. "C-Three."

On the display labeled C-3, militia were moving unimpeded through a corridor.

"You've got to go before they cut you off," the emperor said, breaking the hug.

The empress didn't let go of his hand, then jerked him back in for a hard kiss before she turned and ran back up to the waiting guards and Marines. A young woman, in what looked to be a plain version of the Marine body armor, took her place beside her.

"Fromsky, Delbert!" the guard commander said, and the two guides left through the open doors, the Marines following behind.

Leif took one last glance at the countdown clock: 5 hours, 37 minutes, 13 seconds.

✳✳✳✳✳✳✳✳✳✳✳✳✳✳✳✳

Another blast sounded through the walls. The sounds of battle were evident as they rushed through one corridor after another. These were not the grand and opulent halls of the upper levels, but rather plain and spartan passages with controls, pipes, and ducts running the lengths. Lighting was dim, which didn't bother Leif or Hkekka, but Sousa seemed to be placing her feet with deliberate care.

Either she was having some trouble seeing, or her meds were affecting her.

With the two IGs leading the way, eight Marines were next. Leif, Sousa, and Hkekka were the point, followed by Sergeant Zoran and the Carabao pilot. Manu and his two Marines, were next, and finally Staff Sergeant Antoine. Behind them were the main body of guards surrounding the empress, the major and the rest of the Marines bringing up the rear.

The guides took a hard right into a tiny, constricted corridor, more dimly lit than the one they'd been following. The sounds of automatic fire reached them, sharp and clear. Leif raised his M88, ready to use it, but the two guards didn't hesitate and pushed on.

It seemed as if they were rushing into a firefight, and as they passed, Leif could hear the yells of humans shouting in battle, but the fighting had to be just on the other side of the walls, only meters away. Leif wondered if they were the militia that he'd seen on the C-3 display. Whoever they were, militia or Marines, didn't matter, though. A large enough blast there could breach their passage, exposing the empress, but they made it through, leaving that particular fight behind.

Leif didn't know how long they jogged as they twisted and turned in the bowels of the palace, but finally, they came to a secure door, like the vacuum-tight doors on a Navy ship. The two guards held up, and Leif could see Fromsky . . . or was it Delbert? . . . subvocalize as he reported back.

The other guard activated a screen which displayed . . . nothing. No, not nothing. There was the faint outline visible of what had to be the Carabao. The guard switched the scanner, and the Carabao popped on the screen in the washed-out green of night-vision. Another switch, and the screen went mostly dark again, with only the faint yellowish indication of a seam past the Carabao. That had to be a heat scan. The guard was going through the spectrum of scanners, one after the other.

"It looks clear," Sergeant Zoran passed. "As soon as the door opens, First, take left, Second, take right. Secure the back ramp from any surprises. Wait until I give the order to board."

Leif didn't like the fact that he couldn't communicate with the guards if he had to, but they used different systems. The major, the staff sergeant, and the two sergeants were given small hand-held communicators, and they'd relay messages, but Leif would feel better if he could communicate directly other than by simply talking.

But there was no reason why he couldn't do that now.

"Give us a signal before you open," he told the guard on the controls.

"You've got it."

The guard entered a code, then held up a small device to the receptor-field. What had been a red light turned green, and Leif started forward, ready to move. But that must have only been a lock. The two guards pulled out a recessed wheel, and together, they undogged the door, spinning the wheel until it clicked.

"Now," the guard said, pulling a lever on the right side.

The door hissed as it slid into the wall on the right.

The hangar was far more constrained than he'd expected, the Carabao looming in the dark took up most of the space. The back ramp was down. Leif, Sousa, and Hkekka rushed to the right, stopping by the sides of the ramp, weapons trained forward as the rest of the party pounded past them and into the Carabao. Within moments, the big plane started to power up as the pilot took over. They'd been briefed that it would take four minutes before the Carabao was ready to fly, and that was a huge window of vulnerability. The hangar was shielded, but that didn't mean the Jin Longs couldn't detect the plane powering up. And while this was one of three "secret hangars," not on any publicly accessed palace plans, it was impossible to keep something like that completely unknown. The Jin Longs were probably aware of it.

Time ticked ever-so-slowly as the Carabao came online. Leif kept expecting to see the outer hangar doors explode in with fire and heat. Finally, the fans rotated down, and the plane was ready for flight. Leif felt a wave of relief sweep through him. Their mission wasn't done, but getting away from the palace in one piece was a major milestone.

The outer doors began to recess into the walls, and bright light flooded the hangar, making Leif flinch and raise a hand to shade his eyes. Hkekka slammed down his shades, turning his head.

"Oh, shit!" Sousa said, rising to her feet, bringing her 88 up.

Leif squinted, and his blood ran cold. Three very surprised-looking militia were getting to their feet. One had Borer-20, a small, but powerful, all-purpose missile, that he was raising to his shoulder.

"We've got contact to the front," Leif passed as he and Sousa opened fire. One of the militiamen fell, but the other two, including the missileman, bolted to the side.

"Take them out!" the sergeant shouted as she ran under the fuselage of the Carabao to get to their side.

Hkekka was still recoiling from the light, but Sousa and Leif bolted forward, reaching the front of the hangar just in time to become targets. Rounds whizzed by Leif's head, one creasing his shoulder, as the militiaman without the missile fired on auto—his mistake as the muzzle of his rifle rose to spit rounds harmlessly into the air. Leif double-tapped the soldier, one round hitting him high on his armor, the next finding flesh just under his helmet faceshield.

The missileman, with a look of horror on his face, dropped the Borer and struggled to pull out his sidearm when Sousa took him out, horror turning to surprise as he realized what had happened to him. He sat down, then slowly toppled over.

"Is that it?" Sergeant Zoran asked, coming around the corner.

No one else was right there, but more militiamen could be seen, and they hadn't missed the fight. A round pinged on the palace wall as someone took a shot at them.

"Get back and on the plane," Sergeant Zoran said.

She took a step forward and put several rounds into the missile lying on the ground, sending chunks of it flying. No one was going to be able to use it after that.

The six fans were already lifting the plane, buffeting the three Marines as they ran back. Leif grabbed Hkekka by the shoulder and almost bodily threw him onto the ramp, before jumping up himself. He turned back to offer an arm, then pull Sousa on board. The Carabao started to move forward. Sergeant Zoran, shorter than most Marines, had to reverse course, run, and then jump, arms extended . . . but she was going to come up just short. Both Sousa and Leif reached, and somehow, Sousa grabbed the sergeant's arm, swinging her under the closing ramp as the Carabao started to pick up speed. On the second swing, Leif managed to grab the sergeant as well and together, they yanked her aboard.

"Cover the plane!" Sergeant Zoran yelled.

Leif had placed his 88 on the deck of the ramp to grab Sousa and Zoran, and with the ramp now tilted up, it was sliding down. He hooked it with his foot and kicked it up, snatched it with one hand, and looked for targets as the Carabao cleared the hangar and started to swoop down the slope to the lake.

Militia covered the gardens and paths between the palace and the shoreline. Rounds reached up to them, and Leif sprayed those he could target. He caught a quick sight of another missileman and fired a volley at him. He didn't think he hit the soldier, but he made the woman drop the missile and dive for cover. With six powerful fans and a chatter-jet in the tail above Leif's head, the Carabao quickly picked up speed. Within moments, it was skipping across the surface of Lake Victoria, out of range of the militia.

The empress was still in danger, and their mission was not accomplished yet, but Leif finally let out a sigh of relief. At least they were out of the palace.

Chapter 36

Leif had expected the Carabao to head up the shoreline before banking to the east to Nanni or NIS, Nairobi Imperial Spaceport, but instead, the Carabao skimmed the surface of the lake across a bay, over a spit of land, and to a brown, somewhat barren island. Six minutes after leaving the palace, the Carabao was flaring in for a landing. A single, fortress-like building rose from the ground at the edge of the northern end of the island, a large "Irugwa Imperial Research Station" sign on the nearest side.

What Leif didn't see was a ship. The imperial household fleet was at Nanni, the secured annex of NIS, and this wasn't that.

"Where are we?" he asked the sergeant, who hushed him by waving her left hand, the right holding her communicator.

Staff Sergeant Antoine answered instead. "We were kind of kept in the dark as to our destination. This is a classified imperial spaceport, but nothing has changed as to our orders. The building below is a front. The empress's ride is inside."

It made sense, and that would explain why only so few would accompany her off the planet, but Leif didn't like that they'd been kept in the dark. They'd proven their loyalty, so why the secrecy? He didn't have time to dwell on that as the Carabao touched down. Leif led his team down the ramp, jumping off before it had even finished lowering.

The island was low, with just a few low hills breaking the plane. Brown and dusty in the dry season, a few bushes and trees were scattered about, some going right up to the building. That was evidence that the ship inside had not flown for quite some time. Shuttles could land and take off without damaging the area around, but not a space-going ship. Even a small one would have blasted the island clean with its ion engines—which was why the empress's ship was not hidden at the palace itself.

As the two teams from First Squad pivoted to provide security, Leif looked across the water to the mainland. He wasn't an expert, but it was probably far enough to weather the empress's take-off without damage.

The Imperial Guards ran off the Carabao, surrounding the empress. Ten of them sprinted to the building some 100 meters away, while the rest stopped the empress just past the line of Marines.

Her carefully coiffed hair had become disheveled, several strands bouncing about in the breeze. Her attendant tried to capture the wayward hair, but the empress brushed her off. With her white and gray armor, she made a bright target among the Marines and IGs, but she did look regal. Leif just hoped she had the force of will to bring the empire back from the abyss.

The ten guards reached the building. One held up a control of some type, and a moment later, a section of the front wall started to part. Within a few moments, a squat, ugly . . . spaceship? . . . was visible. It looked like a piece of space junk, not an imperial ship.

That can't be her ship, can it?

But a track extended, 10 meters, 20 meters, 30. The ten guards became grunt labor, pushing the ship along the track. When they got it to the end, a canopy of sorts opened. One of the guards stuck his head in, then pulled back, signaling with a thumbs up.

These guys are not just guards, Leif realized, his opinion of them going up another notch.

The empress turned back to the Marines and said, "I want to thank you for your service. The ship is automated, so all I have to do is initiate the sequence, but I'll hold off until you're on your way."

Leif hadn't thought of that. Even a tiny ship like that would kill them all if they were this close when it launched.

"I'm so proud of you," she said, choking up.

Two of the guards, one being the wyntonan, stepped up to escort her to the ship. They'd taken two steps when a flash streaked in from above, and the ship—and those guards standing by it—disappeared in an explosion of heat and sound. The blast knocked the empress to the ground. A moment later, another streak flashed by, and the building was hit.

Leif hadn't gone down, but Hkekka was blown ass over heels, coming to a stop in a heap. Almost instantly, the two guards on the empress picked her up, slung her like a sack of barley over the wyntonan Marine's shoulder, and started sprinting back to the Carabao, which was hit next. It didn't explode, but it collapsed with a rendering screech. Without pause, the two guards reversed course to the nearest cover, which was the rubble of the building, past the smoking pieces of what had been her escape.

The Marines were exposed, and Major Jespers immediately stepped up, ordering the Marines forward, following the empress. This was why they were there. They had to protect her. Rounds peppered the dirt around them as they ran for cover—but not as many as Leif would have expected. All of the Marines and guards, at least those guards who hadn't been killed in the first blast, made it to what was left of the building.

Coming in low over the water, three bright yellow tour planes came in, "Kili-Tours" still emblazoned on the sides. They weren't military craft, and Leif didn't know what they'd jury-rigged to take out the empress's ship. Military or not, the tour planes were built to carry lots of tourists who couldn't make the summit on foot. Each one could carry upwards of 40 tourists. With three of them, there had to be 120 Jin Longs—and that's who they had to be—landing on the island.

The Marines started firing, but it was too late. The planes disappeared behind the rocks, landing on the shore. A few moments later, the three planes took off, peeling away. Marines started firing again in anger until the major told them to conserve their ammo. Their enemy was the ones on the island with them, not the planes.

"Come on, Leif. Shift left. You're too bunched up," Sergeant Zoran yelled, pulling him by the harness.

Leif hadn't thought about positioning. He'd just wanted to get his two Marines to cover. But she was right. They were Marines, damn it, not just a mob, and if they were going to keep the empress alive, they had to be a unit, not a mob.

Leif grabbed the other two and shifted them to the left, putting Hkekka behind a section of wall that was still upright and Sousa in within a pile of rubble.

"You with us?" he asked Hkekka.

The qiincer shook his head, which almost threw his shades off, causing him to reach up to steady them, and said, "I'll be OK. Just dazed."

"Well, un-daze yourself, because we're going to get company."

He positioned himself as well, with as much cover as he could yet still observe the breadth of the island.

"How the fuck did they know the empress was here?" Manu asked over the squad net.

"I don't think they did," Sousa answered. "But they could have guessed someone, her or the emperor, would try to get out."

"But this island? There's nothing here?" Qaan protested.

"You're forgetting something. The empress is . . . was a Jin Long. If she knew about it, maybe she said something to her family."

"You think she turned traitor?"

"No!" Sousa shouted. "Before—"

"Cut the chatter," Sergeant Zoran barked. "We've got work to do, not gossip."

A moment later, she softly said, "She's the target here, so remember that before you go with the 'traitor' bullshit."

"There they are," Aaron Sribuarin from Second Platoon passed on the mission net.

"Hold your fire," the major ordered as his 17 Marines gripped their weapons. "Let more of them expose themselves."

Which was the right call, Leif knew. He edged back down out-of-sight. If they knew there was some sort of emergency spaceport on the island, the Jin Long commander might have guessed that someone would make a break for it, but it was doubtful that they would know how many or if there were Marines on board. Protocol probably had it just the Imperial Guards, and while Leif was continually impressed with them, they were not designed to operate as combat troops.

Even if they'd guessed there were Marines on the Carabao, they wouldn't know how many had survived. There were blackened bodies out in the open, and that might make them confident—over-confident.

"Watch to the left, Leif," Sergeant Zoran passed. "Make sure they don't flank us."

Five hundred or more meters out, militiamen were appearing as they started to move across the open area. They'd be stupid to commit everyone to that. While it would canalize them, it also made sense to send some up along the shoreline, to come out just 60 meters from the edge of the destroyed building to the left of their makeshift line.

They moved quickly, with decent-enough dispersion. Leif guessed it would be too much to hope for that they'd bunch up for the Marines as they'd done in the main and upper plazas. There, they'd been forced to because of sheer numbers and lack of room. Here, they had much more space in which to disperse.

"Steady," the major passed. "Another couple of hundred meters."

Leif checked his two Marines. Gone was the hesitant, almost fearful girl who he'd first met, to be replaced by a determined woman. He was proud of her.

Hkekka . . . he still didn't know what to make of the Marine. He sat with his back against the remnants of the wall, clutching his M77. Leif half expected to see him unfurl his wings and boogie out of there. He might not have much stamina in the heat and lower O2 of Earth, but he could probably make it to the mainland shore from here.

Hkekka must have sensed he was looking at the qiincer, and he snapped his head over to look him in the eye. Leif just nodded. The qiincer didn't change his expression and simply looked away.

"The empress just passed to me that whatever happens, she is proud of all of us, and it has been an honor to be our empress," the major said.

Hkekka snorted, his take on that plain. Leif felt a surge of anger. The empress could have walked out of the White Room and would probably have retained the throne when all was said and done, but she chose to remain loyal to her oath. That deserved respect, not disdain. He wanted to go over there and slap some sense into that cynical head.

"What I'd do for a few volleys of 205's," Manu said on the 1P.

"Might as well ask for the *Penang* back, and let them burn the field," Leif answered.

"Aw, what's the fun in that, letting the Navy get the credit?"

Leif had to choke back a laugh—even with over a hundred militia just 300 hundred meters away and closing. "Right now, I'd go ahead and let the Navy take all the credit they wanted."

"You always were a pussy," Manu said. "Ever since boot." There was a long pause, then he added in a more serious tone, "You're a good Marine, Leif, and a damned fine human be . . . I mean, a damn fine person. I'm proud to call you my friend."

"Hell, Tank," he said, reverting to Manu's old boot camp nickname. "Don't you get all maudlin on me now. I'll look you up after we take care of these *mintas*, and you can get all gushy with me then."

"Deal."

That was all the time they had. The major passed, "Stand by . . . FIRE!"

As one, 18 Marines rose and leveled one, two, three volleys downrange. The militia were dispersed, but at 200 meters, the Marines could hardly miss. At least a dozen were cut down, and the rest broke into what the Marines referred to as fire team rushes. In this case, instead of four Marines, it was three militia, hitting the deck and firing at the Marines, then bounding up and rushing forward 15 or 20 meters while the other teams fired.

Leif tried to time his shots to hit them, but it was more difficult than he'd thought. As soon as he acquired one of them in his sights, the soldier was down on the deck again. He managed to hit one for sure, then another when he went prone on a slightly raised piece of dirt.

The militiamen had teeth, too. They fired back, the angry zips of rounds filling the air, pieces of rubble exploding as the rounds hit. Leif felt a smack on his face, and he'd thought he'd been shot, but it was a near miss that had knocked loose some small particles of plasticrete. Plasticrete or not, blood started to drip down his face.

"Damn it, Hkekka, fire!" he yelled to his Marine.

The qiincer pointed to his 77, then in the direction of the militia.

"I don't care what your effective range is, fire!"

Leif couldn't see through the Marine's shades, but he just knew the *minta* was rolling his eyes. But he did turn around, rise, and start firing.

The incoming fire was having an effect. Marines started falling. Sousa took yet another round that dropped her on her ass, but she picked her 88 back up and resumed firing. Heinz, just five meters to Leif's right, took a round through his jaw and up into his head, hitting and cracking the back of his helmet from the inside.

Doc Yamata did not make the mission. Two of the guards were medical doctors, but the Marines would have to survive the assault to make use of them. Not that even the finest doctor could do anything for Heinz.

Firing erupted from behind him, and Leif spun around, sure they'd been flanked. But it was six of the guards, adding their fire to the Marines. One of them was almost immediately hit, and he fell back from sight.

The militia was slowing their assault, spending more time down on the ground. For a moment, Leif thought they'd broken the assault, making it too expensive a proposition. That was until Sousa cried out in pain.

They'd been flanked after all, and Sousa had taken a heavy round that penetrated her body armor. Blood welled between her fingers and she tried to keep her guts in. In one bound, Leif was at her side, spraying the 20 or so militia that were rushing up the bank.

"Sergeant Zoran, we've got trouble!" Leif shouted.

He saw a flash of gold and immediately fired on the armored figure, hitting it several times . . . and to no effect.

"I want the empress alive, but kill the rest," the figure shouted out in a familiar voice, his word amplified to reach all of the militia in the field.

Leif knew where he'd heard that voice. It was the empress's brother, the Jin Long heir. Like a god, he stood in gold armor, lights flashing. On his helmet brow, a golden bird-of-prey jutted forward.

Sergeant Zoran shifted Manu and Private Wonstat to meet the new threat, then joined them. Several of the militia fell, but the heir stood tall, encouraging them on while he and four militia ran to the rubble, bypassing the Marines and intent on where his sister might be.

As soon the flanking force appeared, the rest of the militia, those who had gone prone, rose with a yell and started running. The Marines hadn't broken off their assault—they'd been a fixing force, giving the heir and his group the diversion they'd needed to close in on their target.

"Sister, dear. Where are you?" the heir blasted out of his speakers, laughing at his phrasing.

"Damn, like to hear your voice, don't you?" Leif muttered before dropping the two militia who'd closed to within 15 meters of Sousa and him.

"Boris!" another voice shouted out, words amplified across the battlefield.

"Ulysses?" the heir said, for the first time sounding unsure of himself.

"You fucking oathbreaker! I'm going to gut you like a fish!"

"Out of the way, jarheads!" someone else shouted.

Leif looked back. Three Imperial Guards, one the guard commander, had emerged from the rubble in the middle of the Marines' hasty line and were running full tilt at the heir. Sergeant Zoran, who'd wheeled to engage the militia, had to jump out of the way.

The guard commander pulled out a wicked looking blade that flashed in the sun—Leif had assumed the blades were ceremonial, but the guard held it like he had ill will in his mind.

The heir took a step back, then Leif could see the determination return to him.

"Have it your way, Ulysses," he said, his shoulder speaker still amplifying his voice. He raised his weapon, a beautiful, polished slug-thrower that had to cost a king's ransom. Blue lighting ran down the barrel which flickered as the rounds were pulled to hyperspeeds—the lighting was not necessary; it was purely for show—and that incensed Leif. Killing was not a game.

Show or not, the rounds slammed into the guard, staggering him. He fell to his knees, then threw his sword at the heir, tumbling it end-over-end. It landed, hilt first, three meters from the heir, who leaned back his head and erupted into laughter as his militia bodyguards killed the other two IGs.

Leif felt a twinge of his musapha . . . no, not his. He could sense his mistress gathering energy, but this was something else, like when Jordun had finally answered the call.

As the heir roared with laughter, oblivious to the Marines firing at him, a single Imperial Guard climbed over the rubble to the side of him, almost broadcasting deadly intent. It was the wyntonan guard, and Leif . . . just felt, somehow, that he was under the grip of his mistress.

The guard commander had been a feint, a sacrifice to distract the Jin Long heir. Leif shifted his aim to fire on the heir again, knowing that his 88 was not going to defeat the human's armor, but it might capture his attention.

The wyntonan guard ran fast and low, holding a small tube, but he was not invisible. Three of the militia bodyguards saw him and started firing. Leif could see the rounds strike, but the wyntonan barely faltered. He couldn't take much of that. Musapha could push someone into amazing feats of strength, but flesh was flesh and bone was bone.

Still kneeling over Sousa, who was feebly reaching for her dropped 88, Leif spun to face the group around the heir, taking the militiamen under fire. He might not be able to kill the heir, but he could strip him of the militia firing on the wyntonan guard. He hit the first one at the base of the neck, dropping him like a sack of flour. He hit his second target a little lower in the back, making the human dive out of the way. The militiaman crawled on his hands and knees, seeking cover, and Leif let him go.

The heir finally seemed to realize what was going on. He turned to see the Imperial Guard just as the wyntonan triggered the tube he was carrying. A blast, seemingly too big to have come from the small weapon, expanded outwards, striking the heir in the chest, knocking him back off his feet.

The wyntonan kept running, now pulling out a large-barrel handgun, firing into the prone heir. His right leg buckled, a gout of blood and flesh exploding backward. The musapha kept him upright, and he gathered himself, screaming "Die, traitor." Leif's musapha, perhaps spurred on by the guard's, fought to be released.

Not yet.

Leif kept firing, barely aware of the hand-to-hand fighting behind him in Second Platoon's position. In every battle, there were pivotal moments, where the outcome hung in the balance. This was one of those times.

The heir shook his head, and as the wyntonan guard rushed the last five meters, heavy rounds now denting the armor at such close range, the heir raised a hand, almost as if in surrender, or to block the expected stroke. But that was hopeful thinking on Leif's part. A . . . a compression blasted from the heir's raised hand, a visible distortion of the air that rolled at the wyntonan, striking him in the chest and simply removing the torso in a burst of pink. The guard's detached legs and hips fell to the ground in a jumble.

What the name of the Mother?

Leif had never seen such a weapon. He'd never *heard* of such a weapon.

A round hit Leif's M88, shocking him back. He snapped off a round, not bothering to aim.

"Hkekka, where the . . ." he started, looking for his Marine, only to see him hugging the wall and stripping off his armor. "What the hell are you doing?"

The qiincer looked up, then yelled back, "This monkey-armor is too heavy. Can't fly."

His wings were already unfurling, heartbeat by heartbeat, and with a final snap, the last of his armor fell. His forewings spread, his hindwings still expanding, he grabbed his M77, looked at Leif, and sprang into the air, heading to the rear.

"You . . ." Leif shouted, at a loss for words. He raised his M88 to shoot the traitor, but knew that would just be a waste of ammunition.

Another blast shook the air with a crump that Leif could feel in his heart. The heir was on his feet, screaming as he strode forward. Just like his rifle, the air weapon in his armor's arm had lights, this time red, that pulsed slowly from shoulder to hand.

"OK, Jen. If that's the way you want to play it, here I come!" he shouted, his voice reverberating among the ruin of the building.

The red light's pulses sped up in frequency as the heir started climbing the rubble towards the center. The light turned steady just as two guards rose up, firing at him. The nearest had one of those tube weapons, which he started to raise. The heir pointed, and another blast of compressed air rolled forward, killing the guard.

A militiaman jumped over the rubble, landing on Sousa, which made him lose his footing. Leif swung, smashing the downed man with the butt of his M88, shattering it with the force of the blow. With a snap, he detached the butt. The assembly was still whole—it would fire.

Anger flared, and his mistress called out to be released.

"Now, Leif!" a voice called out.

Now what?

Half a dozen militiamen were now targeting him. Two rounds pinged off his armor as he sprayed them, breaking up their advance.

"Corporal Hollow, your musapha. Stop the heir! Now!" blasted his earset.

He jerked his head, almost deafened, looking behind him. Sergeant Zoran, the bottom of her left leg gone, sat on the dirt, M88 to her shoulder as she fired deliberate shots into the militia.

"Now, Leif!"

Of course, now. What am I waiting for? he thought as he released the floodgates and his mistress claimed her due.

Immediately, he felt the rush of power fill his very being. He laughed, wondering why he'd waited, why he'd allowed a monkey sergeant to keep him from letting loose before.

Two more militia climbed over the first line of rubble. Leif shot one, then slammed the barrel of his M88 over the other's head, cracking the humans' helmet. He eagerly started forward to engage more of them.

"The heir, Leif. The heir," a voice kept saying, like an Earth mosquito buzzing around his ear.

The heir!

He fought his mistress and broke away from the fighting. Twenty meters away, the heir was almost casually climbing through the rubble, surrounded by six of his bodyguards while he called out to his sister, telling her she'd chosen the wrong side, that the emperor was dead.

Leif—the rational, every-day Leif—felt a pang of loss when he'd heard that. But the mistress would not let him stop. Like a wasilla on a grazpin, Leif was locked onto his target, and nothing was going to distract him.

Once, twice, three times, rounds defeated his armor. He could feel the damage done, but the pain was like a distant memory. The musapha was coursing strong, stronger then he'd ever felt before. It gave him a focus, a singularity of being.

A militiaman stepped in his way, his weapon wielded like a club. Why a club and not shoot him, Leif had no idea. Maybe he thought that like his commander, Leif was impervious to regular fire. Whatever the reason, Leif didn't care. He caught the swung rifle in one hand and drove his

M88 right through the body armor of the militiaman, burying it in his chest. He left it there. Even if it still functioned, it would be useless against the heir.

And that had been the wyntonan guard's mistake, relying on a personal weapon for the killing shot.

Another Imperial Guard rushed the heir, and almost without thinking, the Jin Long let go another compression blast. The red lights started flashing, and Leif broke into a charge. He was a wasilla, he was an Earth lion.

More rounds hit him, and his right elbow was shattered. He didn't care.

The red lights started flashing faster as the heir's weapon recharged. Leif hit the last bodyguard low and hard, sending the human flying, knocking him into the heir, who turned around in surprise.

When he saw Leif, blood streaming from numerous wounds, he smiled, even nodding at his audacity as he brought up his right hand, the red lights almost continuous. He knew Leif didn't have a rifle that could touch him.

But, he could touch him with something else. Just as the light turned steady, Leif hit the heir shoulder to chest in his best rugby tackle, sending both to the ground. As he fell, Leif pulled Soran's vik from his calf sheath.

The heir fired his compression gun, but Leif was on his chest, and the blast went over his shoulder and up into the air.

"Doesn't matter, casper," the heir said as he reached for his sidearm.

Leif ignored it. With his right hand, he grabbed the ridiculous bird ornament on the brim of the heir's helmet. His elbow was shattered, but all he had to do was hold tight and jerk forward with his upper arm. His elbow screamed in agony, even through the musapha, but the heir's head bent forward.

Begging his mistress for every ounce of strength he could muster, Leif screamed "Jordan!" and drove his vik down at the gold-lit seam between helmet and body armor. The hardened point, carefully crafted by a wyntonan mastersmith, punched through the seam, driving into the heir's neck and severing the spine.

Boris Chen, heir to the Jin Long Clan, was dead.

Leif tired to rise, but he was shot again. And he felt the pain. His mistress was spent, and she was leaving his body. He begged her to stay, and he tried to grab her, but it was like trying to grab mist.

He fell back and rolled off the heir's body. A militiaman hit him with the butt of his weapon, probably breaking his knee. More were stepping into view, ready to beat him when someone shouted "Stop!"

Another militiaman stepped up and shouted to the others, "The empress is still here somewhere. We don't have time for this."

He pulled a sidearm and pointed it at Leif's head . . . and his shoulders were shredded. The three militiamen in his view looked up, then raised their weapons only to get cut down by something powerful. A moment later, a shape swooped from the sky, a small shape with six wings.

Leif tried to shout "Ooh-rah," but all he did was cough up blood as Private NFN Hkkeka pulled up into a wickedly sharp twisted loop and strafed the militia with his close-in defense M77. With extreme effort, Leif turned to follow the qiincer as he chewed up the militia, who fired, but couldn't seem to catch up to him.

Hkekka pulled another roll-whatever, something that didn't seem to be aeronautically possible, and he was coming in for a third time. But there was no answer for gravity, and the laws of physics could not be denied. Enough of the speed from his initial dive had bled off so that when he came in over Second Platoon's lines, his M77 spitting out death, he flew right into the remaining militiamen's fire. His right forewing buckled, then his body crumbled, falling with a thud 15 meters from Leif.

Leif tried to crawl to the motionless Marine, but his body would not cooperate. Bones grated on bones, and he almost screamed out. He turned his head away from Hkekka. Sousa was motionless where he left her. Sergeant Zoran was still fighting, her stump jammed into the mud made with her blood.

It's over. The emperor is dead, and the empress will soon be dead. We failed.

There was a roar behind him, and Leif forced his head around to watch the final assault. But it was the remaining Imperial Guards, led by the empress herself, firing an assault rifle. Hkekka's aerial assault had broken the attack, and the guards were exploiting it. Leif saw two militia raise their hands in surrender as the guards and a few Marines swept forward.

"What's happening?" he croaked out when the firing finally stopped, but there was no one to hear him.

Sergeant Zoran was on her back, motionless. No one was moving in his field of vision. He felt himself slipping into unconsciousness, but he fought it. He had to know.

A whine began to take substance. At first, he thought it was his imagination, or the effects of a concussion. But as it grew louder, he knew it was real. It was too early for the Navy, but he could hope. He finally caught sight of another tour plane, this one bright red, "Serengeti Adventures" emblazoned on the side, and his heart fell. The militia had won, and the empress was either captured or dead. The tour plane was there to pick her—or her body—up and display her to the empire like a trophy.

He leaned back to stare into the blue, blue African sky, hot against his face.

This is a shitty place to die. But we gave them a run for their money.

He closed his eyes and was in and out of consciousness for an hour, a day, or maybe a week. Time lost its meaning. He was vaguely aware of people moving, of people talking, but he couldn't drag himself out of wherever his mind had taken him. He didn't *want* to come out.

"*Rustak mantu ol patat to wyntonak.*"

What? My mind must be going. I can't even hear straight anymore.

He felt arms grabbing him, and he struggled to open his eyes, to stare at his executioners, going out like a warrior should. He tried to call forth musapha for one last fight, but there was nothing there. They lifted him, and his tortured body screamed out in pain before sweet darkness released him.

Chapter 37

Awareness returned slowly, as if Leif's brain was cushioned in cotton. There was a soft rumble, that confused him, and it took him a moment to realize the rumble was human voices.

Fight them!

Leif forced his brain into awareness, managing to open his eyes, and tried to sit up, but two sets of arms restrained him, kept him down. He weakly swung his left arm, connecting with a white-clad chest.

"Easy, easy," one of the humans said as they pushed him back down, as easily as if he was a baby grazbin. "You're OK."

The lights were bright, too bright for his wyntonan eyes, but he realized he was in a hospital, and the two humans were medical personnel. If he was in a hospital, then he wasn't in immediate danger.

Am I a prisoner?

"Why . . . what . . ." he tried to say with a tongue that refused to cooperate.

"He's checking on the wounded, so we thought we'd bring you around a little early," the nurse said.

"Who?"

The fuzziness was fading, but he was still confused.

The nurse slowly released him and pointed to his left.

Leif turned his head . . . and saw the emperor, in a simple jumpsuit, with the empress at his side, both talking to someone in the bed beside him, hooked up to tubes and heavily bandaged.

They're alive!

Leif felt a surge of energy that banished the last remaining grogginess. The empress had a patch of plastiskin on the side of her face, but neither of the imperial couple looked too worse for wear.

"What happened? Did we win?"

"Yeah, we did—"

"Not completely," the other interrupted.

"Here, on Earth, we did, Hank." He turned back to Leif. "It was pretty touch-and-go, but the citizens, they rallied."

"I was there when the tokits came, but they got slaughtered."

The smile faded from the nurse's face, and he said, "Yes, they did. But there were more of them in the Nairobi, and here in the palace. Not just tokits. Alindamirs, hissers, humans. They came however they could."

"Thank God they did," the other nurse said.

"Yeah, thank God. They were able to hold off the traitors just long enough for the Navy to arrive, and then, that was all she wrote."

Leif's memory was spotty, but he seemed to remember hearing something, a language maybe, that he didn't understand.

"Who came to us, the empress, I mean?"

"Well, no one from Nairobi knew about that place. Hell, I sure didn't. But a few of the palace staff, a handful of technicians who maintained the ship and equipment, did, and when they empress didn't take off, they took it upon themselves to grab others and head over."

"Who were they?"

"Who? Tokits, mostly. Calling themselves the 'Dung Brigade' now, of all things."

"There were humans, too," the other nurse said.

"Sure, but they're all using that name. Humans and tokits. But they brought you and the rest back. Good thing, too. Empress Jen," he said quietly, tilting his head at her, "she already had defeated the traitors, but they saved a bunch of you who probably wouldn't have made it if much more time had passed by."

"Like me?"

"Like you," he said, putting a hand on his shoulder. "You especially."

"How many . . ." he started before trailing off.

Jonathan P. Brazee

"The empress is fine. Of the rest of you, two Marines and one IP weren't hurt. Five more Marines and three guards are here with us now," he said soberly. "You'll all make it, I think, but you've got some serious recovery time, my friend."

Who, Leif wanted to ask, but he was afraid to find out.

"Hey, I heard there was a fairy who turned the battle," the second nurse said quietly, leaning in to Leif. "Is that true?"

Leif closed his eyes for a moment, the image of Hkekka strafing the militia, the image of him crashing to the ground burned into his mind.

How could I have been so wrong about him?

"Yes, Private Hkekka. Without him, I don't think the empress would have survived.

"Who would have thought it? A fairy," the nurse said.

"A *qiincer,*" Leif said. "A *Marine.*"

"Oh, yeah, sorry. I didn't mean anything. And you. We heard about you. You took out the Jin Long heir with your bare hands," he said, clearly impressed.

Not quite. I had my vik. Thank you, Soran.

"Hank," the first nurse said, tilting his head.

Both of them stepped back as His Imperial Majesty, Forsythe the Third, Protector of the Empire and Servant of the People, gave the person in the next bed a pat on the foot and turned to Leif. The empress leaned in to the person and gave her a deep hug . . .

"Harper!" Leif blurted out as he recognized her.

Sousa, her face over the empress's shoulder, gave him a wink.

The emperor hesitated, glanced back at Sousa for a moment before stepping up beside him.

"Yes, you're Harper's team leader," he said before slipping into Uzboss with, *"Daya, Leefen a'Hope Hollow."*

He calls her Harper?

"Daya, Your Majesty."

The emperor's overalls were in imperial white and grey, but they were quite understated. The small platinum lion on his collar was the only indicator of his exalted position.

"I'd ask how are you, but I can see. You took quite a beating there."

"I'm OK," Leif mumbled.

"No, you're not. You were at the Mother's Pantry," said, slipping into the Uzboss phrase. "But, the doctors assure me that you're out of immediate danger. You've got a long, long journey ahead of you before you're fit for duty. If that is what you want, of course."

If it's what I want? Of course, I want that . . . I think.

This was almost too much for him. One moment, he was expecting to be executed. The next—at least as far as he was concerned—he was lying in a bed, facing a long recovery, and the emperor was standing over him.

Yes, by the Mother I want to stay. I want to serve again. Too many friends lost to dishonor them.

The empress stepped up to him and took his hand.

"I want to thank you, *Leefen a'Hope Hollow*," she said, somewhat mangling his name.

"I'm sorry about your brother," Leif said.

Stupid! Why did you say that?

Her face hardened, and she said, "He was an oathbreaker. You served the empire well in removing him."

She was conflicted, he could see. No matter that he was an oathbreaker, no matter that he was trying to either capture or kill her, he was still her brother. That had to tear her apart.

For a moment, Leif wanted to sit up and comfort her, like an older brother. This human was someone special.

"You get better, Corporal," the emperor said, breaking the tension. "Later, when you're back on duty, I want to talk. I've got some ideas I want to discuss with you."

Yeah, right. That's going to happen, the emperor just getting advice from a grunt corporal.

Leif knew it was just small talk, intended to buck up the wounded, and it was a nice gesture, but that's all it was.

"Thank you, Corporal, for everything," the empress said as the two moved to the next bed.

"Doctor Liang will come see you after the imperial couple leaves," the nurse told Leif. "Just hold on."

Leif laid his head back, trying to sort through his feelings when Sousa said, "You look like shit, Corporal. With all due respect, of course."

Leif laughed, then groaned as the pain hit. Whatever they were giving him needed to be adjusted. Probably human specs.

"You don't look so hot yourself."

"Hell, I'm OK. Got hit five times. Nothing serious but this one," she said, pointing at her stomach. "Looks like I'll be shitting through a plastic tube for a couple of months, but the doc says I'll make a full recovery. How about you?"

"Don't know yet. I haven't talked to the doctor yet."

"Well, you look horrible. And what did you do? Fall asleep at the beach?"

"What do you mean?"

"Your face. It's as red as a tomato."

A memory popped into Leif's mind, that of him lying on his back in the rubble, sun hot on his face. He hadn't noticed it before, but his face was hot. Despite the nanoblocks, he'd been sunburnt. After all his injuries, this was simply the icing on the cake. Despite himself, he laughed again.

"Yeah, something like that."

"Hey, Corporal. Thanks," she said, suddenly serious.

"For what?"

"For standing over me like that. For protecting me when I was down."

Leif didn't say anything. What could he say? That was just what Marines did, nothing more, nothing less.

"And Hkekka . . . she started before trailing off.

"Yeah, Hkekka."

They were silent for a moment. To his right, the emperor was moving on from the Imperial Guard in the adjoining bed to the next of the wounded.

"Who else?" Leif asked.

"Qaan, Wonstat, Zoran . . ."

Alive or dead?

"you, and me here. Savea, Preter-Smith, and Lopez, they weren't even touched. Corporal Savea was here asking about you just before the emperor came, but they chased him out.

"Savea? As big as he is, how the heck did they miss him?" Leif said, relieved that Manu was alive, then feeling guilty that he'd been hoping for that over the others.

"The gods of war are a fickle lot."

What about Lori? he wondered, not asking because Sousa wouldn't have the answer to that. When things calmed down, he'd ask one of the nurses or orderlies.

He looked over at his surviving fire team member. A year ago, she was a hesitant, scared young human, and Leif hadn't thought she'd deserved the title of Marine. She had developed, though. He'd been wrong to write her off so early.

He knew he wasn't the same recruit that had reported to Camp Navarro. He'd only wanted to prove himself, to gain skills, using the Corps as a tool, nothing more. Now, he was a Marine, first and foremost, and NCO who lead other Marines into combat. Even among the humans, even off Home, he felt like he belonged.

Something about Sousa still nagged at him, though—the empress.

"Hey Harper, so are you going to tell me what the heck the empress said to you yesterday? And now here she is hugging you like a sister?"

Sousa grimaced and looked around to see if anyone was listening in. With the emperor and the empress in the ward, she didn't have to worry about that.

"Not sister," she said in a low voice, barely loud enough for him to hear.

"What? I said 'like' a sister."

"She's not my sister," Sousa repeated. "She's my cousin."

Leif was gobsmacked. His mouth dropped open.

"You're . . . you're a Jin Long?" he asked.

"No! I'm from Mojave. You know that. My mother and Jen . . . the empress's mother were sisters. My mother stayed on Mojave, and my aunt left to marry August Chen."

"So, you and the empress, Empress Jenifer I, are cousins?"

"Yeah, and we kinda spent a lot of time together when we were young."

And that explained a lot. That also probably explained how 3/6 was one of the battalions chosen to attend the coronation. Sure, the battalion's schedule worked out, but other battalions could have been selected. An emperor, however, when asked by his soon-to-be bride, would almost certainly make sure that her cousin's battalion was part of the ceremonies. That would explain Sousa being pulled aside when the company went on the safari. That would explain India being at the command center during the attack, and an under-strengthed First and Second Platoon accompanying the empress in the attempt to get off the planet.

He'd always felt that there was something odd about the battalion getting the mission. It might be a coincidence that Leif and Sousa served together, but given that, the rest fell into place.

"Who else knows?" he asked her.

"The skipper. The battalion CO. The general, of course. Of course.

"You're not going to tell anyone, are you?"

"That's up to you. But if you're some sort of clan leadership—"

"No. I mean, yes, my family runs the Deep Voyagers, but we're quite a ways down the line of succession. Aunt Larissa, well, my mom says she and Chen married for love. Politics, too, I mean. But also, for love."

Leif let that sink in for a moment. First, that August Chen, the man who started this rebellion, would marry anyone for love. Leif had imagined him as some sort of evil devil. Second, that Sousa was part of that world.

Glad I never tried to get her kicked out of the Marines.

"So, if you lived the life, why did you join the Corps?"

"I joined because I lived the life. I was sheltered, with everything given to me. I wanted to prove myself. I wanted to earn whatever I was going to get in life. My sister? She joined a gang. I joined the Corps."

And Leif understood that. he'd joined to prove himself, too.

"Well, you've done that, Harper. And I'm proud to be serving with you."

When she didn't say anything, Leif turned to look. A tear was rolling down the side of her face.

CAMP MARTELLE, NORTHUMBRIA

Chapter 38

"You ready?" Lance Corporal Harper Sousa asked Leif.

"He's a damned Marine Sergeant, Sousa. Of course, he's ready," Manu, a sergeant now as well, told her.

"Yeah, I'm ready," he said, sticking a forefinger under his collar and pulling it out.

I've got to lose some weight.

A decided lack of activity while he was going through recuperation was having an effect. Doc Lyss told him he could be cleared for duty in another month, and he needed to get back into combat shape.

Still, it felt good to be in his blues. He'd worn them a month ago back on Earth when he'd gone back to the Imperial Palace for the first time since the Jin Long revolt when he, along with two other living and six deceased Marines, including Private Hkekka, had been awarded the Imperial Order of the Empire.

He still wasn't sure he deserved it simply for killing the Jin Long heir. He'd been in the grip of his mistress at the time, and he'd done no more than any other Marine. But he understood the optics. Having human, wyntonan, and qiincer receiving the award in a joint ceremony was great optics for the emperor's agenda, and as Leif happened to agree with the agenda, he didn't raise an objection.

This time, it was different. He was not being singled out in the same way. Manu, Sousa, Staff Sergeant Zoran, Lance Corporal Tile "Beast-mode" Qaan, Ophelia Wonstat (now a civilian), Sergeant Erin Preter-Smith, and Lance

Corporal Yarrow Lopez, all the survivors from the Battle of Irugwa Island, were in this with him together.

Seventy Marines and Corpsmen were also going to go through the same thing, but later, at a different ceremony.

He tugged at the bottom of his blues blouse, pulling it flat, his right elbow twinging in protest. His recovery had been slow. The elbow had been shattered, and the doctors had contemplated just replacing it with an artificial one, but with Leif's blessing, they implanted the matrix designed for wytnonans and initiated his stem-cell regrowth. Through hours of therapy, the elbow worked, but it liked to remind him that it had been destroyed only ten months ago.

Lots had happened over those ten months. When the assault on the palace was broken—and from all accounts, it had been a very close thing—the sassares had withdrawn. Without that threat, the Navy and Marines had crushed the Novacks, Jin Longs, and the other four clans that had joined the revolt within three days. Those six clans were dissolved by imperial decree, and their holdings granted to the people, human or otherwise, who occupied them.

Those clans who'd remained loyal had expected the spoils of the traitor-clans, and they'd hadn't liked the precedent of people being completely independent of them, but the vast bulk of the citizenry had rallied behind the brave emperor and empress, who'd personally led their people in the defense of the empire. There might have been some artistic license taken with the images of the imperial couple charging into battle, but from what Lori had told them, they weren't far off with regards to the emperor, and Leif had seen the empress lead the final charge on Irugwa.

The remaining clans were still a powerful force, but their hold on the empire had been irretrievably diminished. They had their fingers embedded in commerce, but the political power had shifted back to the Granite Throne.

And the imperial couple was making use of their political dividends. More people—wyntonans, qiincers, tokits, and alindamirs were being recruited for the military and government. Even tost'el'tzy, who would not raise a weapon, were joining the Lions of Peace, the imperial public service corps that helped those in need, within the empire or without. Leera, the lead race of the Red Hegemony, began to join the ranks of the LOP.

While most of these galaxy-wide events happened without Leif as he went through his recovery, one small change did touch him. He was no longer Leif Hollow. The Corps had long stopped changing Wyntonan names to suit human tongues, but the first two groups of them still had the names assigned to them. The emperor changed that with a stroke of the pen. He was now Sergeant Leefen a'Hope Hollow. On paper. He was still Leif to everyone he knew, and he was fine with that. Leif was his name now.

There was one other thing that happened during the last ten months, not something that affected the empire, but nonetheless affected him. As with the custom of his people, those who'd fallen in the battle were taken from the mourning crypts to the crematoriums, so their souls would be released to rejoin the Mother. His arm immobilized and limping from his other wounds, Leif had journeyed home to honor Jordun, Carlton, Inga, Iden a'Springer (the Imperial Guard who'd charged the heir), and the other sixteen wyntonans who'd fallen.

Leif had stayed in Hope Hollow afterwards for three months, conducting his therapy with off-site guidance and monitoring. On the third month, his tri-year had gone into heat. Only off his inhibitors since his surgery (they would interfere with the stem-cell growth) he shouldn't have entered musth, but nature would not be denied. Soran had been hesitant, given his medical condition. She needn't have worried. And if Leif had thought that his musapha was a harsh mistress, that was nothing compared to the master that was his musth. Crippled or not . . .

And now he was going to be a father.

He wasn't sure how that was going to work with him in the Corps. He and Soran were going to discuss it before he was back on active duty.

"Hey, snap out of it," Manu said, punching him in the arm. "Where've you been?"

"Just thinking," he said.

"Dangerous thing, that. But get ready. It's about time."

A tokit opened the door and said, "OK, you all know what you're supposed to do, so this will be easy. Forget about the cams and newsdrones, forget about the billions watching. Just relax. Any last questions?" she asked. When there weren't any, she said, "Then let's do this. Just follow Grigori, then as soon as you get to the door, Lance Corporal Qaan, you lead to your mark."

Leif was the fifth in line, with only Manu and Staff Sergeant Zoran behind him. As he stepped off, Manu gave him a pat on the back.

When Marines marched, they usually had someone calling cadence, but this was to be silent. Leif, limping ever-so-slightly, focused on Sousa's feet, trying to keep in synch with her. They marched down the corridor to the side entrance of the stage. Grigori pushed open the door and stepped to the side. The eight Marines filed across the stage, halted in unison (almost), performed a right face, and knelt, backs to the audience. They bowed their heads and froze like that, not moving a muscle.

A moment later, Leif heard steps. He could see, from the waist down, two people march out, clad in imperial white and gray. They stopped in the middle of the line, faced the Marines, and one of the figures stepped back two paces.

"If there are any who oppose this, speak now. If there are any who refuse this, leave now," the empress announced.

The theater remained silent.

The Imperial Court loved ceremonies, the more elaborate the better. But this one was different. This one went back centuries, millennia, to pre-space Earth. The words and procedures might have changed over time, but this was between regent and subject, a special bond. Anyone else was merely a spectator.

When no one spoke up, the empress moved to her right, to Beast-mode. Leif watched out of the corner of his eyes as she lifted her sword, gleaming impossibly bright in the lights, and brought in down on Beast-Mode's left shoulder.

"I dub thee a Knight Extraordinaire, Protector of the Empire. She raised the sword, shifted it over his head to his right shoulder, and placed the blade on it. "Embrace the responsibility I give unto you."

Beast-mode raised his head and looked into the empress's eyes. He didn't say a word, no oath, nothing. As a Marine, he'd already sworn and oath to the imperial couple and the empire. This was an honor—and responsibility being thrust upon him.

The empress went down the line, repeating the simple act. Leif's heart started pounding as she stepped in front of him. He felt faint, until the moment the sword touched him. As if imbued with magic power, he felt an overwhelming wave sweep through him, like musapha.

"I dub thee a Knight Extraordinaire, Protector of the Empire." She passed the sword over his head and touched his right shoulder. "Embrace the responsibility I give unto you."

Leif raised his head and looked into her eyes. She gave the slightest of smiles and stepped in front of Manu to knight him. The emperor stood alone, but his smile was broad. He'd be conducting the same ceremony later today, then again at Rostok and Rebirth, where 1/9 and 2/23 were based, but this one was for the empress.

After knighting Manu and Zoran, the empress marched back to her place just in front of the emperor, and said, "Rise, knights, and face those who look to you for protection."

Someone started to clap before being hushed as the Marines stood and conducted an about face. The base theater was the largest auditorium-type building at Camp Martelle, and every one of the almost 3000 seats was filled.

The ceremony was not quite done yet. The imperial couple marched to Beast-mode. The emperor handed his empress a small silver pin, which she attached to his collar. The simple crossed swords with the lion's head was the only emblem given to a Knight Extraordinaire. For the eight Marines, the head was that of a lioness, signifying who had knighted them. For the others, they'd receive one with the head of a male lion. Technically, they were the same, but for Leif, as much as he respected the emperor, he now felt attached to Empress Jenifer. He was her man.

And this somehow meant more to him. His IOE, the Imperial Order of the Empire, hung heavy at his neck, a gaudy medal, and one that signified past actions. The tiny pin on his collar was a promise of the future.

The empress pinned the emblem on the staff sergeant, then stepped back, sweeping an arm to indicate the new knights.

Applause washed over them as Leif stood tall.

****

The reception was another world. Taking place in the base officer's club, the eight new knights had stood in a receiving line for almost two hours as high-ranking officers and worthies filed past, giving them congratulations. Leif's elbow was aching before they finally broke. After a quick head call and grabbing a glass of punch, he gravitated away from the higher-ups to the group of Marines congregating in the corner, out of everyone's way.

"You look good," Lori said. "Or do I have to call you 'Ser Knight' now?"

"You can call me a cab to take me home," he said, taking a long draught of the punch, then making a face.

Why do humans like stuff so sweet?

"Oh, are you hurting?" she asked, suddenly concerned.

He was hurting, but not that badly, and he didn't want her to worry.

"No, no. I'm fine. There's just too much brass around here."

She didn't look convinced, but she let it go.

Leif saw a familiar face, and he gave Kyle a hug. "I'm so glad you could make it, my man."

"Wouldn't miss it," his old roommate slurred.

He looked terrible. A good portion of his head was flattened, temporarily covered with a protective shell. The doctors had put in two lattices so far, and they'd slowly build it up before replacing the skull. Kyle was going to live, but he'd probably never be 100%. Despite all the advances in medical care, the brain still withheld its mysteries.

Kyle was still a Marine, but he was in the process of being boarded out. He'd retire as a corporal, living the remainder of his life in the what-could-have-been.

Still, he'd have a life, not like Jordun, Stone, Hkekka, and too many others.

"What's with Sousa?" Lori asked. "Does the empress have a crush on her?"

The empress and Sousa were over in the corner, heads together. As if on cue, both snapped their heads back and laughed.

Leif had never told anyone about their relations, not even to Lori, so he said, "I think they might have gotten close on Irugwa, and then when the empress kept visiting us in the hospital. It's probably hard on the empress with all her responsibilities, not having someone her age around."

"Well, maybe," Lori said.

"Sergeant a'Hope Hollow," an alindamair in imperial livery said, tapping on his shoulder from behind, "Can you please come with me?"

Leif had never spoken to an alindamair, and his soft voice and odd accent were a little difficult to make out. But the livery spoke volumes.

"Hang around," he told the others. "I'll be right back."

"Congratulations, Sergeant," a general who'd probably had a few too many said, grabbing his arm as he followed the alindamair. "I always said you people would make good Marines."

"Thank you, sir, but I've got to go," he said, pointing to the orderly and pulling away.

He had to fight from rolling his eyes. "You people."

The orderly led Leif to a side room and opened the door. The emperor was inside, sitting in an overstuffed chair talking with a Navy admiral. He smiled when he saw Leif and said, "Admiral Kim, if you can excuse us for a few minutes."

The admiral and the orderly left the room leaving him, a mere sergeant in the Marines, alone with the most powerful man in the empire.

The most powerful man pointed to a seat beside him, and after Leif took it, said, "*Daya, Leefen a'Hope Hollow.*"

"*Daya*, Your Majesty."

"Well, I see you survived the receiving line. God, I hate those."

Leif had been ready for the emperor to say about anything . . . but not that.

He laughed and said, "Yes, sir. It was touch and go there, but I managed to pull through."

"Well, I didn't have a chance to talk to you during the IOE award ceremony. I apologize for that.

You apologize?

"I promised we would talk, but now we can."

Leif remembered the emperor saying something like that back in the hospital at the palace, but he hadn't thought he was serious.

"First, on a man-to-man level, I want to thank you. Without you, the empress would not be here, and the history of the empire might have changed."

"It wasn't just—"

The emperor stopped him. "No, it wasn't. It was Major Jespers, Guard Commander Lake, Iden a'Springer, Private Hkekka. Hell, it was the empress herself. God, I keep looking at the recordings, and seeing her lead that final charge . . .

Oh, boy, this guy's fallen hard. He really does love her.

Which made him feel good.

"It took a lot of people, but if any one of them had failed, everything would have failed. You were necessary. Which sort of highlights what I'm going to ask you."

"What do you want, Your Majesty?"

He hesitated, then asked, "What are your plans, Sergeant?"

"Sir?"

"Your second enlistment will be up in a little more than a year."

"I want to reenlist, sir."

"And then what?"

"Whatever the Marines ask me to do."

"But for you? Do you want to be an officer? Second Lieutenant a'Black is doing well, and I'd like more officers that represent the entire empire.

An officer? Me?

The idea had some appeal, mostly from an ego side, but Leif already knew the answer to that.

"No, sir. I know officers fight, but they usually fight other officers, sitting behind desks, using memos as weapons. That's not for me. I want to stay with the troops."

He knew there should be more wyntonan officers, and there would be—just not him.

"Well, then, if that's the case, I'd like you to consider something. I told you that you were a part of a combined effort. Human, wyntonan, and qiincer all combined to save the empress, right?"

"Yes, sir."

"Well, I'm positive that we need more combined units, where we can make the best use of all our citizens. To that end, I'm forming a special operations unit in the Corps."

The empire had their special ops forces in the Navy, who had recently adopted the old name SEALs. The Marines didn't have special ops. They had scout-snipers and recon, who were in support of Marine units, but not special ops teams who went pooping and snooping on their own throughout the empire—and according to rumor, outside the empire.

"But this is not going to be a human force . . ."

The SEALs were famously all-human.

". . . but rather made up from all the races who can provide a benefit."

"Qiincers, too?"

Hkekka aside, there was still some resistance to the qiincers. Their perceived lack of teamwork was considered something too difficult to overcome.

"What do you think about that?"

"You're saying you want a representative force, but you want this force to be effective, I'm guessing. It's one thing to have qiincers in the Corps or as police, but in a special ops team, where each had to trust each other? Am I right?"

"There has been some mention as to that," the emperor said guardedly.

"I know. I've heard it. But I've got personal experience in that. Private Hkekka had my back. Without him, I'd be dead now, already reunited with the Mother."

"So, you're saying they should be in this new unit?"

"They can fly, sir. And I trust them."

The emperor leaned back and smiled. "I'll take that under consideration. But to you, would you be interested in this new unit? It would mean long and frequent deployments, which would keep you away from your bondmate and child."

By the Mother, what doesn't he know about me?

"And I wish we had time to go about this slowly. But the sassares are becoming a problem. I think we might be in conflict sooner rather than later."

This was something high above Leif's head. The sassares had fired the first volley with the Jin Longs as proxies, but he hadn't heard anything else. War with them could be devastating, but the only way to survive such a war would be to be prepared.

Leif didn't know exactly what this special ops force would entail, how it would be organized. But the emperor wanted it, and he trusted the human. He'd also sworn an oath to him.

This might be rough on his new family, but this was also the life he'd chosen. He reached up to finger the small crossed swords on his collar, just put on a few hours ago. What had the empress said?

Embrace the responsibility I give unto you.

There was really only one response for him to give.

"I would be honored, Your Majesty."

Epilogue

"I realize all of this is new. Hell, it's new to me, but together, we're going to work this out as we go," Lieutenant Colonel Tork Malante, the first Marine Special Operations Battalion Commander, said.

"I'd like to think my staff," he added, turning to the fourteen Marines, one civilian, and two Navy SEALs who were sitting on the stage behind him, "for all the hard work you've put in over the last month. That's just the beginning, though. As we stand up tomorrow, the workload is only going to get heavier. The sassares are not going to give us the luxury of time."

He turned back to the 217 Marines and sailors who, as of 0001 tonight, would be assigned to the battalion, and said, "So, you poor souls have one more night of freedom, so I suggest you take advantage of it, because as of zero-five-hundred in the morning, your ass belongs to me."

There was a scattering of laughs and ooh-rahs. This wasn't boot camp. Every one of the Marines and sailors sitting in the seats were veterans, from the major in the front row to the junior Marine, a lance corporal the CO had stand up to the calls of "boot!" There weren't even any lieutenants. The junior officers were captains.

They didn't expect the casual abuse of boot camp, but as the colonel had briefed them, the next few months were going to be tough, physically and mentally. They were going to be pushed to their limits and then some. Not everyone was going to make it, and that was OK. To sharpen a blade, the rough edges had to be honed away.

Leif still wasn't in shape, and his elbow was not at 100%. This was going to hurt, and hurt big time. But he wasn't concerned. That might be naive bravado, but he'd gut through it. The CO had been very circumspect over the last four hours as he described some of the potential missions assigned to the battalion, but what he had said had sent his pulse racing and his mistress stirring. There was no way in the icy depths of hell that he was going to let this opportunity slip between his fingers.

"Hey, I'm serious. Get out of here. I'm not sure I've ever seen Marines turn down liberty call, so you're getting me worried," the CO said to more laughter.

"Alpha-Two, on me," Captain Rory Dubois shouted from the front row.

Leif hadn't met his new team leader yet, or any of his other teammates except for one.

"It's good to see you again, Sergeant a'Hope Hollow," Gunny Dream Bear, his old DI said, coming down the aisle. "I've been following you, though. Kinda hard to miss," he added, pointing at Leif's IOE.

"It's been a long time, Gunny," Leif said, shaking his hand. "And not too far from here."

The battalion was housed aboard Camp Navarro, adjacent to boot camp. Leif had thought it was counter-productive to have what was still a semi-secret unit that close to the recruits, but it was a secure camp within the base complex. And from what the CO had just said, they wouldn't be spending much time in garrison.

"Do you know anyone else in the team?" the gunny asked.

"No. I heard of a few, but never met them."

"Well, I know the captain. Good people, but he doesn't like to be kept waiting, so let's get over there. Let's talk later, OK?"

"Sure thing."

All around the auditorium, teams were meeting each other. They'd be getting extremely close, but for now, most were strangers to each other.

"OK, Gunny, that's everyone. I'm Captain Rory Dubois, the team leader. Gunny Dream Bear there is the assistant. As far as the rest of you, we won't have positions until we work things out, and that includes you, Doc."

Doc Yeltsov was a tall, willowy HM4. She was the team corpsman, but everyone in the team would carry multiple billets, including her.

"So, we know each other's names from what the CO passed, but let's introduce each other first."

Some of the other teams were breaking up and leaving, mostly in small groups. Evidently, Captain Dubois was a little more hands on.

"I'm Lars Silva," a heavyworlder staff sergeant said. "Just left Two-Twenty-Three where I was a platoon sergeant. And yes, I was at the palace. And no, I never met Hollow there, though. I think we were a little busy at the time."

"Ariel Fruhstuck," a stocky, redheaded sergeant said.

"And who were you with last?"

"Three-Four."

Ariel evidently wasn't much for gab.

"I guess I'm up. Sergeant Anthony Garamundi. They call me Bird." Bird looked like a chestie, one of the subraces of humans. Not many of them were in the Corps.

"Well, we'll see if you get to keep that name," the captain said to the laughter of the others.

"Leif a'Hope Hollow. Three-Six."

Leif realized that he was very well-known in the Corps, and he wondered again if that was going to help or hurt him in the team.

"Welcome aboard, Sergeant," the captain said.

All eyes turned to the qiincer. With typical disdain, she said, "Forintik."

The captain's eyes narrowed at her curt response. Leif wondered if he'd ever worked with a qiincer before. There weren't many in the Corps yet, and there were only three assigned to the battalion.

"Well, as you can see, we're a pretty diverse lot. That was by design. We have some teams that are all female, some all male, one team is half-tokit. Here, we've got six monkeys—four regs, a troll, and a chestie—along with casper and a fairy," he said, using less-than-polite terminology. "None of that matters. What we all are are Marines . . . and a fleet corpsman. So, if you have any problem with working as a team, tell me now, and I'll get you transferred."

Leif had been surprised to hear a captain use those terms—even if Leif had used them on occasion. But now he understood that he'd done it for shock value. He'd been watching each of their faces as he'd said them.

His opinion of the captain edged up a notch. If they were going to mesh as a team, then he had to find out if anyone had problems working with the other, for any reason.

No one said a word, and he nodded. "Look, I'm not officially your team leader until a minute after midnight, but as far as I'm concerned, we start now. So, I'm requesting, not ordering, that we go out into V-town as a team, relax, and shoot the shit. It's your call."

No, not when you put it that way. If we say no, then we'll pay in the morning.

He didn't care though. He'd wanted to catch up with the gunny, but he could still do that if the team went out together.

"Sounds good, Staff Sergeant Silva said. "And I know the place. The owner's good to Marines, and she hasn't seen me since I was a DI. She'll probably comp us the first pitcher."

"Now, that's what I call initiative," the captain said with a laugh. "Are we good with that?"

There was a chorus of ooh-rahs.

"OK, so let's meet in front of the Q at say, seventeen-thirty? Does that work?" No one said anything, so he said, "Seventeen-thirty it is. I'll have us a ride."

****

The "ride" was a four-meter Weimer limo the captain had rented. With hoots and hollers, they boarded, happy to find cold beer and ciders in the cooler. Staff Sergeant Silva, sporting a gaudy flower-covered, orange-and-blue top he called an "Aloha shirt," stuck his upper body out of the open sunroof as they started off, yelling "Suckas, look what our team leader got us!" as they passed several more of the battalion's new Marines who were walking to the shuttle stop.

Leif, half-way through his Dynx, just sat in the back taking in the experience. He'd never been in a limo before, and he kept snapping selfies to send to Soran and Lori.

As they passed through the front gate, a guard yelled at Silva to get back inside, who saluted her with his middle finger before taking a long swig of his beer. Even the captain laughed at that. They were all alpha dogs in the limo, feeling their oats, and reading for one last blow-out before things got serious.

The limo made its way through V-town, past the bars and shops servicing the Marines. Silva rode with his body half-out, shouting directions and spilling beer with each swerve. It would have been easier to just enter the destination, but if the captain paid for a real driver, then they were going to make him earn his salary.

Finally, the limo came to halt, and the driver jumped out to open the door. Too late, though. Staff Sergeant Silva had vaulted out through the sunroof, landed with a thud, and then grabbed the door, opening it with a sweeping bow, forehead close to the muck in the street. The driver rolled his eyes, but stood back.

"I accept tips," Silva shouted and they tumbled out.

Silva's bar was like any other, non-descript and totally forgetable, yet it looked vaguely familiar.

"Watches, genuine Rolexes, sers," a tokit cried out hopefully, rising and rushing forward, hoping to score.

Leif ignored her.

They poured into the bar, leaving the tokit behind. It was dark and dingy like most bars, a small dance floor unoccupied. A Marine sat in a booth, his head between his arms on the table as he snored.

"Oh, yeah, Silva," Gunny Dream Bear said. "This place is happening."

"Just wait, Gunny, it'll get better," he said before yelling out, "Hey Kassie, it's your boyfriend, come back from the dead!"

He grabbed an empty pitcher from over the bar and helped himself to the tap, filling it.

"Sit, sit," he told the others. "She'll be here in a moment."

"I hope you're not getting us arrested," the captain said.

That didn't stop him, however, from taking a glass and letting Silva fill it.

Leif still had a Dynx from the limo, so he waved Silva off before sliding into the booth next to the gunny. The gunny lifted his glass, and they clinked them.

"To Alpha-Two," they said in unison.

"Lars, you bastard," a woman shouted, coming out of the head. "I thought you were dead."

"They can't kill me, old lady."

"Well, you could have let me know."

Something about the lady's voice tickled his memory, and he tried to pin it down. She walked up and looked over the group, her eyes locking, ever-so-slightly on Leif and Forintik.

And it hit him. He looked around the bar. It had changed. There wasn't a pool table, just a shoddy dance floor, and the woman hadn't aged well over the last six years, but he was sure of it. This was the woman who'd refused to serve him and the other wyntonans when they'd graduated from boot camp. That was the first time he'd heard the term "dung races" directed at him.

"We've got to go," he whispered to Gunny Dream Bear.

"Why? It's a dive, but it's not that bad. The beer's cold, at least."

Leif felt small, belittled, which didn't make much sense. Who cared what this human thought? He was with Marines who valued him. The emperor valued him.

So why is my heart beating so fast?

"Well, I see Lars here had already stolen my beer, so I might as well find out what else you want."

"How about a pitcher of Munich Gold," Doc asked.

The woman cackled, then said, "Does this look like Wayfare? You think we serve that highfalutin stuff here? Heineken, Swisher, or Dynx," she said, naming the beer. "Winter Cider. And I can mix up a few cocktails if you don't care much what goes in it."

Lars laughed, raising his hand for a high-five, which the woman ignored.

"Dynx, then."

She turned to Leif and asked, "What'll you have, son?"

Leif had been ready to stand up and leave, but he sat there, mouth open, saying nothing.

"What do you want?" she asked again.

"You'll serve me?"

"No, that's why I'm asking you what you want," she said, rolling her eyes

"You wouldn't serve me before. Any of my people. Six years ago."

She stepped back, lifting her hand over her mouth, her eyes getting big.

"Kassie, what's the matter?" he asked, suddenly serious.

She ignored him.

"I . . . yes, that probably happened then," she said. "And I'm so sorry."

If Leif was surprised before, he was even more so now. He didn't expect an apology.

"I was stupid then. I thought you people were, well, not good, I can say. But, I read about you, hating that you were Marines, but every time I read, I saw what you were doing. First, the poor girl getting killed.

Leif swallowed hard. She was referring to Kaatrn a'Telltell, killed on Omeyocan.

"Then the other battles, where you all did your duty. I asked Sergeant Major Elsworth, you know him?"

Leif shook his head, but the gunny said, "I do."

It was only then that Leif realized that everyone was silent, beer forgotten, as they listened in.

"Well, he used to bitch about you people, but then, not two years later, he said the Marines needed your kind. You were good for the Corps.

"My bar suffered, and I didn't know why. I tried to change it up. Put in a dance floor, you know, to get people in. But nothing worked. Sergeant Major Elsworth, he said that's because all of you Marines hung out together, and if your caspers . . . sorry, I mean wyntonans, couldn't come in and get served, or after that, the qiincers, the whole group would go somewhere else.

"But I'm a stubborn old lady, and I thought too old to change. But then the fucking Jin Longs," she said, venom in her voice, "What they did. Almost killed our dear emperor and empress. But the Marines saved them. Not just humans, but one of you," she said, pointing at Leif, "and one of you," she added, pointing at Forintik, you saved the empress. I seen it on the holo. They even got the IOE, but the poor qiincer boy, he died."

She stopped, tears in her eyes. Leif didn't know if that was for Hkekka or from a sense of shame.

"Oh, look at me, crying like this. Anyway, I may be stubborn, but I'm not stupid. You people saved the empire, you and us humans together. Maybe the emperor is right, and we're stronger together.

"I started telling my regulars that everyone is welcome here, but none of you ever came. Until today. And now, to my shame, I find out I fucked you over six years ago. All I can say is I'm sorry.

"I told everyone if that Sergeant Hollow, with his IOE, ever wants to come here, his drinks are on me. I know you want to leave now, and I understand it. But if you stay, your drinks, for all of you, are on the house tonight."

All eyes shifted to Leif, waiting for his response. He knew they were leaving it up to him, and he knew they would be fine with whatever he decided.

He looked at the woman, strands of gray hair hanging in front of her face, wringing her hands. He shifted his gaze to the bar, run down as it was. This was her livelihood, but it had suffered because of her prejudice.

He'd been angry at her before, for the refusal, for making him feel less than he was. She'd personified the contempt that many humans felt for the "dung races." And now, she was just a sorry old human, even if she was trying to change her worldview.

With a sigh, Leif stood up and scooted out of the booth. She nodded and looked down. Instead of leaving, however, Leif stepped up and enveloped her with his arms. She stiffened, then pushed her face into his chest and cried, hot tears soaking through his shirt.

He let her cry herself out. A few minutes ago, he'd asked himself who cared what this human thought. The answer was he cared. And if this human woman could change her mind, if she could see him, the qiincers, the tokits, as equals, then, as she said, maybe the emperor was right. They were stronger together.

She pushed back, wiping her eyes with her sleeve, then looking up at him hopefully.

"If I ever see Sergeant Hope Hollow, I'll let him know he can come in for a free drink. But until then, how about starting us off with another round?"

Thank you for reading *Unification*. The third book in the series, *Fusion*, will be coming out soon. I hope you enjoyed this book, and I welcome a review on Amazon, Goodreads, or any other outlet.

If you would like updates on new books releases, news, or special offers, please consider signing up for my mailing list. Your email will not be sold, rented, or in any other way disseminated. If you are interested, please sign up at the link below:

http://eepurl.com/bnFSHH

Two books were extremely helpful for me in my research for the *Ghost Marines series*:

The Marines of Montford Point: America's First Black Marines, by Melton A. McLaurin

White Man's Tears Conquer My Pains: My WWII Service Story, by Henry Badgett

Other Books by Jonathan Brazee

The United Federation Marine Corps
Recruit
Sergeant
Lieutenant
Captain
Major
Lieutenant Colonel
Colonel
Commandant

Coda

An Accidental War (A Ryck Lysander short story published in BOB's Bar: Tales of the Multiverse)

Rebel
(Set in the UFMC universe.)

Behind Enemy Lines
(A UFMC Prequel)

The United Federation Marine Corps' Lysander Twins
Legacy Marines
Esther's Story: Recon Marine
Noah's Story: Marine Tanker
Esther's Story: Special Duty
Blood United

Women of the United Federation Marine Corps
Gladiator
Sniper
Corpsman

High Value Target (A Gracie Medicine Crow Short Story)
BOLO Mission (A Gracie Medicine Crow Short Story)
Weaponized Math (A Gracie Medicine Crow Short Story and a 2017 Nebula Award Finalist)

The United Federation Marine Corps' Grub Wars
Alliance
The Price of Honor
Division of Power

The Navy of Humankind: Wasp Squadron
Fire Ant
Crystals

Ghost Marines
Integration (2018 Dragon Award Finalist)
Unification
Fusion (coming soon)

The Return of the Marines Trilogy
The Few
The Proud
The Marines

The Al Anbar Chronicles: First Marine Expeditionary Force--Iraq
Prisoner of Fallujah
Combat Corpsman
Sniper

Werewolf of Marines
Werewolf of Marines: Semper Lycanus
Werewolf of Marines: Patria Lycanus
Werewolf of Marines: Pax Lycanus

To the Shores of Tripoli

Wererat

Darwin's Quest: The Search for the Ultimate Survivor

Venus: A Paleolithic Short Story

Secession

Duty

Semper Fidelis

Seeds of War (with Lawrence Schoen)
Invasion
Scorched Earth
Bitter Harvest

Non-Fiction

Exercise for a Longer Life

Author Website
http://www.jonathanbrazee.com

Made in United States
Orlando, FL
30 November 2021

10983074R00137